Green Heritage

John R. Allan

Illustrations by
Ruth Smythe

Ardo Publishing Company
Buchan

John R. Allan c.1936

Published by Ardo Publishing Company, Buchan
Printed by Famedram Publishers Ltd, Aberdeenshire

Contents

Foreword

THE PUBLICATION of "Green Heritage" will be welcomed by the many admirers of John R. Allan. This substantial novel adds considerably to our knowledge of a fresh and individual talent.

This volume was written in the late 1930's while the author was living near Stirling. It is not known whether he attempted to publish it; the lack of correspondence on the subject suggests he did not. Perhaps Allan felt that the concerns embodied in "Green Heritage" would seem dated to a post-1945 readership. If so, the passage of time has brought its own vindication. It is a tribute to Allan's artistry that the work speaks so clearly to us in the 1990's.

John R. Allan writes a prose which is free of affectation and obscurity. For that very reason, perhaps, his work has not attracted "the prelections of university professors". But there is no doubting the literary skill which animates such passages as the depiction of the storm and its aftermath (chapter seven). Each reader will have his own favourite episode. It is characteristic of Allan to fuse external description and internal debate, as the following extract indicates:

"It would be a life of steady effort, of good money, of reasonable amusement. Then he won to the top of the hill, and stood looking down on the lower world. Up there, away from the sight of harvest, the uncertain day had its own swift glories. The wind had rent the banks of cloud, and the sun was sweeping the land with slanting shafts of light. Here was shadow, there the light; and, in between, the light and shadow blended...

4

Down by Lendrum where the valley widened, the cloud shadows rolled across the haughs, now darkening the pale drowned fields; now obscuring the reflected lights from farm windows. And eastward, over the high ridge of the land, through a channel cut by the ice in a prehistoric age, there was a line where the horizon darkened to a deeper blue, the sea... these elemental things played havoc with the young man's mind. Their magnificence challenged him.

The way that passage moves from the everyday to the spiritually splendid is breathtaking; at a stroke the claims of prudent self-interest evaporate. The turbulent cloudscape is in Allan's best "elemental" vein. Another passage which I particularly admire is the close of chapter nine. The author's control is absolute as he recounts the winding-down of the harvest celebrations – "our revels now are ended". The stark final sentence ushers in the winter.

Readers of "Farmer's Boy" will find much that is familiar in "Green Heritage" (not least the presence of an indomitable old man). Indeed, "Farmer's Boy" part II supplies an epigraph of the novel:

"I climbed the steep ascent towards a morning coat and an English accent, and managed to wear both with distinction... But it was no good. I was merely one among a million climbers, parasites that had their roots in thin air and aspired to a place in the sun... So I said good-bye to the morning coat... and returned in all humility to the place where I began... I have at least one thing that is worth all the gentility and aspirations I forswore – I have one tremendous reality behind me, the tradition and loyalties of my fathers."

"Green Heritage" presents a fictional working-out of this theme. Stephen Lees, like the "I" of "Farmer's Boy", forsakes gentility and commercial aspiration and returns to his roots. But the journey from breakfast in Dulwich to possession of Hillhead is no pastoral idyll. The novel catalogues the hardships and difficulties

5

inspearable from farming. Financial instability and ruin are never far away. None of this is shirked by Allan, who depicts vividly the rapacity of financiers and the parasitic dependence of lairds – see for example the indictment of banking practices in chapter five. The exchange between Stephen and Tam in chapter seven is merely one of a series of reflections on the harsh conditions which very often defeat the most industrious farmer. In Allan's world the imperative is to survive; and survival at Hillhead depends upon change. Stephen shows his loyalty to his inheritance, not by slavish adherence to the practices of the past, but by a courageous capacity for adaptation. The last chapter is "The Beginning"; the tractor has come to Hillhead. The amiably cynical Mr Elphinstone prophesies that:

"For every Tam you find in the countryside you'll find a hundred Willums (sceptics)"

But Stephen said, "I don't care. I don't care a damn. This is my place and my living; it's my living and Tam's. We'll make it thrive in our own way and them that don't like our way can go and starve in a corner. This is my work. I'm going to do it the best way I can, and freedom and tradition and everybody that thinks I'm a fool can go to hell."

This is Stephen's climactic statement; he has earned the right to be master of his place. This is his heritage – not the fruit of acquiescence but of determination (against all odds) to bring new life to his patrimony. By abandoning 'tradition' in the narrow sense of agricultural custom he shows himself to be the possessor of the true 'tradition' to which the narrator of 'Farmer's Boy' laid claim. Stephen Lees has the authentic robustness and spiritual independence of the North-East tenant farmer. His story deserves to be read.

Charles Calder, Department of English,
University of Aberdeen.
30th August, 1991

Editorial Note

I REMEMBER my mother saying, when I was quite young, that my father's career as a writer had been damaged by the war against Hitler. There had been books which had been ready to go but had been lost. I imagined bombs falling on the presses loaded with great books. After the war and up till the illness which finished his serious writing in 1956, I was aware of a struggle to finish some major literary work and I was aware also that the work was always being sabotaged by highly paid commissions from the BBC and others. Those clearly had to take precedence over art.

It was not, therefore, a complete surprise when, after his death in 1986, I discovered among his papers, not fewer than seven novels and bits of novels, by John R. Allan. If they are all published it will double the number of his books. He will have to be reassessed and may yet be remembered not so much a journalist but as a novelist. I find it almost unbearable to think of my father spending years of his working life writing novels but (as I believe) never trying to publish them.

I am now engaged in a labour of love and admiration. I am sorting them out from among the garage bills, the cancelled cheques and the hoarded press cuttings, with a view to publication.

Green Heritage is published first because it had been completed and was intact. But more than that, it has a direct bearing on the farming community about which it is written, as it struggles with change in the 1990s. It is a beautifully crafted account of a peasant's instinct for his land, an instinct which John R. Allan helped nurture in me. I could not be more moved by this written testament nor by the circumstances of its publication.

I hope he will not be angry with me but he was unavailable for consultation and I have therefore had to take some editorial decisions without his help. He has a somewhat eccentric punctuation style. He doesn't like the apostrophe except where there may be confusion. He only uses a capital G in God when there is a genuine reverence. Blasphemies only warrant a small g.

Some cuts have also been made. I believe most of those were done with the author's approval as they were indicated by square brackets in the manuscript. If anyone doubts my sagacity they can consult the original which has been deposited in Edinburgh with the National Library of Scotland.

Bringing the book out has been a team effort. Fiona Allan, Susan Allan, Alison Mutch and Bill Williams have all helped. But I would like to thank Eleanor Stewart particularly for her skill in desk top publishing and for her cheerfulness.

My old boss, Sir Kenneth Alexander, once told me that the priority in writing should go, not to getting it right but to getting it wrote. If errors remain they will be my fault (and perhaps Sir Kenneth's) because I have seen it as a matter of urgency to get this volume to you.

Charlie Allan, Little Ardo, Methlick.
10th September, 1991

Three Persons

The persons in this history are: JOHN BREWSTER of Hillhead in Lendrum, a Scots farmer of a type that is now
rare and soon may be forgotten. A square-built man of
seventy seven with a short white beard and a hard blue
eye. For fifty years he had been the brave companion to
his pleasures, but now he was a little tired and bent with
the weight of years. His wife, who had run a hard race
with him, was dead. His children had left Hillhead.
Many of the friends with whom he had gone roistering
in his youth were dead and others had grown too old for
anything but death. The old man was alone and yet he
was not lonely for there remained to him the one thing
that he had always valued above all else – his farm. It
was a long time since his ancestors had come to Hillhead.
They had been there at the rebellion of 1745 but there
was no record of their beginnings. For one hundred
and eighty years the six generations – the three Alexan-
ders, the three Georges and John had farmed the land.
In the lease of 1803 there had only been 45 acres of arable and 190 acres of waste ground, with the right to a
lair of peat in the moss. In the lease of 1879 there were
235 acres of arable and no waste. Seventy-seven years of
mighty labour had gone to make that change. Acre by
acre the rough ground had been brought in to the
plough, till the peats were cast from under the very roots
of the corn. The Brewsters had never made money;
they had made land instead. What increase remained
after their pleasures were paid for went back into the
land from whence it had come. Though the farm was
only rented it was more truly theirs than the laird's; and

each Brewster, having served the land for a generation, handed it on to his eldest son in better heart than he had got it from his father. But now old John Brewster had no son. There had been two but one had been killed in the war of 1914 and the younger had been gored to death by a bull. The other three children, being daughters, were of no account.

Old John was the last of the Brewsters. He had no heir who would carry on the farm when he was dead. He was old and it seemed that he had nothing to work for. Yet he kept on working. He cared for his farm as his father had done before him, because the Brewsters had made Hillhead, and life could not have meaning apart from it. He had grown on those gently sloping fields and his pride was all in them. They had always carried the best of nowt and corn; and so they would as long as a Brewster lived to serve them. Thus old John lived by and for his fields and awaited in a grim humour that day when he must die and the Brewsters come to an end.

ELIZABETH DAVIES, born Elizabeth Brewster, is the second person of the story. She was John's only sister and a widow; and his housekeeper since the death of his wife. She was an old lady of incomparable presence. Her white hair was thick. The red of good living had taken the place of the delicate rose on her cheeks. A pair of gold-rimmed glasses shone before the eyes that had themselves shone so brightly. She was old but she was still the mistress of her life. The swish of her black silk dress and the set of her shoulders proved her dauntless spirit. The way she toyed with the gold-rimmed glasses on their thin gold chain, showed that she had known and loved a life far different from that of the cold North East.

Old Brewster and Mistress Davies were magnificently matched. Both had a great strength of spirit. His was the spirit of the land that had bred him; hard, unyielding and with a passionate heat that was seldom revealed. She was the female counterpart: her strength was no less and her passions had been as warm; but they had spent themselves more furiously and had so permeated her in the spending that now she had the rich harmony of a great sunset. All the wild elements of her life were resolved into peace and beauty. The brother and sister had grown old and very wise. They had lived in the grand manner. They had pursued their pleasures far beyond the bounds of caution. Now he had learned to despise all follies, and most men, because he had outlived them; and she to love and understand all foolish mortals because she in her day had served so many mortal follies.

Together they lived at Hillhead, carrying on a tradition that had endured two hundred years and now must end with them. Never had that tradition been more glorious than in its end.

The third person of this story is STEPHEN LEES, old Brewster's grandson. His mother was the old man's eldest daughter, Anne. She had married Edward Lees, the son of a small chemical manufacturer in the nearby town. Edward, a well-doing but not very enterprising young man, had inherited the family business; and, just before the War of 1914, had sold it to a large combine that had retained him in a not very important position. That position had led him first of all to Glasgow and then to London, where his wife died, leaving him alone with his sons Stephen and James.

The boys had both been taken into the company where they were doing very well. Stephen in particular; for at twenty-five he had a salary of £450 a year as a salesman. Several mothers looked on him very kindly and so did their daughters. He was five foot ten and strongly-built, not bad looking, and knew his own mind. Everyone was sure he would be a great success in business: but he himself was not so sure that he wanted to succeed. His friends and his father's friends lived for business and the things it could bring them. They wanted bigger net sales, bigger profits, bigger houses, bigger cars, more expensive women. It was no matter how those things were attained. Good was something that raised net profits; evil was something that lowered them. That was a simple and sufficient morality and they never thought beyond it. Stephen did. When he was a small boy he had been delicate and and had spent a long time with his grandparents at Hillhead. Perhaps he had acquired something of his grandfather's skeptical mind during those impressionable years. Often he found himself asking if his way of living was really worth while. Was anybody any better when he stole a rival's market for lipstick in a Lancashire town? Yet he seemed to be committed to lipstick for life. He was a success, of course, and would be a still greater success: he would stop peddling lipstick and direct the peddlers. But would anybody be any better? If the answer were no, then what would his success be worth? But it was a stupid world anyway so why worry? He couldn't afford to worry. He was going to marry Jane Dorman, and Jane had no doubt about the value of success. She liked men who were effective and did things. She intended they would do great things together. She could help him. Her father was the managing director of the company, and his son-in-law would get every chance. There could be little doubt about Stephen's future, and Stephen knew it; but yet he was not happy.

These three, old Brewster, Mistress Davies and Stephen are the three chief persons in this story: the old man and the old woman representative of a simpler world; and the young man representative of a world in transition. The story will tell how they came together; how they acted upon each other; and how a young man fared in the land of his fathers.

CHAPTER ONE

Morning in Dulwich

IT WAS a fine morning in the middle of July. The sun shone impartially on the green fields of Kent and the great disaster that is London. It even shone through the Gothic windows of Sandringham, that quaint house in Dulwich where the Lees had lived for seven years. At eight o'clock it was shining on the bald head of Mr. Lees as he ate his bacon and eggs at the head of the table with the *Daily Telegraph* propped up against the marmalade. At one side of the table his younger son James was eating bacon and eggs with the help of the *Daily Mail*. A third place, still empty, was laid at the other side and three letters waited there.

The Lees ate in silence.

The father was a nice little man with a fringe of white hair round the bald dome of his head. His close-cropped white moustache was deeply stained with nicotine. He looked a serious and hard-working man, the kind that is always ready to pay for bigger men's mistakes in the name of some philosophy such as the team spirit or playing the game. He was reading the *Daily Telegraph* as if every word were gospel, which indeed he believed.

His son was the image of what he himself had been at twenty-three. He was rather less than middle height. His fair hair was carefully parted, his moustache neatly clipped and his tie the correct pattern of blue and red. He looked a serious and hardworking young man, one of those who get what they want because they never want the unattainable. He was reading the *Daily Mail* on the iniquity of France and agreeing with every word of it.

When they had got to the marmalade stage, the door opened and Stephen Lees came in, wearing a dressing gown. He was quite unlike his father and brother for he was dark where they were fair and he looked bigger in every way. You would hardly have thought they belonged to the same family. The difference would have been greater if he had not looked so pale; for he was recovering from a severe pneumonia as a result of a chill on top of long overwork. There were dark hollows under his eyes, and a weariness in his manner, as if he were tired out by maintaining a precarious hold on the world.

His father and brother greeted him as if glad that he had joined them.

Stephen sat down in his place and slowly opened his letters.

"I couldn't stay in bed any longer. I wanted to see if it were possible that people still caught the 8.41 to town."

"Never been known to miss it," James said, that being the kind of thing he was in the habit of saying.

"You'll be coming with us soon," his father said.

Stephen looked up from the letter he was reading.

"Not for a bit yet anyway."

"What does Clarkson say?" his father asked. He wasn't the kind of parent that opens his children's letters but he always had a look at the outsides of the envelopes and he had seen one from the company on Stephen's plate.

"'Don't hurry back. Things are slack just now. Go away and get well till the middle of September,'" Stephen read from the letter. "Very decent of the man."

His father nodded, very pleased. "The company like like you. If you stick to them they'll stick to you. Besides after that selling campaign in the North you're a made man."

"Pretty hot," James said, for he admired success even in his brother.

Stephen laughed, pleased by his compliments, and

14

opened his second letter.

"Where'll you go?"

"Paris," James said. "That'll put you on your feet."

"No," Mr. Lees said. If I were you I'd clear off to some quiet place where you'll meet some good people. Might make some useful contacts. A young man should never lose a chance."

Stephen looked up from his letter.

"Well, here's one. The Dormans are going to Provence and Jane wants me to go with them. At the end of the week."

James and his father sat up with something like awe on their faces.

"The Dormans," Mr. Lees said as if he were speaking of deity. "You're a made man."

"Two months' holiday from the sales manager; an invitation from the managing director's daughter to go to Provence. Looks like a wangle to me," said James. "Some chaps have all the luck."

Mr. Lees looked earnestly at Stephen. "Dorman must have every penny of seven thousand a year."

"And two Daimlers," James said.

"You'll be going, of course," Mr. Lees said.

"And don't forget to tell them all about me," said James. "Boy, if only Jane had a younger sister."

Mr. Lees considered the situation. "What you should do is to take a taxi into town and order anything you're needing, in the way of clothes."

"And don't forget a book on 'How to Behave in High Society,'" said James.

Stephen smiled at their excitement.

"You two seem quite carried away by the occasion. Maybe it's a pity you're not going instead of me."

James rose and looked at his watch.

"Oh we're going, my son, for the 8.41. Cheerio. See you in Provence."

His father rose to follow him. As he passed Stephen he put his hand on his shoulder. "It's the biggest chance

you've had yet. Play your cards for all you're worth –
and win." He walked away quickly for the 8.41.

Stephen remained thinking, till they had left the
house; and then he rang the bell. Mrs. Sledge, the
housekeeper, brought in the breakfast and he began to
eat. After a bit he opened the third letter and read it
slowly. It was written in a fine old-fashioned hand and
was in these terms:

Hillhead,
Lendrum.
July 12.

My Dear Stephen,

*We were very sorry to hear through your
Aunt Mary that you have been ill. London is a
poor place to get better in. What you need is the
fresh air of Hillhead, fresh eggs and milk, and a
glass of toddy to make you sleep sound at night.
Won't you come and stay with us for a while? You
were fond of Hillhead when you were a little boy –
don't you remember the golden weathercock on the
gable end. I'm sure you'd still like Hillhead though
your grandfather and I are lonely now and the
house is very quiet. They are going to cut the hay
tomorrow and the tea roses are out in the arbour
where I used to play with your mother when she was
a little girl. If only you would come you would give
your grandfather and myself a world of pleasure.
Please give my good wishes to Mr. Lees and your
brother.*

I am,
yours afftly,
ELIZABETH DAVIES.

*P.S. You don't need to have linen sheets unless
you like them better than you used to.*

Stephen read the letter three times, then laid it

beside the others on the table. He did not consider it
seriously. It would of course have been very pleasant to
have looked in at Hillhead and spent a few hours with
the old people whom he had not seen for ten years. But
there was Jane's invitation; and anyway Scotland was out
of the question. There could be nothing there for him.
His future lay in London and ...

Then he remembered how they had led in the hay
from the Lady Park at Hillhead. He was seven and it
was late July. The sun was burning hot. There was
hardly a breath of wind. All day they trailed the coles to
the corner nearest to the steading where the ricks were
built. He remembered how Dan the second horseman, a
giant of a man who was always whistling, put him on
Bess the mare, and led them across to the coles. There
he got down, slipping a monstrous distance over the
glossy coat of the quiet mare. A thick rope was run
round the foot of the cole and fixed to Bess's harness.
Dan cried, "Come up." Bess heaved. The cole rocked
into motion and slid away over the stubble that was
already darkening with the first young leaves of the
aftermath. Then Dan would lift Stephen and, swinging
him high in the air, set him down on top of the cole. So
they, the boy and the cole, bumped along behind the
round quarters of the mare till they reached the growing
rick and Stephen could ride on the mare's back again for
the return journey.

They were brave days of hot sun and cool wind, days
of endless pleasure. When he grew tired and thirsty he
would tell his grandfather and the old man, setting his
fork carefully against a rick would lead him to the Lady
Well for a drink of spring water. The well was in the
corner of the drystone dyke and always reminded him of
a little fireplace with a rudely carved lintel. Where the
fire should have been there was a shallow trough of
water that silently brimmed the worn stones and seeped
away into the field among lush grass and cresses. There
was an old tin for drinking from, a tin that gave the

sweet water a delicious rusty flavour. But those who
were young and supple of the joints got down on their
knees and drank from the face of the living water. That
was exquisite pleasure on a hot day. The cresses and
other green things that grew out of the water wreathed
the small boy's face as he stooped to drink; their cool
wet fingers restored the life that the fiery sun would have
destroyed. When he stood up again the thrilling cold
streams of water ran down his face from his dripping
forelock. He was renewed and the afternoon was his
again, for pleasure.

There had never been such pleasure since.

Straddled across the Clydesdale's back – she was so
round he feared his legs would never come together
again – he could see the men building the ricks. The
coles were drawn in one by one, to Sandy, the third
horseman and Mr. Leslie, the odd-job man, who dug
their shining forks in them and pitched the hay onto the
rick where Dave, the foreman and Uncle Sandy laid it in
order and trampled it down with the heavy, impeded
steps of men walking in deep snow. Thus, all day, the
work went on steadily till all the various operations
seemed to blend into one continuous movement. The
old farmer supervised the work with a fork in his hand.
Not that he did very much. However hot the others
looked, he was always cool enough in his wide-brimmed
straw hat and his flannel shirt with the sleeves rolled up
to the elbows. His job was to see that others worked and
he kept them going with sharp dry remarks that the little
boy did not fully understand but which made him feel
glad they were not addressed to him. The air was full of
warmth and sweetness. The smell of the hay, like strong
China tea, was mingled with the savour of the green sap
from the clover crushed by the heavy passage of the
coles. A million wild flowers growing by the dykes
yielded their sharp fragrance to the heat of the sun. And
at half past three there was added the stronger, sweeter
smell of the harvest ale which the old man dispensed

from a brown stone jar. Then evening brought the dew and the thin mists that rose from the moss. The smell of the hayfield then came over like a mist into the small boy's brain. He grew sleepy. His mother carried him upstairs to his bed in the attic room and his grand-mother sat beside him and laughed about the adventures of the day, and cried baloo to him in a quavering voice. Before the end of the song he had fallen asleep.

Stephen came to himself with a start as if he had wakened from a fair dream. It was a moment before he could realise that he was still in Dulwich where people caught the 8.41 to town.

He poured some more coffee and read Jane's letter again. He tried to think of Provence, or of what he imagined Provence to be like, but the dream was still en-chanting his mind. And suddenly he wanted to be at Hillhead again.

Bright images crowded up out of his memory till their beauty, at the distance of time past, blurred his vision with tears. Brightest of all was the attic room whose walls, distempered a bright blue, met above his bed like the lift of heaven. Night had come gently there with quiet sounds – slow footsteps down in the house, the murmur of distant voices, his mother singing; as if the old house were pleasuring its child. Outside the wind rustled the ivy by the wall, a wandering teuchat cried and an owl uttered its shuddering call from the shadows. Stephen lay warm and safe between his cotton sheets, for he could never abide the unfriendly cold of linen, and told himself fantastic stories of the great world beyond the darkling window. Knights in armour, kings and heroes, moved in the pride of their high estate before him and when he opened his eyes he could see beyond the dark blue window panes the lonely stars wheeling in their courses through the heaven.

Stephen sighed and, collecting his letters, went up to his room to dress. But he made little progress for his thoughts were still with Hillhead and the people who

19

had been so kind to him when he was a little boy.

He thought of his mother dead those five years and
almost forgotten. She had been a gentle creature who
abode in silence and served her household because that
was her duty. She had been kind but she had never fully
understood the value of rugger or the importance of the
cosmetics by which the family lived. She had moved
about her house rather like a ghost; and, as the house
grew always more comfortable, more genteel, she had
been more ghost-like; not insubstantial, but as if she did
not belong to a world where success was stamped with
silver teapots and motor cars were the marks of a sound
morality.

Now Stephen remembered her as she had been in
the summers they had spent together at Hillhead. She
had been bright and happy then. She had laughed with
him and chased him down the garden paths, played
hide-and-seek among the raspberry canes and sung the
old country songs in the evenings underneath his window. She had danced like any girl. When Donald the
second horseman played his melodeon, she and Sally the
maid had danced a reel on the green beside the garden
gate with uncle Andrew and another. How lightly she
had moved over the grass in her long wide skirts, how
rosy red and happy she looked under her dark hair
when the reel was ended.

Stephen, remembering, was suddenly stricken, for
he now realised that she had never been truly happy
away from home. Her body had been in Glasgow but
her spirit had been at Hillhead. So in London: and the
distance between her spiritual and her bodily life had so
weakened the vital union of body and soul that her first
serious illness had killed her. Her children had not been
enough to hold her to life; love for its fruits could not
preserve the tree cut off from its roots.

Stephen felt a profound pity for his mother, a
deeper emotion than he had ever felt before. Pity
changed to love, to an urgent wish to hold her close to

him and tell her how cruel he had been that he had never understood her. His body ached with the sudden access of love and there for the first time he really knew that she was dead. She was dead and there was an end of it. He could never find her and tell her that the golden weathercock was swinging in the west wind and lead her down among the yellow roses where they could laugh together and stand close together, silent and at peace in their perfect love. At that moment, being weak and far beyond himself, he wanted above all things to go back to Hillhead and find his mother there.

Jane called to see him at twelve o'clock.

When she entered the drawing room she looked, as she always did, very up-to-the-minute and pleased with the world. Her hair was waved as if it had been cast in bronze. Her tweeds had been made by an excellent tailor. Her scarf looked careless and expensive. She had the air of having taken pains to do the right thing. Everything about her was in admirable proportion. She had good looks that did not amount to beauty and a fair intelligence that could never be mistaken for talent. She was the efficient daughter of her age.

She went to him quickly, holding out her hands.

"My dear," she said, "you look ever so much better."

Holding her hands, Stephen smiled down on her.

"But don't tell anybody or I may have to go back to work."

"Not before you come to Provence."

"Not even if I have to get pneumonia again."

They laughed and sat down on the sofa.

"There'll be eight of us - Dad and Mum and Dennis and Beryl, the Samsons and ourselves. We're taking both the cars and the Samsons will have theirs. We'll drive all the way to Avignon where Dad's taken a Palace that once belonged to one of the wickeder cardinals. Lots of people will be coming later, very important people with their fingers in all sorts of interesting pies."

21

"Far too good for a commercial traveller," Stephen said with a smile.

She frowned a little. "You're not. Or you won't be long. Dad likes you. He thinks you deliver the goods. After a month at Avignon he's going to like you a lot more."

"The industrious apprentice?"

She replied gaily, "And the master's daughter."

Not so gaily he said, "How we go on and on and up and up."

She looked at him slightly puzzled.

"What a strange thing to say. It doesn't sound like you. Anyway I can't help being my father's daughter, can I?"

"I'm sorry. I shouldn't have said that." His voice sounded tired. "But I suddenly felt that Avignon was all part of the lipstick business and I wish it wasn't."

"You're not going to turn romantic on me, are you?" she said reproachfully.

"Heaven forbid. But it's a holiday, and nobody wants business at a time like that."

"Of course it's a holiday, but it won't do any harm to get in good with people that can be useful to you. Clarkson will be getting an assistant soon, you know."

Stephen did not reply. Taking out his case, he offered her a cigarette and lit it for her. There was a short silence between them. Suddenly she put her hand on his arm.

"What's wrong with you today? You seem to be in a queer mood, I don't understand you."

"I don't understand myself. Don't mind me. I'll get over it."

"But are you coming to Avignon?"

Stephen took a long time to reply. The experiences of the earlier morning came back to him with greater force. The Dormans and their friends seemed unreal; their talk of mergers and loans and selling campaigns meaningless – as if they existed only in the financial columns of a newspaper. A wave of weariness came over him when he thought that he must go on speaking their language and impressing his personality on them. Memory betrayed him; for he felt that he was again the small boy in the hayfield and that the Dormans were native to a different and too formidable world. Then he wished that he were indeed at Hillhead. But Jane was sitting beside him, and she must have her answer.

"I don't know," he said. "I'm sorry."

"And that means you aren't coming." No affected brightness could hide her disappointment.

Stephen caught her up and kissed her.

"My dear. I love you. I'd go to Avignon or the end of the earth for you. But I've been remembering things. When I was very young I lived with my mother and her people on a farm in the north of Scotland. She was very fond of the place and none of us understood that. Now she's dead and I'm sorry. Jane I want to go back there before I forget everything."

"I think I understand," Jane said. "But couldn't you come to Avignon with me first, for a week or two?"

Stephen shook his head. "I must go now, or I'll never go at all."

Jane rose. "I'm lunching with some people at one. Goodbye just now, Stephen. I'm sorry you won't come with us, but if you change your mind..."

"My dear," he said, "you're very kind and I love you very, very much."

He kissed her and she said, "That'll be something to remember you by."

Then she left him.

After he heard her drive away Stephen began to feel that his memories had made a fool of him. Five minutes ago Hillhead had seemed the only real thing in the world. Now he began to doubt it. He had disappointed Jane for – perhaps nothing at all. He had practically committed himself to a visit to Scotland. He had almost thrown away a chance any other man in the office would have given a year of his life for. He felt tired again. He couldn't think, couldn't do anything but stare at an armless Venus on the mantelpiece till, mesmerised, he fell asleep.

When Mrs. Sledge wakened him to lunch he had made up his mind. Before going to the dining room he rang up King's Cross, and booked a sleeper on the night train for Aberdeen. He sat down to lunch, happy.

When his father came home on the stroke of six Stephen was ready to leave. He wore an old suit; his bag was packed; and he had enough ready money to last him a month.

His father noticed the bag in the hall.

"That's right. You're not losing any time," he said, as he came into the drawing room in the quick, fussy way that was his business manner and which usually lasted till dinner time when he became almost human again.

"It's the family motto," Stephen replied.

"When are you leaving?" Mr. Lees asked, straightening the fire irons in the fireless hearth through force of ritual.

"Tonight, at seven-thirty."

"That's quick work. Victoria or Waterloo?"

The answer seemed to mean a great deal to him, judging by the earnest way he asked the question; but Stephen felt the answer he was going to give would mean far more.

"Neither. King's Cross."

Mr. Lees frowned as he did when his typist was stupid.

"But you can't go to France from King's Cross."

"I'm not going to France. I'm going to Hillhead."

His father grew red with anger and surprise.

"Are you mad?" he just managed to say. Then he repeated, angrily this time, "Are ye clean mad?"

Now he had said Hillhead, Stephen felt much

more confident; to his surprise the fact that his father was angry meant very little.

"No," he replied. "Maybe I'm getting sane again."

His father stamped about in rage. "Queer kind of sanity. You get the best chance you're ever likely to get and you throw it away for an old man and an old woman that would be dead if they'd any sense of decency left in them. And what d'ye think *they* can give ye?'

"I don't know. I'm going to find out. And you needn't be angry with me. I've been doing the wise thing so long that it's maybe time I was doing something silly."

"Ye couldn't do worse."

"Maybe not. But I'm going to do it all the same. My mind's made up. My seat's booked. And I'm going."

His father threw up his hands in despair.

"If your seat's booked and paid for, you mean it. I can't stop ye. But let me tell ye this; you're a damned sentimental idiot and if there is a god in heaven ye'll live to repent this day."

"I don't think God'll worry very much what I do," Stephen said with a laugh.

His father's anger changed to pleading.

"But think of your career, man."

"It can surely wait for a week or two."

"Wait. O heavens, man, think what you're doing. With that assistantship coming on, ye can't afford to wait."

"Then I'll be extravagant for once. It's time to go now, father. Won't you wish me luck?"

His father gave him a look of sorrow and disgust. Then he said, "I'll wish you luck – the luck to get sick of the place in a week. And if I know that damned old grandfather of yours, you will. The man's a confirmed bankrupt."

Stephen laughed. "Don't worry, father. It isn't contagious. And I'll be back."

A taxi stopped outside.

Stephen went out into the hall, took up his coat and his bag and opened the door.

His father went after him quickly to make a last appeal but he was prevented by the arrival of James.

"Cheerio, Jimmy. Cheerio, father," Stephen cried. "Be good." He waved his hand to them and ran down to the taxi.

"What's it all about?" James asked.

"About?"his father replied. "Stephen's raving mad. He's going to Scotland."

"To Scotland," James replied incredulously. "And what's he going to do in that god-awful place?"

CHAPTER TWO

Rediscovery

WHEN STEPHEN stood on the platform at Lendrum
and watched the North Express disappearing round the
corner, he ceased to doubt the wisdom of the impulse
that had brought him north. Just as the notice board on
the high embankment was bowered about with rambler
roses, so all the land was fresh embroidered with the
early summer. Not drowned as the south country is
drowned with the excess of its own fertility, but wearing
summer with a comely grace, fitting to its spare though
not ungenerous nature. Down in the haughs the river
twined, silver between the green of the fields. The high
road crossed it by the three arches of a bow-backed
bridge, slipped round a curve to pass beneath the railway line and then followed the gentle rise and fall of the
land to disappear under the western sky. There were
fields on every hand; some pasture where cattle fed in
the young grass; some corn that dipped and flashed in
the sun as the light wind passed over them. On the
higher slopes above the river, plantings of beech and fir
made shelter against the summer's heat and the winter's
cold. Beyond these plantings stood the hills, now delicately veiled with blue; yet never veiled enough to hide
the granite rocks that mocked the softness of the season.
Farmhouses stood scattered across the land; some shel-
tering by great old trees; others set on the steep braes
and torn at by the wind. Everywhere a balance between
man and nature, a balance won by unremitting labour
and often desperately maintained. Looking across the
fields from the high embankment Stephen felt a challenge in that countryside. It was a challenge to action,
to set the pattern of his will upon the fields. For there

on a round hill beyond the river the parish church raised its slender spire from a ring of trees. The men of Lendrum lay buried by its walls; the land stood very fair around them; and they had made it so. They had drained the hollows, they had gathered the stones and built the houses. Generation by generation they had driven the waste land nearer and nearer the stony limits of the hills. Now they were dead and even their houses were dust, but the bright fields proclaimed their immortality. Thus to die must be a little less than death when something one has made lives after. Stephen felt the men of Lendrum challenge him from their graves. They had given him life; let him in turn preserve their heritage.

As it was a mile and a half to Hillhead, Stephen left his bag at the station and set out to walk along the river bank. For half a mile or so the path ran along the side of open fields. Then came the woods of Lendrum House where the old beeches grew out of the river's brim and shadowed the brown water with their sweeping branches.

He seemed to be walking along that path as he had so often walked in summertime when he was eight. Just for a moment he was the small boy in the boots and the corduroy trousers who stood at the foot of the beech tree and cried to the squirrel to come down. But the brown squirrel, who may have known little boys only too well, sat on a high branch, high out of reach, and looked down at him with manifest contempt. More than that, when he tired of pleading and turned to threats, the beast put up its paw to its face. The gesture was one that he understood and resented. He lost his temper. Sticking out his chin as he had seen his grandfather do when things were going wrong in the hayfield, he addressed the beast in powerful words that ill became his piping voice. The pigeons suddenly were still; the wood seemed to hold its breath with horror; and even the impudent squirrel fled into the topmost branches of the tallest tree. Stephen in triumph turned to his mother who was sitting on a rock with her feet in the cool water.

"That settled him, the cheeky devil," he said, trying to imitate Brewster's deep dry voice.

His mother shook her head at him sorrowfully, but she could not hide the laughter in her eyes.

"I'm glad your grandfather didn't hear you," she said. "You've been a very wicked boy to say such things; but he would have been so pleased he would have given you sixpence."

"I'll tell him when I get hame," Stephen said. And he did and he got a shilling. Then his mother pretended to be angry with her father too, but in her heart she was laughing, and Stephen knew it.

On this day seventeen years later Stephen saw her as she had been sitting on a stone with her white feet in the water. She had laughed and cried to him to come out to her across the warm shallows, but he had hesitated on the bank, being afraid of the nameless beasts of the river. Then she dared him and he couldn't bear it any longer. He too had sat on the stone in the crook of her arm, with the river running swift and brown right under his bare feet. The sun warmed them; the wind cooled them and the river sang its unending song. No people had ever been happier since the world began and no one had ever looked more beautiful than his mother. Her short dark hair hung round her pale cheeks from which the rose had all but died away. Her dark eyes were starred with pleasure. Her long bare arm was soft and comforting. They talked and played for hours by the river side. They watched for the noble salmon in the pools. They spied on the brown trout that stayed against the current with a careless motion of their tails. They hunted nests in the prickly undergrowth. They dug arnotts out of the soft earth with their fingers and ate them till their faces were smudged with loam. They bathed and he ran naked through the woods shouting in a frenzy as the west wind ran over him. Sometimes, and best of all in the evenings, they made a little fire of leaves and dry twigs. When the night was drawing in and the last red was dying on the gentle clouds, the small flames leapt beneath their hands and a thin pillar of smoke rose high above their heads. The woods grew dark and eerie; the noise of the river grew upon the stillness. The world stretched away in the shadows towards unimaginable and tremendous shores.

Stephen dared not look across his shoulder. But there beneath his hands was the brave fire leaping through the smoky twigs and there beyond the flames was his mother with her black hair falling about her face and bright lights kindling in her dark eyes. In the circle of the fire she had sung to him, her voice sounding small and thin and sweet as it trembled away into the vastness of the night. Sometimes she had told him stories of the old time when the snow lay six feet deep at Candlemas and the fairies danced at Midsummer's Eve. And whiles he lay in her arms, half asleep by the fire; as they thought their own thoughts in silence. Then the dew began to fall. It was time to go. They stamped out the fire, sorry to kill such warm beauty, and then hand in hand they walked through the wood and over the dewy woods to home.

Stephen came back across the seventeen years to the intolerable sense of death. There were the trees and the river, the dry leaves and the twigs that cracked beneath his feet; there was the hot sun on the water, and the cool west wind and the damp sweet earth. But his mother was dead and he could not show her them that she had loved so dearly. He saw her sitting in their house in Glasgow, in that dusty and decorous terrace where everyone had tea and walnut cake at four o'clock; he could see her, who should have been so gay, sitting silent in the midst of company. He saw her in London, the year she died, moving slowly like a woman in a dream, seeking something she could never find. They had given her doctors, they had given her cures, they had given her all except the one thing on earth that she desired. And when she died they buried her in Dulwich. Now he understood what she had been seeking all those years. In Glasgow and in London she had had before her eyes a vision of those woods and fields. Now he understood, but she was dead and he could never tell her. Nor could he himself recapture the lost years. They were not the old woods, now they were empty of her laughter. It was she who had drawn the impulse to delight from them and he had caught his own delight from hers. But now she was dead and how could he hope to find his way back to the heart of the woods and the fields without her. He seemed to be reaching out to his childhood across the seventeen desert years, with only a ghost in his memory to help him. It seemed impossible that he would ever make contact with the child he had been; impossible that he should ever find his way to the heart of the things his mother had so greatly loved. Almost he would have turned back, but he knew the thought was treachery. The challenge of the men in the kirkyard at Lendrum came clear into his mind and would not be denied.

As he came out of the wood he saw Hillhead on the slope above him, with its gilded weathercock riding triumphant on the gable end.

The farm lay within the sweep of the Lendrum woods. On the east the Holme Wood sheltered it against the sea wind. The river flowed round a wide curve in front; and, beyond the river, row after row of fields swept up to the hills. There were fourteen fields on Hillhead, ranging from the Lady Park of thirty acres to the little Rabbits Run of ten. The steading would have been about the middle. The house stood in front, with its broad garden before it and then the Lady Park sloping gently to the river. It was a tall house, a plain house of three stories and many narrow windows. It was bare of porches or dormers or any such adornments but it was so old that it might have grown out of the earth like

the grim hills that it so nobly fronted. The house and
the garden were enclosed in a low wall. The farm
buildings ran out behind – the byres and stables built
round a covered court, with the barn next the cornyard
and the cartshed beside it. It was a compact place
shaded by a few beech and ash trees. A burn, coming
down out of the wood, filled the mill dam and then
leaped down a stony course by the garden wall. In
everything it was as it had always been and, the defiant
weathercock on the gable seemed to say, as it would
always be.

The Lady Park was in hay that year. About half of
it had been cut, some that morning. The hay, thick with
clover, lay drying quickly in the hot sun and filled the air
with a heavy sweetness. Stephen missed something at
first. It was the sound of the mower. Then he saw it
standing at the corner next the steading and he realised
that it was the dinner hour and that the men and horses
were taking their rest. Dinner would be ready at twelve.
He looked at his watch. It was five to the hour. Instinc-
tively he smartened his pace and walked quickly round
the mown hay to the garden wall. He climbed over,
feeling guilty as he had always done, for there was a
wicket gate round the corner; crossed the flower bed
and the small lawn and walked up to the parlour window
in the west gable of the house. The window was open.
Looking in, he could see a table laid for two. A great jug
of roses glowed on the dark sideboard against the far
wall. And in the easy chair beside the window his grandfather sat reading the morning paper. There was a
frown on his forehead and his mouth looked grim above
his short white beard. He was not enjoying the paper. A
maid came in with a bowl of soup. That made the old
man look up. He saw Stephen at the window, gave him
a long searching look and then said to the maid –

"Babbie, set anither place."

"Good morning, Grandfather," said Stephen.

The old man gave him another look then nodded.

"Come in, man, Stephen. Ye've been lang in comin hame."

Though Stephen did feel strangely at ease, as if he had indeed come home, the meal would have been a difficult one had Miss Elizabeth not been at the foot of the table. Stephen was curiously shy of the old man; perhaps they were shy of each other. There was so much that might have been said and words did not come easily. Fortunately there was nothing that Aunt Elizabeth loved better than such an occasion. She had the nature that glories in a crisis. Now she did the honours of the table like a great lady. She asked Stephen about his father and brother and regretted she had not seen them for so many years. She talked about the West End of London where she had been in service with her husband. She recalled his mother as a beautiful girl and told a story about him as a little boy. All the time she saw that his plate was filled and that he had everything he could wish for.

Stephen fell in love with her. She had such dignity, there was such warmth in her husky voice. They became friends at once, to remain friends for ever. At the same time she brought Stephen and the old man out of their shyness, by casually recalling adventures which they had shared. There was the day when they set fire to the great bush of whins by the mill dam. It was a mighty bush of Saharan dryness and it had gone up in a tremendous roar of flame. Stephen had cheered it with all his power and his short hair stood on end with the thrill of it. Unfortunately a poor hen had been nesting in the heart of the bush when the flames broke out around her. Giving an agonised screech she burst from the bush and flew over the dam with her tail feathers on fire. Stephen and his grandfather looked at each other in the deepest consternation, as they saw the foolish bird being consumed before their very eyes in mid air like a fearful omen. However her flight came to a sudden end in the waters of the dam which quenched her burning tail. As the dam was low she scrambled ashore without much difficulty and staggered away to the henhouse in a sorry state indeed. Her life had been miraculously saved, but Stephen and his grandfather knew that the mistress would want to know all about why one of her pet Minorcas had lost her tail. So they had a long consultation in which it was decided that Stephen should take the blame because his grandmother was fond of him and would let him off scot free. Stephen didn't like the idea very much, but they tried it and it worked, and ever after he had a great respect for his grandfather's wits, but little for his morality. The story made the young man laugh and the old man smile.

Aunt Elizabeth put her arm on Stephen's arm and said, "Your grandmother was very fond of you and would have forgiven you anything." Then she looked at the old man and added, "Both of you."

"She had plenty of practice," the old man said.

Stephen did not reply. For a moment he was conscious of his grandmother in the room – the grey haired woman with the worn hands who was always so kind and always a little tired. The ghost seemed very slight between the old man and the woman in the room, for she had never had their splendid lust for living, but he knew that her love had been no less than theirs though it had never been spent on foolish things.

Suddenly the old man turned to Stephen with something like warmth in his eyes.

"Will ye tak a dram?" he asked.

"Wi pleasure," said Stephen.

"We'll all have one," said Aunt Elizabeth.

She went to the sideboard and brought out the old square whisky bottle and the glasses. With a slight ceremonial gesture she set them before the old man. He poured out three good measures of whisky.

"Well," he said looking over the glass at Stephen, "here's good health."

"And welcome," said Aunt Elizabeth with a gracious smiling bow towards their guest.

The old man drank his whisky down in one long deliberate mouthful. Aunt Elizabeth did the same with a look of perfect joy upon her face.

"Here's health to both of you," said Stephen and drank down the neat spirit that gripped him by the throat.

When he put down his glass again there were tears in his eyes, and he could not be sure that they had been caused by the whisky.

"And now we might walk in the garden," said Aunt Elizabeth rising from the table. "Your grandfather has a few things to think about and would like to be alone."

"Aye," said the old man grimly, "she means I'm gaun tae sleep."

Stephen did not know what he could say for he was sure the old man was not in love with growing old. However Aunt Elizabeth saved him.

"If you come with me, Stephen, she said, and led the way out of the room.

Stephen looked back and nodded to the old man who nodded shortly in reply. Stephen closed the door and went after Aunt Elizabeth.

The broad-shouldered young man and the stout old lady made a slow promenade of the garden under the high noon sun. Out through the yellow roses by the front door they walked arm in arm and across the wide gravel walk to the lawn. Down one side of the lawn they went, admiring the hollyhocks, the irises, the black-eyed susans and a dozen others that grew in the broad east border. Along the end they walked by the strawberry beds and the raspberry brake. Now and then they stopped to watch the mower cutting round the Lady Park and filling the air with its whirr and clatter. The horses strained against their collars; the driver sat far back with the reins gripped in his hands and the man on the tilting seat flourishing his rake with a regular motion

as he swept the heavy swathe on to the cutting board.
Stephen felt a little ashamed to be idle in the garden
while such brave work was being done in the field below.

"You'll spare me this one afternoon," said Aunt
Elizabeth. "There'll be plenty of work for you before
that heavy crop's won home."

He squeezed her arm gallantly. She smiled like a
Cleopatra of old and toyed with the gold spectacles
hanging at her breast. They walked on slowly along the
west border where the small herbs and kitchen vegetables grew. Then the flowers began again and continued round into the north west corner. And in the recess
formed by the wall and the gable end of the house there
was the arbour overhung with honeysuckle in flower.

They walked into the arbour and sat there in silence
and peace. Bees from the hives at the foot of the garden
worked contentedly in the flowers above their heads. A
pert robin looked at them curiously, then hopped away.

"Your mother loved this place," said Aunt Elizabeth,
and there are few left now who care.

Stephen realised the loneliness of the old people
who had no one to come after them.

"When I got your letter I couldn't stay away," he
said.

Aunt Elizabeth pressed his arm to her side. "I'm
glad you came. Your grandfather is lonely. I'm afraid
he's losing heart. He has only the farm now, and what
does it matter, since he won't have it much longer. But
you know Hillhead and you can get him to speak about
it. We're very silent sometimes, for you see our plans are
all behind us. It will be pleasant to have someone who
loves Hillhead and is not preparing to die."

There was no self pity in Aunt Elizabeth's voice; her
pity was all for a greater thing.

"It is so sad that all this must end," she added and
she made a small gesture with her hand that seemed to
include the whole life of Hillhead and all that it had been
for its two hundred years.

"There's no one?" Stephen asked, though he knew the answer.

Aunt Elizabeth shook her head. "Andrew is dead. Sandy is dead. Your mother is dead. Mary and Ann never cared for the place. They were glad to get away to the towns and they will never come back. Nor will your cousins."

"That leaves Jimmy and myself."

"And you have your own work to do."

"Yes," Stephen answered. "I suppose I have."

"All things come to an end," said the old lady, "and ten years after this what will it matter? We have been a long time here."

She said it as if she were confident that the dead don't mourn, and that the passing of one family was a small thing in the greater sorrow of destroying time.

But Stephen was young and it hurt him to think that what had seemed eternal should take on the habit of all mortal things.

"It is fate," Aunt Elizabeth said. "Now I must go inside. I always waken your grandfather with a cup of tea. We will have it in the parlour and then you can ask him to show you the farm."

He rose and gave her his arm. Looking up, she said with a smile - "I'm glad you've come."

After tea Stephen and his grandfather went for a walk. The old man moved slowly, stopping every now and then to look at the fields or the hills or the sky. He said little, but Stephen felt he was quite pleased to have his company. Though it was a brilliant afternoon, Stephen could not enjoy it, for his mind was full of Aunt Elizabeth's words and he could not help seeing the contrast between the old man and the prime of the year. His grandfather was very square but his broad shoulders were bent, and he walked with one hand in the hollow of his back, heavily, as if his spirit were too tired to meet the fiery challenge of the season.

As they walked along the side of the Lady Park they heard the mower stop. There came the sound of swearing. The driver reined in his horses sharply, pulling them back on their haunches; the man on the tilting seat jumped down; and the machine was dragged out.

"Something broken," the old man said, annoyed. He wrinkled up his eyes as if trying to guess what could have happened and thinking how to meet the occasion, so that no valuable time might be lost.

The horsemen cleared away the hay from the cutting board. Stephen could see them detach a bit of the machinery and then examine it leisurely, as if they had all eternity before them.

He looked at the old man, expecting some violent action; for he remembered how he had loved to ride the whirlwind and direct the storm twenty years before.

But the old man did nothing.

"We'll be haudin on," he said. "There's aye something wrang wi that lot. They were born wantin."

He turned away and walked slowly towards the house.

My God, but he's growing old, Stephen said to himself and followed sadly after him.

After supper in the little parlour the old man said; "Ye've a bag at the station? We'll yoke the gig and gang doon for't."

So they yoked the bay pony into the gig and set out through the woods to Lendrum Station. The old man drove, leaving the reins slack and letting the bay trot at her own sweet will. Sometimes he passed a word about a field of oats; sometimes he recalled an old neighbour with "Auld Jimmie's deid", or "Sammy's dafter than ever"; but mostly he just sat quiet, looking steadily before him from under the brim of his square felt hat. It was not an unfriendly silence. As the old man and the little boy had driven together on many social occasions about the countryside, so once more they were driving out together on a fair evening in July, and to Stephen it was as if the lost seventeen years had never been.

He got his bag from the station and they set off home again by another road. This led them through the village of Lendrum where the war memorial stood on an island of dusty grass. The pony was walking as they passed and, turned to gold by the last rays of the sun, the long list of names on the granite shone out, with this one at their head:

4TH GORDON HIGHLANDERS
ANDREW BREWSTER ... SERGEANT

"Bloody fool," the old man said dispassionately.

Stephen felt his bones grow weak; for the whole tragedy of Hillhead seemed to be summed up in those two words.

The sunset was filling the Glen with rosy light when they got home. Long shadows lay across the fields. The air was full of the heavy smell of the clover. There was hardly a sound but the distant cry of the rooks in the Holme Wood and the mumbling song of the river.

Dead tired and drunken with the need for sleep, Stephen drank the mixture of whisky and honey and cream that Aunt Elizabeth had prepared for him. Then, saying good night to the old man, he followed his aunt upstairs to the big east bedroom.

When Elizabeth had seen that everything was in order for him, she took him into her arms and kissed him.

"Good night, my dear," she said. "I am very happy now that you are here."

CHAPTER THREE

The Old and the Young

STEPHEN SPENT the next few days in a strange sweet melancholy of present and recollected pleasures. Hillhead had a thousand corners - the dark dusty chambers under the mill, the green forgotten thickets of the wood, the secret warm places hedged about with whins along the burn side – where he had played as a child and which still had the power to make his heart beat faster and his head turn fearfully at the sound of his own footsteps. Loitering in those still places, he found the memories of the earlier years. Then he would feel a boy again and suffer all the fears and exultations of a child alone in the tremendous size of the world.

On the day after he went to Hillhead his grandfather and Aunt Elizabeth left him to find his own amusements – the old man because it was not in his nature to make a fuss of anybody and Aunt Elizabeth because she guessed his memories would be his dearest friends. It was a pleasant exercise but sad, for the last thought was always that something very gracious had passed and could never return. Round any corner he met the ghost of his mother – hiding from him in the gooseberry bushes during their long afternoons of play, sailing his boats on the dam under the arms of the old beech trees, or dancing on the green in front of the house when the wind was shaking the petals from the yellow rose. It was a sad thing that those could never be more than joys remembered. One sadness begot another and he found himself pitying the old man whose time was so nearly run. There was nothing at Hillhead but sadness, for all powers and bright immediate pleasures were in the past. But there was something so big in

the old man and in the long story of the farm that it took
away the sharper edge of sorrow. At the end of two days
Stephen was regarding Hillhead in an elegiac mood, a
grave sweet sadness.

Aunt Elizabeth was always delighted to talk to him
about anything in the world and the old man would
sometimes cry him in to speak about the strange ways of
the English, whom he regarded as a comic race. But
when Stephen went downstairs on the third morning, he
was a little shy of approaching the old man, for he realised the great difference in their age and he was afraid
he might be a nuisance. He need not have been afraid.
The old man, having examined him thoroughly for
three days, had decided that he was worth his company.
He invited him to walk up to the wood side to look at the
swedes in Sandy's Park and on the way he talked to him
about the fields and the crops they were passing. Then
he got on the subject of drains, for draining was his great
enthusiasm. As he talked about the drains on the farm
he came nearer to emotion than Stephen had thought
possible, from his usual air of dry detachment. He drew
plans of them in the dust. He followed them down the
fall of the land, stopping every now and then with his
head to the side, as if he could hear the small voice of
the running water five feet down under the earth. He
followed them and made Stephen follow them to their
mouths in the deep sedgy ditch that ran along the sides
of the fields.

When he got to the ditch he said, "Man, she should
come oot at the third post tae the left o' the roddin tree."

They found the rowan tree standing in solitary
grace on the bank, but, looking down, they saw no trace
of the drain among the rank growth in the ditch. The
old man stood thinking for a minute; he looked back
along the field with eyes that took in the exact shape and
significance of every hillock; and then said, "Man, she's
got tae be here, for here I put her."

He climbed down the bank with a lot of damning

under his breath. Standing in the ditch with the water over the tops of his boots, he searched about in the long grass till he gave a shout and called Stephen down beside him. "There she goes, man," he said; and Stephen, now well down in the ditch beside him, saw the end of the pipe running a trickle of cold pure water. With their feet against one bank and their backs against the other, they looked at the ceaseless miracle of the drain.

"Thirty year since I laid doon that drain," the old man said, "and many's the quarter o' corn she's meant tae me. Look at her, man – runnin as clear as the day I made her."

"You might well be proud of it," Stephen said with awe and admiration in his voice.

"Proud," the old man replied with a laugh. "I couldna be prouder if I had made the water tae."

When they got back to the house for dinner Aunt Elizabeth spotted their wet feet as soon as they entered the parlour.

"Drains and ditches," she said to Stephen, shaking her head at the old man. "I might have known it. But that's always the way with your grandfather. There's nothing in his head but drains and he's never happier than when he's poking about in them. He's a fair disgust. If I didna ken him for my ain mother's bairn I'd think he had been misbegotten on a mole."

Then she rounded on the old man and told him that it ill became his years. "Puddling in ditches at your age, man. Ye should hae mair sense. You'll get rheumatics again and be groaning in your pain and crying for hot cloths and whisky. All for the sake of a drain. Get off your boots and your stockings this minute, John – you too Stephen."

She stood over the old man with her arms folded and a chastening gleam in her eyes. The old man hung his head till she had had her say then he looked up at her with a cozening smile.

"Daena be sae hard on's, Betsy," he pleaded with

42

great meekness, like a little boy who knew he had been bad.

Aunt Elizabeth uttered a Royal "tchach" and went out of the room.

The old man looked round at Stephen, gave him a quick wink and then bent down to take off his boots.

When Stephen laughed out loud, the old man looked up again and said;

"Aye, laddie, ye can laugh; but ye maun aye lat them hae an antrin rage if ye want tae hae peace aboot the house."

"You know a lot about women," Stephen replied.

"I should," the old man said.

As they took off their wet boots, *There was a lot in that reply,* Stephen thought to himself.

The small incident of the drains brought Stephen and the old man into greater intimacy; for the old man had, as it were, made him free of his great enthusiasm. At the same time he had invited him into conspiracy against Aunt Elizabeth – the delightful conspiracy of two men against one woman. Hitherto the old man had been pleased enough to have his grandson about the place; now there was a warmth in his manner, a dry warmth but heartening, which made Stephen remember the old days when they had conspired against his grandmother in raiding the strawberry beds.

Late in the afternoon, when the old man had been wakened from his sleep with a cup of tea, he proposed another walk. This time they went across to the young corn in the Holme Park. As they walked through the corn, Stephen tried to remember something that was in his mind, something associated with that field. Then suddenly he said, "Of course. There used to be a road through this park that we walked on the way to school."

The old man said, as if pleased that Stephen remembered, "Aye there used tae be but we ploughed it up. There's nae bairns gaun this wye noo."

Stephen did not know what to say, for he did not

know what the old man might be feeling. He himself was smitten with the sad state of the childless farm and he was sure that the old man could not be less.

Therefore he was more than surprised when the old man began speaking about the road as one who marvels on the strange chances of life.

"It was a queer thing when we ploughed up the bairns' roadie. Man, it didna seem richt. As lang as there's been Brewsters here there's been bairns, for we've been a michty race tae breed, both in o' bed and oot o't."

That was an aspect of his family's history that Stephen's father and aunts mentioned with every disgust; and he laughed to hear it spoken of with appreciation.

"The bible commands it," he said.

"Aye but we were aye willin tae dae't for the love o' the thing. Yet time's brocht us low enough. I ploughed up the roadie. It was wasted. I didna like the mockery o't."

He laughed a dry laugh, mocking at his splendid amorous youth that had left so little good fruit to his old age.

Stephen felt then, as he was so often to feel not only with the old man but with other people of the countryside, that their words always implied more than they said.

"If Andra hadna been a damned fool and gaen tae that war it micht hae been different," the old man continued. Then he went on with a touch of anger in his voice, "What had he tae dae wi their wars? They tell me he was killed savin civilisation – as if the bit that's left was worth the trouble. Well, he cam by a fine end but it would hae been a sma loss tae the world if he'd bidden at hame and taen a wife tae his bed and farmed his ain laan like a' the Brewsters hae done before him."

He waved his stick impatiently, dismissing wars and glory and all that nonsense. Stephen felt surprised beyond thinking; then he was relieved that the old man could speak so easily of what would have been thought his heart's sorrow. Being accustomed to mothers who had given their sons for their country (lives not theirs to give) and the vast communal sorrows of the English, he found it a little heartless, a little strange and more than a little exciting.

"But you have other children," he said. "Aunt Ann and Aunt Mary."

"Aye," the old man said casually. "There's Mary and there's Ann."

Stephen felt himself challenged. "They're your daughters," he said.

The old man cocked a wicked blue eye at him.

"But they daena think me respectable."

"They just would," said Stephen for he disliked his aunts.

"O – ye daena like them?"

Stephen hesitated, then dared to say it – "I daena."

"Neither dae I," the old man replied with complete agreement, "and wha has a better right than me that am their ain father?"

They walked on together in the silence of perfect sympathy for a minute or two, then the old man said with considerable feeling –

"Upsettin bitches."

Stephen could only answer, "yes." His aunts' epitaph had been written once and for ever more.

After a bit, "Six generations o' bairns hae gaen up the roadie tae the school," the old man said, "and what's at the tail o' the lang procession – Ann's bairns and Mary's bairns wouldna step aff the pavement in case they fell in the glaur. Dammit man, the bairns that used this roadie grew up tae be big men that set the countryside in a roar o' rage; but Bella's loons and Mary's loons gae ye naething but a cheep frae their clippit tongues. Eh, it's a guid job the auld Brewsters are deid, for they'd be sorry tae see what we've come tae."

Stephen protested, "But dammit, there's me."

The old man gave him a look that made him feel as if he were stuffed with straw and very poor straw at that.

"Ye was game eneuch aince," he said. "But that was a lang time ago."

"We'd maybe better change the subject," was all that Stephen could say.

"O aye," the old man said. "There's some things that'll no' bide thinkin' on."

But dammit, Stephen said to himself, *I'm not going to stand this from anybody.*

"And who's to blame for what we are?" he asked, hotly.

The old man laughed with amusement. "Ye would fight would ye?"

"Indeed I will. When I'm miscalled I fight back."

The old man looked over the green tops of the Holme Wood along the ridge.

"Why should ye?" he asked.

"Didn't you?"

"Na," the old man said. "I've aye been ower busy daein things tae worry what folk said about them. Though I'm sure they said plenty," he added in appreciation of his neighbours.

Before Stephen could say anything the old man went on;

·"But what folk think is nae worth bothering about. It's mostly jealousy."

Stephen had heard people say that before, but the force with which they said it had shown that they really cared a great deal for public opinion. The old man dismissed public opinion as something to which he was wholly indifferent; and Stephen felt that he himself was included in the public opinion. His anger changed to wonder and admiration. *It's amazing,* he said to himself, *there the old devil stands, as old and as square as his house. The winds can blow through his beard but he doesn't care. People can hate him and rage at him but he laughs at them in his own mind. Men can die but he thinks no more of them than of last year's corn that went to the mill. He loves nothing on earth but this farm – it's the one thing that keeps him human; for it is inhuman to stand so far apart from the rest of human kind.*

They had reached the Holme Wood by now. This was a long planting of ancient beeches along the brow of the land, great tall stems that rose straight for fifty feet then branched out into a firmament of bright green leaves through which the sunlight blazed in brilliant stars of the afternoon. At the roots of the beeches there grew only small thickets of rowan about the height of a man.

Old Brewster climbed the dyke into the wood and began searching in one of the thickets. After a bit he cried on Stephen to help him uproot a sapling.

"Ye maun hae a staff if ye're tae be countryman," he said.

When they had pulled the rowan they sat on the mossy dyke in the sun while the old man shaped the staff with his knife. He cut away the branches and all the roots but one, till a straight stem was left with a natural bend at the top for the hand. Very carefully he whittled away all roughness. He was so completely absorbed in his job that he did not speak a single word for half an hour.

Stephen sat on the warm dyke and looked across the farm. At first he was uneasy because the old man did not speak to him, for he had lived so long with people who could not leave each other alone. But in a little while he became grateful for his freedom. It was so pleasant to be with someone who didn't want to make him do anything or believe anything or be anything except himself. More than that, in the old man's detachment, in his independence of spirit Stephen felt a challenge to be very much himself, to show a like detachment and independence. *Dammit,* he said to himself, *I'll do both. I'll go my own way, thinking my own thoughts and doing as I please. I'll...* But then he realised he hadn't any thoughts in particular and didn't know where he wanted to go; so he just lay on his back and watched the dance of the green leaves against the distant blue of the sky.

The old man having finished the stick, presented it to Stephen with a grim little speech. "Now daena ye be usin it tae chase the cattle."

Stephen was highly honoured by the present, for he knew it was a proof that the old man liked him. Curiously, all that he could say was, "Thank you"; but as they walked homeward again he thought to himself, *He's maybe not inhuman after all. He's pleased to have me here for company. And I'm pleased to be here.* But while he thought that, he knew the words did not begin to express the effect the old man's company was having on him and the new friendship that was growing between them.

They walked home slowly, each leaning on his staff; and anyone seeing them would have known them to be of the same blood; for Stephen was so completely at ease with the old man and so much in harmony with the rural scene that he took the old man's slow, deliberate country motion, and walked at the old man's side as if he had never been away from his native fields.

That night before he fell asleep Stephen wondered if he had been right in thinking of his grandfather as the poor old done man and next day he had yet more reason to question his judgment. In the afternoon they took another walk. This time they crossed the Lady Park between the heavy bouts of the mown hay. Then they passed into the lea park beyond, where forty young cattle were grazing on the thick white clover. Over among the cattle the old man pointed his staff at this one and that, saying, "There's a good stot," or "Nae timmer there." Stephen, because he was naturally curious, asked why the beast was good and the old man explained its points. Stephen soon found himself deeply interested and the old man, sensing that interest, made him free of the experience of seventy years. He had sympathy as well as knowledge. He moved quietly among the beasts.

The square black heifers raised their heads from the grass when they heard him coming; but a word or two, spoken in a low caressing voice, laid the fear in their shining eyes and they returned to their grazing, assured. Then the old man went up to them cautiously and, still murmuring to them, ran his hand over their quarters, They stood for him, as if pleasured by his touch, while he told Stephen where the flesh should be firm and the bones sweetly set each to the other. But when he invited Stephen to see for himself and Stephen, going forward, set his hand to the beast's flank she became uneasy and moved away, leaving Stephen with the thrilling touch of the warm body and the living hair.

"They don't seem to like me very much," he said, disappointed.

The old man laughed. "Och, they need a lighter touch than a woman."

So they went round the cattle one by one and Stephen could only marvel at the way the old man seemed to lose his age. His voice grew stronger, more easy, as he spoke about his beasts. He knew all their history from the day he bought them and he seemed to know exactly what he would make of each by the day he sold it. The weariness that Stephen had fancied he saw in him was now quite gone. It was as if his hands could draw some strong life from the beasts to refresh his age; and the green sap of the clover under his feet were renewing his brittle bones. Stephen saw him as the little boy had seen him seventeen years before, the master of fields and cattle, and he thought what a fine thing it was to be a man.

When they had made the round of the beasts they went down to Jamie's Well in the corner of the field.

Set at the meeting of three fields so that it served all of them, the well was a valuable amenity on a farm where water was scarce. But it was more than an amenity; it was a legend. The Jamie who had dug it was the old man's uncle. It had been the great enterprise of his life, and he had been so proud of it that he had spent all his spare time looking down its fifty feet to the gleam of the still water. One night Jamie had been to market where he had drunk too much strong porter mixed with too much stronger whisky. On his way home he had made his pilgrimage to the well. No one saw what happened there; but when the cattleman drew water next day he found Jamie's hat floating in the first bucket. His body was recovered a little later. It all happened a long time ago and it had become a legend which the old man had often told to Stephen when he was a boy.

The well was enclosed by a stone wall about three feet high and long troughs radiated out into each of the three fields. Stephen leaned on the wall and looked down to the face of the water. Ferns and other green plants grew far down the well maintaining a precarious and secret life in the crevices of the stones. Far away there was a circle of reflected light on which vague shapes half formed and disappeared. When Stephen was a child he had imagined the face and drowned corpse of Jamie and they struck him with such wild terror that he jumped down from the well and ran for home. Now, seeing these shapes again, something of the old fear came back but so diminished by the passing of the years that he only shook himself to remember that they were not true.

"Are ye mindin about Jamie?" the old man asked. "It was a great day when we hauled him up and a lot o' whisky was drunk by even."

Stephen looked at the well set so cunningly at the meeting place of the three fields and giving life to each. It was beautiful, being so perfectly adapted to the end it had to serve, yet it had been the death of the man who had made it. And because Stephen feared death he felt a sudden loathing, almost hatred of the well.

"It's a wonder they didn't fill it up," he said, turning away quickly.

The old man threw away the match with which he

was trying to light his pipe, then he laughed and said, "Man, man, it would hae taen mair than Jamie tae spoil that sweet water."

He let the bucket down, then pulled it slowly hand over hand till he held it dripping before him.

"It was maybe death tae Jamie," he said, "but it's been life tae generations o' nowt sinsyne."

He poured the living water, water that fell shining through the sunlight, into the dry cattle trough. A black heifer, hearing the clank of the bucket and the noise of the water, came towards them with her long tongue licking her dry nose.

Stephen took the bucket from the old man and, forgetting all about Jamie, drew water till the trough was full. By that time the black heifer was drinking in long noisy draughts of pure animal delight.

"That's what Jamie made it for," the old man said. "Come lat's be steppin on."

They walked along the Stane Park by the narrow footpath which the children of the district used on their way to school. Halfway along the bottom of the field they came on the great rock from which the park took its name. No one could tell how great the rock was, for only a broad shoulder heaved out of the young surrounding corn like the back of a whale from a quiet green sea. On the highest part of the rock the old man's grandfather had hollowed a round shallow cup and in it he had placed a ball carved out of granite. The ball must have weighed a good three hundredweight and stood on the tip of the rock like some memorial of a far older time. Some people thought it a religious relic, a phallic symbol or something of that order. And indeed it might have been, for the old man's grandfather had put it there to keep in mind his wedding day.

"Auld John did that," the old man said. "And ye'd wonder why. They say he was so fond of it that he wanted to be buried aneath it."

"But he wasn't."

"Na," the old man replied as if the idea was unthinkable. "They couldna bury him aneath the stane for nae man has ever come tae its foundations. And they wouldna bury him aside it for the plough would hae gaen rivin through his banes."

"But they could have fenced him off."

"A sinfu waste o' guid black laan," the old man said.

Stephen looked at him, puzzled by his manner. *A sinfu waste,* he had said and there could be no doubt that he meant it. Yet Stephen suspected something else, a slight dry mocking laugh, and he could not be sure if the laugh was meant for himself who would have wasted good land or for them who would have thought it waste. It was something new in his family to find a man who could believe a thing and at the same time laugh at himself for believing it. *The old devil laughs at everything,* he said to himself.

They walked along to the end of the field. When they came to the gate the old man looked back at the twenty green acres over which the wind passed lightly in shining waves.

"I've seen worse," he said. "If we get the weather we'll get the corn."

He turned and led the way onto the Stane Dyke.

The Stane Dyke was one of the greater glories of Hillhead.

When the first Brewster went to Hillhead most of the land had been waste. Year by year each Brewster had won it acre by acre. Millions of stones of all sizes had to be cleared away before the plough could pass and these, as they were gathered, had been built up in a great dyke that ran between the fields. The labour that had gone to the making of that dyke passed imagining. It was eight feet high, twenty feet broad at the top and ran straight for six hundred yards between the fields. It was a finished work for the sides had been squared off, the top had been levelled and a flight of narrow stone steps had been built in to the end. Over all it had been turfed, or wiry grass and moss had taken root with the passing of time. After the grass and the moss came small plants and shrubs – whins and broom and the wild flowers of the countryside. Now it was a long promenade from which a Brewster, standing on the labour of his fathers, could see the fields that labour had adorned and which he held in trust for them that might come after him.

Stephen and the old man walked along the dyke till they came to the upper end which was finished in a high mound. Climbing by a flight of narrow stone steps, they sat down on a big flat stone from which they had a clear view of the whole farm, the river and the hills beyond. The old man sat in silence with his hands on the top of his staff and his eyes intent, under the brim of his bonnet. When he had examined the whole farm, field after field sloping gently down to the Lady Park and the river, he pulled out his pipe and, while filling it, said –

"The day my father died, as soon as I kent the last breath was oot o' his body, I cam up here and sat on this stane and lookit aboot me and then I said, 'Man it's mine – a' mine.' And I've come up here ilka day since, and it's still mine."

Stephen felt a little shocked – or thought he should, "You weren't sorry for your father?"

The old man hardly bothered to reply. "He was deid."

Then, having lit his pipe, he began again the long intense survey of the farm.

Stephen looking with him understood, a little, why it should have meant more than a dead father. Gently the land fell away below them within the arms of the woods. The house stood in the middle of the fields with the byres and the barn behind it and the planting of beech and fir by the garden wall. It looked very old and settled as if it were one among eternal things; very bien and comfortable with its cornfields and its cattle in pasture and the small figures of men working among the hay. It was a desirable kingdom guarded from the world by the river and the trees, a kingdom that Brewsters had made, and the gilded weathercock on the gable end proclaimed their sovereignty. What young man, succeeding to that fair kingdom, could waste his thoughts upon the dead? For in those fields that mortal men had made there was a life greater than the life of any mortal man. What the Brewsters had begun could never come to an end. Stephen felt proud, splendidly, absurdly proud, that his own people had thus magnificently wrought. He remembered all that the old man and his mother had told him long ago about his ancestors who had cleared the waste; of the unending labour, the ditching, draining, and dyking, of the stones that were gathered and the trees that were planted, of the bad times when all the labour seemed for nothing and of the good times that hardly repaid the losses of the bad; of the men and women who had spent their lives on something that they were born to serve and who died when they could serve it no longer. He was proud, almost beyond bearing, when he thought of the men who had fashioned Hillhead after the pattern of their own wills, who had tilled the fields and enjoyed the increase and made proud vain displays in the glory of their nature. They had served their fields; they had been good husbandmen but they had never been slaves; they had taken their pleasure wherever they could find it. Secure in the knowledge and the wealth of their fields they had been their own masters, admitting death their only equal; and they had drawn the game against him in the end for they had left sons to live as they had lived.

But Stephen remembered that Aunt Elizabeth had said it all must end. Looking at the old man, he felt a sorrow as great as his pride had been. For the old man who had had two sons now had none and the kingdom of the Brewsters in Hillhead must fall to nothing. The emotion stirred the young man more deeply than anything he had felt in his life before, far more deeply than

he had the power to bear. So he did what he could to
escape that sorrow. He wanted to think of lightsome
things; or better, to lie among the broom in the heat of
the sun like a dog tired of hunting. But he could not
escape so easily. His vision of Hillhead had changed in
the last few hours. He no longer dared to pity the old
man for there was nothing weak or pitiable about him.
His emotion was all for his family, for the Brewsters who
must be parted from Hillhead. And most of all his
sorrow was for himself for he had already begun to
suspect that away from Hillhead he would be less than a
man. Once again he felt the challenge of the dead men
in the kirkyard at Lendrum, a challenge to impress his
will upon those fields as they had done, a challenge that
he could not deny and yet dared not accept. He lay on
the warm grass and shut his eyes, but he still saw the old
man sitting alone on the hill.

Gradually there came a change in Stephen's idea of
Hillhead...

On Saturday afternoon, as he lay among the grass
by the mill dam, listening to the trickle of water from the
sluice and the grasshoppers purring in the high noon's
heat, he ceased to remember his childhood and could
not think of London. He could not lay hold of his later
years for they had no substance. They slipped between
the fingers of his thought like the tangled ends of a
tiresome dream. He let them go willingly and was content to lie in the sun. It was a great joy to lie still, listening to the small voices in the grass, while a fair white
cloud was blown across the upper sky. Maybe because
he had a fanciful turn of mind, he could almost feel the
sun drawing up the life out of the strong earth and some
small part of that life pass into his own weary bones. He
rose feeling strong as a young tree after the rain. His
feet were light as if they had come alive at the touch of
the young grass beneath them. He was all a quick sensation of pleasure at the light on the fields, the shadows on
the hills and the pricking of the sun on his face.

Come evening there was a cold swift shower of rain which passed quickly, leaving a clean jewelled world under the golden sunset. Stephen went out into the garden and walked slowly over the wet grass. He could smell the wet earth and the high savour of a thousand flowers refreshed by the rain. A tiny breath of wind passed over the garden. It shook the drops from the laden branches and made a low rustling sound which moved Stephen profoundly. He felt a rise of life in his bones. He wanted to leap over the garden wall. *By God, he said to himself, I can't bear it. I can hear things growing myself in this damned garden. I'm bewitched. I'm enchanted. I'm mad.*

He felt that things far too great to be understood were happening to him. He became conscious of forces far too great to be reduced to words. He seemed to grow till he was twice the size, till he was as big as all the world. *I could play ball with the earth,* he said to himself. *By the living God I could stot it on the roof of hell and make it dird against the stars.* Then he heard a blackbird singing overhead in gratitude for the cool mercies of the rain. It was a new song to Stephen, the song of a full wame and a merry heart. He listened but before he could learn its secret he heard the river going down through the darkling woods. Now the sound of the many waters was high in the stillness of the evening, a high calling sound that came to Stephen like the voice of his enchantment. He ran out of the garden and followed the voice down to the woods. There in a grassy place he threw off his clothes and dived into a pool. The water flowed over him cool and brown, or fell from him in a rain of dull gold when he broke its surface. The light wind played with his bare body, making him shiver and dive back again into the kind dark of the water. As he played there night came swiftly, the woods grew dim and still. Warm winds succeeded the cold; the smell of the hay came down heavy and sweet as a woman's cloak from the Lady Park. Stephen made a little fire and dried himself and

56

lay there naked on the the soft earth as he had lain in the old days when he was a tiny boy and his mother had laughed at his fat round belly. But he did not think of his mother, for the thought of her was no longer essential to his pleasure there. He was alone in his world with the small flames of the fire, the fluted tower of smoke, the river, the dark wood and the small owls that hoo-hooed unseen in the branches. *And here I am,* he said to himself, *here I'm playing like a young dog in the spring. The wood's mine and the river and all the hours of light and darkness. They're all mine for my own pleasure, for me and for me alone.* He was light and renewed as he walked across the fields to home. Those last few days he had been living in the company of ghosts, of all the Brewsters who had set their landmarks on the farm, of the old man as he had imagined him, of his dead mother and of himself in his thoughtless years. Now he had got free of ghosts, to be himself. A few days ago he had gone into the house as a child after long wandering through the dark seasons of the year. Now he went as his own man, to all the adventures that he might find there.

The change was due to the old man, for even in that short time he had shown Stephen the way to his own splendid independence, and indomitable spirit. Tam, the foreman had spoken to Stephen about the old man that afternoon. "He's a hardy auld devil. Though he's growin auld and bent o' the back, there's something in him that keeps him tae the road. Some men that hae lived the life he has wouldna be able tae spit ower their whiskers at his age. But Hilly's still the mester."

Stephen could feel his mastery. As in the field among the young cattle the old man seemed to draw strength from the land and the creatures round about him. His powers had diminished but his spirit was as strong as it had ever been and he never risked despair by trying himself beyond his limits. When he could do he did. What was beyond him he let go with a laugh as if denying its importance. He never pretended that he was

57

not growing old. He accepted the passing of his vigour as he had accepted the full glories of his prime. It was all in a man's life and all life must end. He would enjoy what he could as he had always done. So with Aunt Elizabeth. She regretted nothing for herself. She had had her pleasure and paid for it. She would still buy her pleasure as long as she had breath to spend. Together they were above pity. To Stephen they were the figures of great tragedy marching towards an heroic end.

Going home that night he had no thought but to worship them and serve their memory for ever.

An old lady of incomparable presence

CHAPTER FOUR

Hay Harvest

STEPHEN WAS soon drawn yet more deeply into the
life of the farm. It was grand haymaking weather, for
the rain kept off and the heavy dews that fell overnight
were soon dried off by the sun that blazed all day
through the cloudless heaven. But everyone knew that
the good weather would not last. The Howe might be
fair in the noon-day sun but no one thought thereby that
the gods were showing their love for men. It was all
chance and every morrow might bring the rain that
would batter the lying hay into the muddied earth. So
the old man looked at the fair but capricious face of the
sky; then at the forty acres of hay; and fell into an
anxious fever to have it gathered. Stephen, catching
something of the fever, asked if he would be allowed to
help.

"Ye may indeed," the old man said, "for he would
be less than a man that could stand idle at sic a time."

Stephen, being still convalescent, was given the
raking as the easiest job in the field. Now that was a fine
ploy, one to make a man's heart glad. Seated high up on
the rake behind the round quarters of Bell, the young
roan mare, Stephen gathered the hay into long rows
across the field. The east wind came up the Howe from
the sea, a dry salt wind with the tang of distant places.
The fields and the woods and the blue hills swam in the
haze of the bright afternoon. Grasshoppers purred, the
river added the burden of a drowsy song and a lark
uttered an incredible sweet rhapsody, like a singing star
hidden in the eye of the sun. It was good to drive the
roan mare on and on, to listen to the dull tread of her
hooves in the stubble and the rhythmic clank of the rake

as it rose and emptied and fell again. The sun burned
the back of his neck. The wind cooled his body like
flowing water. Seeing, hearing, smelling – every sense
gave him a keen new pleasure; and as the hours wore
on they wove themselves into a harmony to which he
moved in time as to an old country measure.

Meantime the rest of the men were building the
hay into coles. They looked much alike at a distance –
stocky men well set into their corduroy trousers, with flat
bonnets on their close-cropped heads and the sleeves of
their dark shirts rolled up above their elbows. Their
movements seemed leisurely almost to the point of
laziness yet they made good speed with their job and
they soon built a long row of coles along the side of the
field. Then Stephen, having decided too soon that they
were lazy, had to change his mind and study them more
closely. After a bit he saw that their ease really came
through art. They made no useless movements as they
gathered the hay onto their forks and placed it on the
growing cole so that it fell immediately into the correct
shape. In their leisurely but efficient actions there was
the flowering of a technique perfected through a
hundred years.

Like any man in a new job, Stephen felt very shy of
those who knew so much about it and he wished not only
to impress them with his own competence but also to
become friendly with them. So far he had not made
much progress. During his five days about the place he
had spoken to them casually; and, while they had always
been civil enough in reply, he knew that they distrusted,
perhaps disliked him as a stranger. So far he had not
found the way to their friendship.

When he had set out on the rake that day he knew
that they watched him with an intense interest that was
not all friendly. *And why should it have been,* he asked
himself, for he was an amateur trying to do their job. So
he swore to win their good opinion by making no mistakes. As a horse rake is not a complicated piece of

machinery, he acquitted himself competently at least, and when they stopped for dinner he noticed that they were more friendly to him than they had been so far.

After the coles were built Stephen had to rake about them, to gather up any hay spilled in the building. That brought him into close contact with the men and he soon began to appreciate the rich diversity of their natures.

Tam, the foreman, was a serious-minded man who was determined to get on. The pride of his work was in his bones. He liked things done right and he damned well saw that they were done to please him. Being the foreman he was the pacemaker; and, being an intelligent man, he set a pace that the others could maintain with comfort. Occasionally he would tell Stephen to drag the hay nearer the cole and Stephen was surprised at the easy way in which he gave the order. *Well, well,* Stephen said to himself, *there's evidently going to be nothing of the young master about me as far as they're concerned.* He obeyed the order as nearly as he could and took a pride in trying to please the foreman. He recognised Tam as a keen spirit, a man who knew his job.

Willum, the second horseman, was a complete contrast to Tam. He was a comfortable snoozy man with short legs and a great broad bottom that was obviously made for sitting on. He was good at his work and, as he had immense reserves of energy, he was capable of endless exertion; but he preferred to lean on his fork, to gossip about the countryside and tell long bawdy tales about kitchen maids and the harvest moon. Tam was a masterful man and his mind directed his actions; Willum was all appetites and a coarse, rich love of kind.

The third of the elderly hands was Davy, the cattleman. He was thin and wiry but by way of compensation he had a magnificent red dragoon's moustache that completely overshadowed the lower part of his face and a pair of ridiculous feet that pointed east and west. "A wee mannie hung on to a muckle moustache and feet"

he had been called by old Brewster and there was indeed
something inadequate about him. His awkward gait
always made him seem to have difficulty in keeping up
with the others; and looking at him, you would have
said that life was a little too much for him. He seldom
spoke but worked on steadily, smoking a very short and
very black clay pipe that gave his red moustache the
appearance of a burning bush, that yet, miraculously,
was never consumed.

Jock, the third horseman, was a careless young
devil of twenty-two. He was handsome in a way for,
though his features were rather blown-about, he had the
splendid ease of youth. The land had not broken him to
its own slow measure yet. He had no wife but several
sweethearts. The road was never too long; the roof
never too steep for his adventures. He had no mind
beyond his pleasures; no ambition except to tell a better
story than his neighbour. The girls loved him and
feared him and could not resist him. He was a great one
for singing and whistling for he had a native music in
him. He played the melodeon too and the penny whistle
and the trump. He was everything that Willum liked to
think he had been when he was twenty-two and free of
women.

The youngest of the men was no man at all but
only a halflin. Sam was seventeen and growing quickly,
so quickly that he was all length and no breadth, like a
straight line. His red hair was clipped short except
above his brow, where a tuft stuck up on end as if he had
been badly scared. Indeed, Stephen thought he might
have been, for the talk that went on around the coles was
enough to frighten any youth come but lately into the
world of grown men.

They kept up a great speaking in their slow voices
but Stephen noticed that the talk dried up when he came
past. However he had not been a commercial traveller
without mastering a certain technique and at the first
chance he told them a story that had gone down very

well in the broader parts of Lancashire. Bawdry being universal, it was no less appreciated on Hillhead. Willum followed it with a detailed account of a merry mating in a churchyard and Jock capped both with a personal experience that would have sent Casanova back to school. When they had all enjoyed their laugh – even Jock the loon, for he was learning quickly – Stephen felt a change in their attitude towards him. Their suspicion of a stranger had abated. He was on the way to being accepted as a man and brother. Willum in particular having got his shoulders comfortably settled against the wheel of the rake, was looking forward to a long and pleasant exploration of this new source of stories; but Tam, although he liked a story himself, remembered that there was work to be done.

"Weel, come on, boys" he said. "Haud on there wi the rake. We've nae time tae lose on sic a day."

Stephen gathered up the reins and stirred the mare into action, too quickly for Willum who lost his balance and fell on the stubbles. However as he fell on his well-appointed nether end, he was able to join in the laughter at his accident. He was a simple man with a simple sense of fun.

Stephen heard the laughter as he drove the rake across the field. It was not a very kind noise, yet it pleased him, for he felt that he had made friends with the men. And Willum, looking after him regretfully, before he returned to his work said –

"He's nae sae bad though he daes come frae a toun."

And Tam said, "Aye but ye maun mind that he was country-bred."

The foreman's word settled it. Stephen was accepted.

Bawbie the maid brought them their piece at midyoking, an old Hillhead harvest custom. Down she came from the house in her bright print dress with a can of tea in one hand and a basket of scones in the other. *How charming*, Stephen thought, *she completes the picture. This jolly afternoon. The wind. The sun. The smell of the hay. The rustics toiling with their forks as if they were creatures grown out of this their native soil. And now neat-handed Phyllis tripping down with her basket and her can. It's like a pastoral. A pastoral with bagpipes instead of a beribboned flute.*

A very rude pastoral he found as they sat round among the hay eating the floury scones and drinking the strong tea that she had brought them. She was a beautiful girl after the country style with a spring in her step and a rare weight in her bones. Her black bobbed hair shone sleek with brushing, her grey eyes and her uneven teeth were bright with health. Her cheeks were ruddy; her bare breast freckled by the sun; her body firmly knit under her tight print dress and her legs as round in the thigh and tight in the ankle as the legs of a young blood mare. By no means unconscious of her beauty, she stood in the centre of the ring of men and every one of them, even Jocky the loon, thrilled at her power. She was a woman, young and desirable, the finest game on earth. They began to tease her with her own womanhood.

"That's a braw dress ye've on," Tam said. "It's like a gairden o' flooers."

"Heh," said Willum squinting up at her with his merry brown eyes, "and I wouldna mind bein' the gairdner."

The girl flushed a lovely dark red like a deep rose in bloom.

"Ye'll never get the chance," she said and Jock said, "You" with a laugh that consigned Willum to the dustheap along with all old married men.

Willum retorted with a sly insinuation, "Maybe somebody's been there afore me wi their shears."

And so the game went on. Stephen, listening, felt that it was a game played for high stakes. It was more than that. In the immediacy of impulse and reaction it was an essential part of country life; like the excitement of a ring of stallions around a young mare. When

Bawbie returned to the house he noticed that all, and Jock in particular, looked often at her across their shoulders. And how, he asked himself, should he explain the new zest with which they all worked during the next half hour. Could it be that the tea, strong though it was, had been so potent?

As he came to know them better, it seemed to him that they were obsessed by women.

Jock and the loon took their meals in the kitchen and lived in the bothy, a two-roomed cottage on the edge of the cornyard. There was a stone seat at the bothy door where you could sit in the evening and look along the Howe to the west where the brave peak of the Ben stood out against the fire of sunset. Sometimes the married men came up from their cottages in the lythe of the Holme Wood, or the boys from the neighbouring farms came in. Then they would all sit around the bothy door and speak for hours about the way of their world. Because he knew some good stories and because he could tell them of a world that was far different from their own, Stephen gradually won a place in their society. Because he talked freely to them, they talked freely in return and he learned more about them in that hay harvest than another man would have learned in a month of Sundays.

They had a great sense of character. They would talk for hours about their horses evoking the character of this beast and that as if they had been human beings. *Bell now was a lazy bitch that would hae likit her feed in her bed in the mornin. The muckle roan on the other hand was that inquisitive he slept on his feet in case anything might pass him. Sall was a hard-workin dacent craiter like a crofter's wife, wi aye anither foal in the spring, as canny as a man could wish for.* They had great stories of the beasts' sagacity – how one would never pass a public house and how another always hurried home when rain was coming because she didn't like to get wet: they had a passion for them. They cared for them better than they cared for their children.

They talked a great deal about their work. Some jobs they hated, such as pulling neeps on a frosty morning. But of others they talked with pleasure and pride. They liked the harvest, the reeshle of the corn in a drying wind and the fine sight of a cornyard full of comely ricks. They boasted of the harvests they had gathered and they praised the good farmers with whom they had worked. For most of them were real countrymen and they would have been unhappy away from the land.

But most of all they talked about their neighbours and about women in particular. Their passion for horses was nothing to their passion for people. Nothing happened in the countryside that was not discussed at the bothy door. They went into committee over every event and appraised its worth. If somebody had brought off a smart deal they enjoyed the superior wit that had won the advantage and derided the inferior that had had to pay. They loved stories about bluff and strategy; and sharp practice, provided it was not too smart, won their highest admiration. Especially if the sharpness were shown in the pursuit of women. What stories they told of pursuit and capture, of desperate adventures upon housetops, of beds that creaked in the night and brought out fathers with loaded shotguns in their hands. *My god,* said Stephen to himself in awe and wonder, *their lives are nothing but a monstrous begetting of children. They travel the roads like stallions. They creep along the dykes at night like Tom cats. They jump upon the hillsides like goats, wagging their beards in the face of all morality. Begetting and begetting and begetting till the land is full of their bastards and there isn't a maid left under the wanton moon.* They made a rare talk of the old sport and there was great laughing at the bothy door. But what happened to the women? Stephen asked. O they had their bairn and if they were clever enough they got the man as well. If they didn't get the man? Then some old woman took the bairn for a few shillings a week, the mother went her way, the father went his (though he had likely done so five months before), and then they set to partners again. Again, again and again for generation upon generation, begetting upon a broom bush in the fiery heat of the blood. A man will be young and hearty and what comes of it but bastards. Well, let them come; there's always the open road to another parish and all's to do again as keen and fresh as twenty. Stephen had heard a lot of talk about women in his time, from the wistful imaginings of the adolescent to the confidences of the super-salesmen adept in chambermaids. But he had never heard anything like those stories of tempestuous passion told in slow voices that rose and swelled in rich appreciation of rowdy lust while the day went out and twilight filled the Howe with a softly veiled beatitude.

Well, it's a queer world, he said to himself as he went in to bed. *Here's this garden of roses and carnations and fifty other flowers whose names I'll never remember. The dew is gathering on them and filling the air with a sweet smell. Intolerably sweet, for I cannot bear it. The things it would bring into my mind are beyond imagining. Divine shapes and forms that pass just outwith the eye of my brain and tantalise my blood with strange desires to do, to be, something, somewhere. But are those shapes divine or evil? Willum and Jock and the lads from the Mains have walked abroad on nights as gentle. They have heard the little wind that runs through the leaves and smelled the sharp savour of the thyme. But they were stallions and Tom cats and lecherous goats. The beautiful small voices of the night so exquisitely quiet whispered to them only of the ruin of maids. So why not to me for I am a man of these woods and these fields as they are. I move quickly across the green because the pulse of my rising blood demands relief in action. Now I smell the sweet honeysuckle subtly intertwined with the scent of roses. God but it's a damned tormenting world. It is so beautiful, so full of flowers and green shady walks through the woods and fields of young grass blown up by the west wind. Surely if nature could speak to a man and a man had ears to hear her there would be no more suffering in the world. Willum lives among the hand-*

*some proud young beasts and the gallant graceful birds and the
plants that grow to flower yet he is only a bag of tripes and
appetites. There is nothing I can see within the compass of my
eye that is not beautiful yet the men who live here can be gross
and wanton. And this excitement that is stirring my blood to a
strange desire for action what shall I call it? God? or a
Woman? Will I jump over the fence and go adventuring across
the dewy fields. O, God knows. I think I'm tired. I'm not strong
enough for this ruthless way of living. I think I'll go to my bed
and Willum if he wants can go adventuring alone.*

Taking a deep breath of the tantalising night
Stephen went up to bed.

Willum, however, would go no more adventuring.
He had a wife and eleven children at home. Stephen
often walked down by the two cottar houses where he
and Davy lived with their multitudinous families and was
heart sorry at the poverty he saw there. They were
mean cottages to begin with – each a but and a ben with
a little room behind – and their tenants had done nothing to improve them. Such amenities as they had – small
gardens enclosed by thorn hedges – had been so
neglected as to increase the general disrepair. Nothing
grew in them but a few old stalks of kail, a fine collection
of weeds, a broken bedstead or two and the ruins of a
bicycle. However there were plenty of children, all of
them ragged and dirty. They could hardly have been
anything else, for the cottages had no bathrooms and all
water had to be carried from a spring a hundred yards
away.

One evening Stephen saw Willum lying at the foot
his garden while half a dozen of his smaller children
played around. Poor Willum was trying to rest after a
hard day in the hayfield, but the children gave him little
peace. They climbed onto his chest, they pulled his hair,
they punched him and pulled him and tormented him,
they turned somersaults on him while their little brown
bottoms affronted the sunset sky. All he could do was
growl at them and smack any round bottom that pre-

sented itself to his hand. He was overpowered by his own fruitfulness. *So that's what it comes to,* Stephen thought. *Poor devils.*

When Stephen had been a fortnight at Hillhead and had become almost as friendly with the men as if he had been one of themselves, Willum invited him to a spree in the cottar house.

"Aye," Willum said, "it's my auldest loon, Bob. He's gaun tae be mairriet. Like mony anither he's been haein a bite afore the grace was said and the lassie's needin mairryin."

"Hard luck," Stephen said, for it seemed all a little sad.

Willum laughed. "Ach what aboot it. Aince he's mairriet he'll maybe bide at hame. Weel, the lassie's a kitchen quean at the place where he's fee'd and he's bringin her hame the nicht tae lat her see's. This bein' the first mairryin in oor hoose, the wife and me thocht we should mak a spree o't. We're haein Tam and his wife, and Davy and his wife, and Jock and the loon in. And there'll be a bottle and a mealy pudden and maybe a reel tae settle the drink. And man, Stephen, we jist thocht ye micht like tae come tae. It maybe willna be muckle aside the nicht life o' London but I promise ye it'll be a richt country splore."

"Man, it's an honour," Stephen said.

Willum smiled all over his brosy face. "Fine man, fine. Come and bring your best thirst wi ye. Man o man what a nicht this nicht will be." He went away licking his lips at the thought.

When Stephen told his grandfather that Willum's oldest had stepped aside with the kitchie maid, the old man just laughed and said, "He's daen nae mair than his father did afore him. If it wasna that the bairns keep on comin there would be little mairryin in this countryside. Weel, see and enjoy yoursel; and ca canny wi Willum's daughters. They're a' het in the bluid, the hale lot o' them."

"O, I think I can look after myself," Stephen replied with a laugh.

"So ye think," the old man said, "but there's something aboot a warm quean and a dewy nicht that wiles awa the wits frae a man."

Well you should know, Stephen said to himself; and to the old man, "I'll take care."

He got a keen ironical look which seemed to sum up all the mischances of our mortal life, then the old man said, "Ye'd better tak something else. There's never enough to drink at a cottar's party, so look in the press and see if there's a bottle."

Stephen found a whole bottle of whisky.

"Tak that in your pouch," he said, "and if ye speak Elizabeth fair she'll maybe gae ye a hen for their table."

When Stephen told Aunt Elizabeth about the marriage she shook her head.

"Another of Willum's? That's the second in a few months; but the last one, poor girl, didn't get married."

"What's happened to the baby?" Stephen asked.

"Mrs. Willum has it. Only three years since she had the last of her own and now she has to begin nursing a new generation. And she's got four other girls. You know, my dear, babies come far too easy in this part of the world. If nature had made it more difficult to get babies, the quality might have been better. O well – have you told your Grandfather?"

Aunt Elizabeth nodded in approval of the bottle. "He always does. There never was a man who enjoyed a party more, whether it was a marriage or a christening or a funeral; and I think by the look in your eye that you'll be fit to take his place."

"I'll try."

Carrying a parcel of cake and sandwiches under one arm and the bottle of whisky under the other, Stephen set out for the party in the evening, ready to enjoy a new and, he hoped, diverting experience.

Willum met him at the door and took him into the

kitchen that seemed to be full of men, women and children, packed in behind a table where an oldish raivelled woman was cutting sheaves of loaf.

"Good evening," said Stephen. He laid his parcels on the table. "Here's something from Miss Brewster with her best wishes to you all, and here's a bottle of whisky from my grandfather in the hope that you'll all drink his health."

Mrs. Willum flourished the bread knife. That and her fleeing grey hair made her look like one of the witches in 'Macbeth'.

"There now," she cried, "ye ken the wye tae come tae a pairty. Haud ower some o' ye and lat him sit doon."

She waved the breadknife at the mass of people sitting on the bed in the corner. They parted and she pushed Stephen down among them, between two young women who giggled hysterically.

Then there came the sound of footsteps outside and a young man put his head in at the door. The company greeted him with a roar of welcome.

"Mither," he shouted back. "We've come. What hae ye for the tea?"

"Mealy puddens," his mother cried. "Come in and bring the lassie."

He entered, half dragging a pretty girl who looked very frightened.

"This is her – Jean," he said pushing the girl face to face with his mother. The rest of the people in the room held their breath as the old woman and the young one stood over against one another. To Stephen it seemed that the girl found something hostile in the silence. She shrank as if the whole world were passing judgment upon her.

Then the old woman, having looked her over from head to foot, flourished the breadknife again.

"So ye're the lass that's gaun tae mairry Jock, are ye? Weel, I'm his mither and that's his faither. And

that's Elsie and that's Bob and that's Jimmie, and that's
Mary and that's Kate and that's Alec and that's Erchie
and that's wee Jess and the baby there's Mary's ain wee
Nell that hasna gotten a faither yet and is never likely to
hae ane. Noo that ye've had a look at's a', what d'ye
think o's?"

The girl looked dreadfully confused in the heat,
the crowd of faces and the dim light from the paraffin
lamp. She could only get out –

"O, I think ye're fine."

Willum smacked his lips delighted. "Boys," he
said. "She thinks we're fine."

Mrs. Willum laughed not unkindly. "It's a good
job, lassie, because ye'll see a lot o's yet. We're great anes
for keepin together."

"Aye," said Willum, "We're a' here together like
the wifie's ae coo."

Out of sheer nervousness the girl joined in his
laughter and the others followed.

The family seemed to have decided that she would
do.

They made a place for her beside the fire. Then;

"Stir aboot, boys," Mrs. Willum said, "and we'll hae
supper."

They steered aboot, Stephen doing what he could.
He found their shyness of him soon disappeared in the
confusion. When they were all seated round the table
the mother brought a lump of beef and a string of mealy
puddens from the pot. While she divided the portions
she kept up a run of conversation mixed with threats.

"It's nae ilka nicht we hae a spread like this and it'll
be a lang time afore we hae anither. Tae tell ye the
truth, we're clean subbed-up till the term, but when we
heard Jock was gettin' mairriet, – Jess, ye little devilock,
keep your thoom oot o' the butter – I jist said 'Tae hell
wi poverty and gaed straight doon tae the Lendrum
butcher. So here we are. What this nicht'll cost I daena
ken and I daena care for I haena the money tae pey

for't. Erchie, gin ye daena stop suppin the jam I'll gae ye a clout wi the tattie chapper. So neighbours fa tae and mak the maist o't and then we'll hae a rammy."

No shyness remained by this time and the noise grew in proportion as the meal progressed. The Willums were letting themselves go. Everybody talked at full pitch, banged plates, fought with each other and had a good old time – all of them, even Mary the seventeen-year-old mother of the month-old baby. When the supper was over Stephen found himself admiring the bastard child along with its mother and Jean. After they had discussed its bonny face and all that, Mary suddenly held the child close to her.

"Ye're ane o' the lucky anes," she said to Jean. "I'm gaun back tae my place on Monday."

"O it's a shame," Jean said, "And the wean'll bide here?"

Mary did not reply. She suddenly rose with the child in her arms and went through to the back room.

Jean and Stephen exchanged a quick glance. "Puir thing," Jean said, as if she were thinking more of what might have happened to herself than of what had happened to Mary. Then Jock slipped his arm around her waist and whirled her away.

The girls had cleared away the table. "Come awa noo," Mrs. Willum cried, "there's only five pence in the hoose till term time but we've meat and drink tae laist till mornin. What say, lads? Throw the table intae the bed and hae an echtsome."

"Aye, aye, aye, Mither," they cried. They threw the table on the bed, Jock struck up a tune on the melodeon, and they set to partners.

A cottar room is not a big room and the amount of floor space is sensibly decreased when it contains a double bed, a dresser, some chairs and twenty people. Yet a space was cleared and the eightsome began. It was dancing in the raw. The dancers shouted and whistled. Their boots dunted and scuffled on the hard stone floor.

Dust rose in clouds. The spectators clapped their hands in time with the music. The dance seemed to last for ever, because when one fell out another was ready to take his place. Bob played on and on, changing the key and slipping into variations of his own until his very soul danced upon the keys. The father and mother sat upon the bed immensely proud and delighted with their sons, their daughters, Jean, their friends, the rammy and everything. They had few comforts and fewer moments of magnificence but in the very splendid love which they gave their children at need and in such nights of roaring riotry they found justification of their glaury days.

When the reel stopped through the exhaustion of the dancers one of the boys produced some bottles of beer, Jock brought out a bottle of whisky to toast his girl, Willum opened the other bottle to toast the master, and Mrs. Willum with great parade discovered a bottle of pungent port for the women. They drank and they danced and they drank till Stephen grew dizzy and drunk and shouted with the rest of them. The whole world was full of a riot and madness, a glorious din that went on and on like eternity and time had become a mad melodeon that mazed their tireless feet.

Sometime in the morning Stephen went out with one of the older girls. It was a cool night, wet with dew, and they shivered after the heat of the room. The girl went close to him in the crook of his arm. She was warm and cosy against his side and young and eager and mad. When he kissed her she grew warm and enfolding. "Goodbye night," he murmured to the stars with his face among her hair. But then the door opened and spilled out Willum with Tam and Davy and a bottle. The girl broke away from him with a short laugh and left him swaying under the ample night. The men, seeing him, came up with the bottle and insisted that he drink with them. They returned to the house singing "Annie Laurie." The bottle was empty.

Stephen went home at half past three. When he

came to the spring where the cottars drew their water, he soused his head in the chilly pool and took a long drink to wash the taste of whisky from his mouth. Now sober enough, he walked home slowly through the dead still night. He was utterly tired and empty of all sensation. Like a small child that had been making a great play in the fields he was already half asleep and he could think only of the cool mercies of his bed.

When the hay was all in the cole they cut the peats. The moss belonging to the Lendrum estate was at the furthest corner of Hillhead in a low-lying fold of the land away up beyond the Holme Wood. Each tenant had his lair from which the peats had been cast for generations. Now the moss was going done; modern fireplaces were not suited to burning peat; and only a few of the older tenants still worked their lairs. So the moss was overgrown with heather and saughs and small shrubs. Old workings had filled up with slime over which the grass grew so thickly that a man might not know what he had stood on till he was in it up to the shoulders. Only the Hillhead lair and a few others remained in decent order.

The casting of the peats was Stephen's introduction to real hard work. The men went in pairs. One of the team cut the peats from the bank with a long flat spade, slicing them out from the bank in wet black slabs of a uniform size. He placed the slabs deftly in a flat barrow without sides, so that their ends were all in a precise alignment. When the barrow was full the other member of the team spat on his hands and wheeled it away to the far side of the lair from which peats had been cut in past years. There he deftly tipped the barrow so that the slabs of peat fell out and stood on their ends. The next barrow load was tipped against the previous one, thus beginning a row of peats that was continued along the side of the lair. When that row was finished another was begun, and so on till the floor of the lair was full. Both the cutting and the barrowing of the peats was hard

work. Stripped to his shirt, the man with the spade
sweated with the force of driving it into the wet peat.
Stripped to his shirt or further, the man with the barrow
sweated with driving the draught of sodden earth over
the uneven ground. And, as if the heat of the sun was
not enough, there were a million insects to plague them
– midges that rose in clouds from the moss waters and
the vicious clegs that stabbed them to suck their blood.
Jock barrowed for Tam, and Stephen and the loon for
Willum. All day they kept at it, with an hour off to eat
their piece, since it was too far for them to get home at
dinner time.

Though Stephen had only half a man's work to do,
he found it was more than enough. His arms ached as if
the weight of the load were tearing them apart. His back
and legs grew sore and his feet grew tender with the hot
uneasy ground. Times without number he went to bathe
his head and shoulders in a pool of wine red water and
each time he felt he could not rise from the ground
again. But he knew that the others were watching him.
He could not give in and by the exercise of his will he
did not give in.

At last the evening came and he went home be-
mused with tiredness. Aunt Elizabeth had a bath waiting
for him and that took some of the weariness out of his
bones; but after supper he could hardly rise from the
table and as soon as he sat down in a chair by the parlour
window he fell sound asleep. It was with great difficulty
that Aunt Elizabeth could waken him at ten o'clock for
his bedtime drink of whisky and cream and honey; and
it was with even more difficulty that he dragged himself
up to bed. At five next morning when Bawbie wakened
him he felt he would never rise again. But *Dammit, I'll
not be beaten,* he swore to himself, and not without many
deep groans he won to the moss with the rest of them.
There Willum, as if to try him, began cutting peats with
incredible address and Stephen for pride's sake had to
spit on his tender hands and bend his back to the bar-

row. It was agony; but even such agony comes to an end; and by eight o'clock the worst of the pain had disappeared. As the day turned over he began to take pleasure in the exercise. Strength that he did not know he possessed came into his bones. He straightened his shoulders and made the barrow jump over the heathy tussocks. Often he was back before Willum had filled the loon's barrow and then he had a precious minute to fan his face with a docken leaf and pass a joke with Tam and the others. *By God,* he said to himself, *this is the life...*
This is the life to sweat the fat from you and bring your belly in. When you're hot and the sweat is running off your shoulders, the west wind comes flowing down the moss like an invisible bright sea to cool you. There now I'm swimming in the waves and they smell, as an island sea should smell, of heather. Sink me, but I could jump on the back of the wind and ride him like a young horse across the silver birches. By the Lord God in his Holy Heaven I'm strong. I stand upon the earth. I am its master. The blood is running swift and strong in every vein of my body and every pulse of that blood is life. By the Living God I am alive.

CHAPTER FIVE

To Church in the Morning

ONE SUNDAY morning the old man said, "Stephen, laddie, what about you and me gaen tae the kirk?"

"Well," said Stephen rather embarrassed, "I'm not very much of a one for religion."

The old man laughed. "Gaun tae the Kirk o' Lendrum has naething tae dae wi religion."

"Then what is it?"

The old man thought for a minute then he replied slowly, "A custom o' the countryside maybe, like fairs and markets, and it never daes a man nae ill tae keep the customs o' his country."

Stephen went to church.

Going to church was no common occasion for the old man and it involved an elaborate ritual. His preparations began as soon as breakfast was over at nine o'clock. Calling for Aunt Elizabeth he went upstairs to his bedroom. There, having settled himself comfortably in a chair by the window, he lit a sixpenny cigar (It was only on Sunday mornings that he allowed himself such a luxury): and, while blowing out great clouds of smoke, he inspected his wardrobe. This inspection was carried out with a high seriousness which Aunt Elizabeth enjoyed just as much as he did. First she brought out the white linen shirts from the long bottom drawer of the wardrobe. They were dazzling white shirts with glossy starched cuffs and fronts and they crackled when they were unfolded. After infinite deliberation the old man chose the one he wanted and the others were replaced in the drawer. Then Aunt Elizabeth produced the socks. Then the collars – broad old-fashioned collars with points four inches long, rather like those the Eton boys wear. Then the boots – four pairs of old and faithful servants, graduated to the severity of the season. Then the ties – silky blacks and greys, to be drawn through a gold ring instead of being tied in the modern way. Then the handkerchiefs in size and design like a Paisley shawl. Then the suits – the black and the grey, the broadcloth and the tweed. And last of all the hats, each a hard square felt and each just five years older than the next. When the old man had made his choice of each separate apparel, he took a big puff of his sixpenny cigar and departed in a cloud of smoke for the bathroom. While the hot water was running, he trimmed his whiskers with a large pair of scissors and sometimes stood for three minutes before the glass in profound contemplation of the upcurl of his moustache. Now and then he would make little experiments, snipping a point here and a fringe there, but always in the end he made a ruthless sacrifice of such vanities, cutting his moustache square along the line of his mouth and his beard square across his chin. Having made sure that the water was luke-warm if it was summer and tepid if it was winter, he took off his clothes and entered his bath in the dignified manner that became an old gentleman of seventy-seven. No one knew what he thought of as he lay naked like a little child. When he saw his toes peeping out of the milky water he may have thought of the strange roads that they had carried him on – but there is no reason to think that a man who had spent so much of his time in the present would have wasted his last few years in thinking about the past. At ten o'clock, now enjoying the last precious inch of his cigar, he returned to his bed-room and dressed himself. At twenty-nine minutes past, the loon brought the gig to the door; and at the half hour, washed, brushed and shining, the old man drove off with his square hat well down over his brows and the whip at the present in his hand.

The harness jangled, the mare stepped out smartly and the wind blew cool on their faces as they drove to

Lendrum Kirk upon its round green hill. The old man was gay that morning, gay in the style of the hard North East, as if his spirit had a keener edge.

"Look at them," he said when they came near the kirk and saw the worshippers in their decent blacks and greys moving up the roads and paths in a sober Sabbath stride. "Just look at the good and godly o' Lendrum walkin in confident anticipation o' the Judgment Day."

"Are they so very good and godly?" Stephen asked.

"Na," said the old man, "But they're michty canny."

"Canny?"

"Aye there's nae a man on the Kirk Road the day but walks in the licht o' his neighbour's good opinion. O we're a weel-daein lot in Lendrum noo."

"Ye say that as if they belonged tae a lower species."

"Aye. Man, I sometimes think their fathers must hae been crossed on white mice."

There was a silence in which the old man meditated on the decadence of the time. Then he gave a short delighted laugh.

"But sometimes the Auld Adam comes jumpin up and then ye'll see them slippin oot and in by the back doors wi the licht o' mischief in their eyen. Ye never ken what a man may be thinkin aboot in the kirk on the Sabbath Day."

Stephen, looking at the old man beside him in the pew during the service, doubted if he had fixed his thoughts on heaven.

The Hillhead pew was in the North West corner and at right angles to the body of the kirk, so that the old man could keep his eye on the whole congregation. Sitting up very square with his hands on his knees this Sunday morning, he took a slow deliberate inventory of the worshippers. His eyes, very blue and frosty, travelled along the pews, sizing up each man and each woman. Like God at the Judgment, a God long since

80

disillusioned by the ways of men, he read their characters in their actions and saw beyond their masks of douce humility to the gnarled pattern of their thoughts. One by one he took them up and examined them; then set them down with a silent laugh. "Fools," he seemed to say, "fools ye may think tae cheat God wi your fine white shirts and your braw black gowns but ye canna cheat me. I ken ye, my friends, I ken ye, and I think little o' ye."

Dash it all, Stephen said to himself, *You'd think it was his kirk not the minister's. It's true that the reverend Corbel isn't much apart from his Presbyterian snarl and his long white hands, but he's surely a little more than the old man allows him to be. My respected grandfather doesn't admit that he exists, except as one of the fittings of the kirk, a little more than the steeple perhaps but definitely less than the bell. The old devil is reducing the whole institute of public worship to a public mockery.*

Just then, it happening to be a missionary Sunday, Mr. Corbel made some reference to the Christian duty of carrying the light of the Gospel to the heathen in foreign parts. Having finished that admonition with a passage of resounding hollowness, he rested on the open Bible and looked meaningly at the upturned but vacant faces of the congregation. The old man took up the look and with a satirical cock of his left eyebrow, carried it right round the assembly of Lendrum folk, so long abandoned in the jungles of their own canny virtue, till it came back to the Reverend Mr. Corbel who was grasping the Bible with both hands preparatory to launching into his secondly. Then having raised both eyebrows at the man of God, the old sinner gave a short dry cough that shattered the pious calm of the kirk like the satirical bleat of an old he-goat. The congregation started, turned over in its sleep, and Mr. Corbel flushed as if a sacrilegious act had been committed under his very nose. The old man then fixed the parson with both his cold blue eyes; and he, calling up all the resources of his long career, began a statistical survey of the fruits of faith. But he never got back into his stride and that sermon was an even greater failure than usual. Mr. Corbel went on and on, a little uncertain perhaps but quite determined, through his secondly, his thirdly and his conclusion that a farthing a head for the heathen was not enough from a prosperous community. Then Mr. Bourdon, the organist, flicking his elegant black coattails and flourishing his hands so that a beam of red light from the tortured brow in the East window struck a reflection of fictitious richness from the imitation ruby in his ring, led the elect of Lendrum into that song of extravagant faith which says:

> Take my all and let it be
> Consecrated, Lord, to thee.

At that verse and at that alone, the old man joined in the singing with a voice of considerable power which rose into a passionate affirmation of total disbelief at the words

> Take my silver and my gold
> Nought from Thee will I withhold.

Then he was silent, for indeed there was nothing more to sing.

Going home the old man waited till they had passed all those on foot and had been passed by all those in motor cars. Then he said, in a voice that was dry and sparkling with the keenest intellectual delight:

"Man, Stephen, it was a grand service."

"Aye," said Stephen with some of the old man's own dryness, "I notice that ye like the Kirk."

"I wouldna miss it for a world o' markets. It daes me guid tae see the fowk o' Lendrum sitting there sae sure o' their immortal souls. O they're sure, of course, for God's a Lendrum man, ye ken. Och jist ane o' oursels."

"All very nice and homely," said Stephen.

"Sae homely we never need tae think o' Him till we're in the claws o' death and then we're sure He'll dae the richt thing by Lendrum men. Though I have heard that some o' them misdoubted Him whan they heard the worms came channerin efter them frae the cauld kirkyaird."

"They've maybe cause."

"Them," said the old man and there was a world of scorn in his voice, "if their God was sic a michty man as mak the hills of Lendrum, and the Ben, and the stars and the birlin warld, He's nae likely tae waste His powder and shot on the like o' them. There was Geordie Simpson o' the Byres – maybe ye noticed him three seats afore ye, him that hung his head at the prayers. And weel he might. Geordie's never sworn an oath or drunk a dram in friendship a' his life. A crawlin body – he'll never stand up in case he fa doon. A cauld man wi a cauld wife and a cauld hoose and three cauld lassies that'll never get men. He's never wanted onything but tae be safe. He's safe for he's been deid thae thirty year, deid at the hert and only waitin for the cauld bones tae be swept awa. That day canna come ower sune for he's chillin the hert o' the guid laan at the Byres that used tae bear heavy corn and hearty men in the aulden time.

"There's my neighbour Mains, a man o' great ambition but little wit. Ye would like him – there's a touch o' the big business man about him. The Mains is the biggest place in Lendrum, and noo that the Laird's fallen intae decrepitude wi drink and weemin, Mains would fain hae been the Squire wi leggins and a saft hat an a'. They tell me he was hopin for a title because o' his services in the War. Nae that he was a sodger, bein' indispensable tae grow five quarters o' corn on the laan where his father grew eight afore him, but he was maist invaluable on tribunals and the like. I think he maun hae helped to send the best part o' five hunder men tae glory but he aye managed tae keep a few stoot chiels aboot the Mains. It was a guid war. Some o' us made money that never made money in our lives afore, and Mains was ane o' them. It was a grand thing for Lendrum. A lot o' men began the war as plain honest fairmers that suppit their cabbage brose wi a horn spoon and they finished it gentlemen that ate their denner at seven wi electroplated silver. Mains, the son o' a decent mannie that was never happy awa frae his ain midden heid, shot richt up among the gentry. He took tae cocktails instead o' beer, his wife came all oot in furs like a heiland cow and his lassie was sent tae a maist expensive school. They made a lady o' her and there were great plans for mairryin her tae ane o' the lesser gentry – though which o' them it was we were never rightly sure. But I some doubt they hadna made her lady enough, for she had tae rin awa tae England tae hae a bairn by the orra man. Puir lassie. England they tell me is a big place and she maun hae been lonely there with only an ill-got bairn for company, for she gaed oot ae day and laid her heid in front o' a railway train. Aye, naebody came very well oot o' that except maybe the orra man was a lucky chield tae hae the preenin o' that expensive education.

"Ye would have noticed Jamie Smith o' the Leys, that fine big place across the river. A hard workin man, Jamie, a guid neighbour and ane o' the kind that gather a bit o' money because they daena ken the wye tae spend it. Now Jamie had fancied a pair o' brown shoes for the best part o' ten year, and ae market day, being merry wi a dram, he got reckless and bought them. But whan he was hame and sober again he found he couldna wear them for fear o' what Lendrum would say. They micht think he was gettin uppish, for only the gentry and them that would like to be, wear shune and brown shune at that. Whiles on a dark nicht he would put them on and tak a walk as far as the top o' the road; but if he heard onybody comin he joukit back tae the house in case they'd see him. That went on for the best o' a year till he could stand the waste nae langer and had them black-ened. Eh, there never was a man mair carefu o' public opinion than Jamie."

Driving the pony along the quiet roads, walking slowly across the fields or sitting on the mound at the top of Brewster's Dyke, the old man often spoke about the countryside, for he had an endless interest in people. He spoke as one who had lived so long that he had grown apart from them and could look down on their comic tragedies from the heights of contemplation.

"Ach," he said, "they're a feart lot; they're feart tae dae what they want and what they want is nae worth daein. Man, there's been a woefu change in the country-side since the war. The sap seems tae hae gaen oot o' the men and the weemin. Maybe it was that they spoke sae muckle nonsense in that four daft years that they canna believe in onything but nonsense noo. But there's nae sap in them noo and nae enterprise like there used tae be. Man, I mind o' Saunders Young that fermed up by the loch. Times were bad; I'm speakin o' fifty years ago, and Saunders, seein that there was nae money in nowt and grain, cast roon for something that would put a penny in his pocket. Now there were a lot o' black-headed gulls that used tae come aboot the loch, sae mony that that their dung lay thick on the shore. Well, Saunders, mindin on the great guano trade, thought this was a gold mine at his ain door and set aboot attracting as mony gulls tae the lochside as corn and fish guts would bring. Gulls cam in plenty but they brocht wi them all kind o' gutsy birds that ate nae only the corn on the shore but the corn in the parks as well till Saunders was nearly harried oot o' hoose and hame. It was only a sharp rise in the price o' nowt that saved his reason. Aye he was an ingenious man, Saunders, and the country-side's in sair need o' his like the day.

"They're wee men, Stephen. There was a friend o' mine ca'd Murdoch, a big swearin man, wha's folk had been in the Hillocks for generations till they scattered and gaed abroad whaur he made a fortune. In his auld age he cam back tae Lendrum – maybe seven years ago.

85

He bein sae weel ballasted wi siller, the folk o' the Howe
made a great fuss o' him and were aye runnin after him.
Till the last time. It was a concert that he was to be
chairman at. The hall was fu and whan Murdoch rolled
on tae the platform it was easy seen that he was fu tae.
The guid and the godly a' took a reid face at sic an
affront tae decency but it was naething tae the affront
they got whan he stood up tae speak. 'Ladies and Gentlemen,' he said, drawin himsel up tae his six feet three,
'Ye think I'm drunk. Well I am drunk. And why?
because it's only bein' drunk that I can bring myself
down to the level of the folk of Lendrum.' Man,
Stephen, would ye believe it, the puir sheep sat there as
mim as maids and never a man o' them dared tae send
him tae hell above his breath. In the aulden time he
would never hae been spared tae see anither day.

"There were big men in the aulden time, men that
would gang tae a market and bide for a week and then
tak a week tae come hame, drivin their gigs through
corn and clover, singin and roarin fu. Man, there was sic
a lot o' rivin life in the countryside that ye had tae be a
strong man or you'd be smoored amon't. But we've
fallen on thin times and even the Laird's grown as ragged as a last year's scarecrow."

Stephen remembered George John, the nineteenth
Laird of Lendrum. The Laird had been a splendid
figure to the little boy, so tall and straight, with brown
moustaches that curled like horns above his square,
clean-shaven chin. His brown boots, his white gaiters,
his tweeds, his gold chains, his cigars and his air of being
far above the cares of the working world made him seem
like a god. And he had been a god to the countryside, or
at least a superior being who enjoyed the licence of a
vague morality. His drinking, his gambling, his wench-
ing, which would have damned a lesser man to eternal
fires, were regarded as the idiosyncrasies of ancient
lineage. The good and the godly loved him because he
was rich and because he was allowed to do the things

they might only dream of, or enjoy only under the privy cloak of night.

But now, alas, he was no longer rich. Indeed he was about the poorest man in Lendrum. His rentroll of five thousand pounds was mortgaged to the last penny and further. For that he blamed Lloyd George, the Death Duties, the War, the Socialists and his tenants – anything rather than his own stupidity. What he had not squandered in an endless round of silly entertainments that had ended as habits quite devoid of pleasure, he allowed to slip through his hands into the pockets of land agents, stewards, lawyers, tradesmen and shameless parasites. He had been born to be the fine flower of aristocracy, to a position of ease devoid of responsibility that seemed to have been created by heaven to last till the end of time. But heaven had changed its mind or grown tired of the lairds. Times changed with a devastating rapidity but George John and his friends, thinking themselves and their state eternal, or being like the eternal above the need of thought, refused to change. Their fine state had fallen into disrepute; where they had once scattered their money and their favour like kings they led a circumscribed life by the mercy of their creditors. They were anachronisms withering, for they had no place in the changing world and their roots could no longer draw life from the land of their fathers.

It was an old and withered man who came on Stephen and his grandfather through the Lendrum woods one afternoon. The sap which had made him so splendid to the little boy had gone out of him. His once martial figure had drawn in on itself. His shoulders drooped; his moustaches, once so brown and curling, drooped over his hanging chin; the whole man drooped as if the burden of his years was too great to be supported by the feeble spirit within him.

"Good day, Brewster," he said to the old man, then looked down on Stephen with a querulous stare.

"My grandson," the old man said, "on holiday from

87

London."

"Your servant, sir," Stephen said with a slight bow.

"Fool to come to this god-awful country if you
could be in London," said George John looking with
disgust at his ancestral acres. His little eyes were yellow
between their wrinkled lids.

"Imphm," the old man said in comment on this
interchange of courtesies. Then to George John, "We're
well met for I was wantin your opinion on a sma matter
about the place."

"No, no, see Duncan. He's my agent and it's his
job. I can't be bothered by you people who are always
trying to get more than you are due."

The old man paid no attention to George John's
reply; but, standing up from the dyke against which he
had been leaning, he said –

"If ye'll step doon tae the house I'll let you see
what I'm thinkin about – mind your feet on that bit o'
wire; the stile's a bit unchancy."

Seemingly against his will, George John climbed
into the field and followed the old man towards the
house.

"Not a sign of game. Hardly a pheasant about the
place. The poachers have got them. It's all those
damned Socialists," he concluded in a burst of senile
rage which yet had a faint ring from the bygone patriar-
chal tradition.

"Aye," the old man said with no more mockery
than a dry look at Stephen. "The Socialists are gettin gie
good shots. It's maybe as weel they daena gang after
bigger game than pheasants."

"If I had my way I'd hang them by their necks
along my avenue," said George John, jabbing his staff
into the ground before him.

"That would mak a braw show," the old man
replied appreciatively. "But maybe we shouldna be sae
hard on them. They haena had oor advantages."

"In my young day people were taught their place

and to have a sense of duty."

"Aye," said the old man, "A grand thing a sense o' duty . . . There's a fine park o' turnips comin up there."

George John inspected them. "Good cover for the partridges. I will say this, Brewster, you've always been a good tenant."

"Thank ye. Thank ye," the old man said, as one receiving a great favour.

George John blew his nose with a flourish and walked on a little better pleased with himself.

The old man led the way into the garden and began to propound a scheme for leading a pipe of water from the stream that ran outside the wall, so as to make a pond for lilies. George John listened to the scheme with great impatience till the old man made it plain that it would not be charged to the estate. Then he gradually became quite enthusiastic and offered three suggestions of unparalleled fatuity which the old man accepted in the spirit in which they were offered. The conference then proceeded in the greatest harmony with George John taking complete charge. So well did they agree that he ended by giving the old man permission to go ahead with the scheme. Stephen, who had become quite interested in the technical problems involved, went on discussing the matter but George John had suddenly lost all interest in it. He began looking towards the house, and clearing his throat and blowing his nose impatiently.

The old man listened to the end of Stephen's plans, then, without making any comment, he said to George John, "It's a warm day. Would you like a drink?"

"Drink? Drink? O well now that I'm here . . ."

The old man nodded to Stephen who fetched the bottle and glasses. He poured half a tumblerful for George John and a little for himself and Stephen. Then he set down the bottle at George John's elbow.

They drank; and the old man, seeing that George John's glass was empty, filled it half full again. Emptying the glass at two mouthfuls, George John wiped his moustache with his handkerchief, lit a cigarette and trailed away with a few almost gracious words.

The old man and Stephen watched the long withered figure dawdling across the pasture towards the Lendrum woods, then the old man turned to Stephen and said, "Eighteen generations hae come tae that – and he's only sixty-two. It's an ill thing for a countryside whan the heid decays. But that ane was maybe born a bittie saft."

Then Stephen asked him when they would begin on the lily pool.

The old man laughed, "What would I dae wi a lily pool?"

"Then what did you ask the laird about it for?"

"Tae flatter him a bit, puir man, and mak it easy for him tae get the dram that he cam across for. It's little enough o' either that he gets, and they're the staff o' life tae the likes o' him."

"Well, well," said Stephen with a slight mocking laugh, "I never thought you had such a kind heart."

"Vanity. Jist vanity, tae see that the michty can be brocht sae low."

There was no day in which Stephen did not learn something about the countryside and gradually the details shaped themselves into a completed picture. There was little in it for pleasure. Perhaps it was, as the old man had said, that the sap had gone out of life since the war. Times were changing rapidly. Not that there was much difference in the ways of husbandry: farmers still ploughed and sowed as they had done for generations. Nor was the fall in prices so very important; bad times had always succeeded the good as surely as winter succeeds harvest. But people were worried in their minds and the zest had gone out of living. A certain splendour had gone out of life. There was the fall of the Laird for instance. George John's magnificence had been paid for by his tenants; the money they earned bought his wine and ponies. But just because he was magnificent in his follies, because he gave them something to speak about and marvel at, because he lived in defiance of all morality and caution, because he seemed to assert that one man at least can be master of his destiny, they held his expense as worth their labour. But now the man who was high had been brought down. The one power in Lendrum that had seemed to be more than mortal had fallen into shameful toleration before its final passing.

The lairds were often bad enough but the power that took their place was worse. Many estates had been broken up in the good times at the end of the war. The farmers had to buy their places or clear out. Many of them had bought, and at greatly inflated prices. Most of them had to borrow from the banks on a mortgage which covered half the value of the farm. But now prices had fallen; the farms might only be worth a third of what they had paid for them; the farmers found themselves owned body and soul by the banks. Not by the old fashioned banks where business was carried on as man to man in the traditional country way; but by vast impersonal bodies with inviolable rules. For the first time the farmers found themselves in the hands of big business. Progress and Rationalisation were squeezing the sap from their bones.

Sometimes the dry bones cracked and another farmer went down into bankruptcy. Now farmers had often been in difficulties. Many of them had been worth no more than ten shillings in the pound before. But if they were good men they were seldom ruined. There was that pleasant instrument the Trust Deed by which the farmer assigned his property to the trustees on behoof of his creditors. The trustees engaged the farmer as their servant, paying him a small wage, and with his help they carried on the farm till they had got all, or almost all their money back. Then the trust was wound up and the farmer took back his farm in reasonable order. The essential thing about the Trust Deed was that men trusted each other. But now the banks trusted no one who borrowed less than a hundred thousand pounds and that distrust had spread itself through the country. When nobody knew when they themselves might be in danger of the screw, they had small courage for trusting their neighbours. So although more farmers than ever were signing Trust Deeds the new instruments were all deed and little trust. Led by the banks, every creditor demanded as much as he could get as soon as possible. No attempt was made to save the estate. The trust was wound up in a six months, the creditors took their half crown in the pound and another family disappeared from the countryside. There was nothing but change and no change was for the better. The ruin was not universal; indeed the bankrupts were few in number; but the psychological effect was great. It put caution in the place of courage. Those who had no money thought uneasily of the day when they might go down in turn, and those who had money lived in a quiet aping of gentility and never dared the gods by any splendid folly of the proud flesh.

"Aye," Tam the foreman said when Stephen found him weeding the garden before his house one Sunday afternoon, "it's as weel that the deid men in the kirkyard o' Lendrum canna see the countryside this day. It would send them hurryin back tae their graves again. The Laird's fallen low and the fairmers are genteel and the laan full o' naesty crawlin bodies that think o' naething but whaur they can fill their ain bellies."

Stephen looked at the cottage, in no way different from those lived in by Willum and Davy, except that everything about it showed signs of meticulous care. There were flowers behind the shining window panes and roses, sweet peas and vegetables grew in well-ordered profusion in the small garden. It was so unlike the ordinary cottar house that Stephen marvelled at it.

"But you," he said, "you at least cultivate your own

garden."

Tam's long brown fingers never ceased their swift and confident work among the tender plants.

"I'd aye see a man's hoose was keepit in order though it wasna my ain."

"You're not like most cottars."

Tam looked up with a flicker of contempt in his shrewd brown eyes.

"Ach them," he said. "They're a shiftless lot. They canna bide in a place. A year here, then awa tae a new parish. Aye cluttered up wi bairns, aye in debt and aye in fear o' the parish. It may be enough for them but it's nae enough for me."

Stephen, thinking back, caught a hint from a previous remark.

"You want a place o' your ain?"

Tam nodded. "And I'll get it. Maybe nae a place like Hillhead. A sma place at the back o' beyond wi a pair o' horse and a score o' sheep. But it'll be a beginnin, and wha ken's what a body can rise tae. If I gae them the start, the loons can haud on tae better."

So-ho, said Stephen to himself, *you'd start a family would you, Found a house. Make a little Hillhead at the back o' beyond You've ambition to rise and be your own master. You'd be an ancestor and be looked up to long after you're dead, as I look up to those old dead Brewsters.*

"You've been a good while here, haven't you?"

"Seven years past the term."

"You like the old man?"

Tam stood up, rubbing the dusty earth from his hands.

"There's nane like him," he said. "The rest o' the countryside are bairns aside him. He kens ten times mair about the laan than ten other men; and, better than that, he kens his ain mind. If the rest o' Lendrum were tae fall, your grandfather would bide standin. Near a'thing I've learned I've learned frae him. Man, he stands above this countryside like the Ben above the

Howe; and we – we run among his feet like bairns."

Stephen and Tam looked at each other across the hedge, gripped fast by the old man's power. They knew each other for true men in acknowledging something greater than themselves. Then they fell talking about ordinary things,

There was a rising ferment in Stephen as he went home across the fields. His words with Tam had excited him. They had, as it were, precipitated all his impressions of his grandfather out of the solution of his thoughts. Now they took a clear shape and he could see the old man walking serenely by the light of his own mind far above a country devastated by the greater fears and the smaller proprieties. And as the Ben, that brave blue peak, seemed to draw herself all the beauty of the Howe, this commanding vision of the old man drew all Stephen's emotions of the past few weeks into a significant pattern.

By the good Lord, he said, *the old man is free. Others abide all sorts of stupid questions but he just laughs and goes his own way. What a tradition he has behind him - all the Brewsters that made this farm, and all the pleasures he took because he wanted them, and all the things he has done because they seemed good to do. With all that behind him a man need have no fear, for they're real things and they'll never betray him. And by God, they might be mine.*

In a moment of intense excitement, Stephen felt as if he could take Hillhead and all the Brewsters within the grasp of his two arms. Exalted, he went forward to something that he did not yet dare guess.

When he got to the house he found the old man in the garden, looking over the oats in the home field.

"Aye, Stephen," he said. "We'll start cuttin the hairst a week the morn."

CHAPTER SIX

Three Friends

WHATEVER WEAKNESSES of the flesh may have been
bothering the rest of Lendrum, the long summer days
brought nothing but peace to Hillhead, and to Stephen a
grace in living that he had never known before. Much of
that felicity was due to Mr. Jeremy Elphinstone, the old
man's friend. Mr. Elphinstone was an agreeable man of
fifty-five whose short white beard, coupled with the
adventurous way in which he had made a fortune on the
London Stock Exchange, gave him a delightful air of benevolent amorality. No one knew exactly who his father
was; perhaps he did not know himself; but ladies with
generous and romantic minds agreed that he belonged
to an old county family. His mother on the other hand
had been a maidservant in Old Aberdeen and everybody
knew about her. However, she was dead and might be
forgotten, in consideration of the hundred thousand
pounds with which her son had returned to his native
town. Whatever else she was, she must have been a
woman of some imagination. Since she had no name to
give her fatherless child she chose that of the good
bishop William who had founded the college near which
he had been born. The name had been an inspiration to
the child; to bear the name of that great statesman, the
saintliest prince of the mediaeval church, may have been
a challenge to magnificence. However it happened,
young Jeremy left the gutters of Old Aberdeen for the
pavements of London that were reputed to be ankle
deep in gold. There his wits, long hardened by the cold
east wind, carried him triumphantly through a long
series of financial adventures, few of them conspicuously
honest, until they enabled him to return to his origins in

a very comfortable state indeed. Now he lived in Dunelm, a small eighteenth century house at the back of the cathedral, half hidden under old beech trees and quite embowered in roses. His wife who had been French and a ballet dancer, was dead, and his only household was his daughter, Susan, an amiable person of twenty-three.

At least twice a week he drove his long grey Sunbeam into the close at Hillhead. Miss Elizabeth came out from the drawing room where she had been taking her little rest on the wide gold-brocaded sofa. Bowing he took her hand; and she, playing with her gold-rimmed glasses on their chain, smiled down on his white head and the elegant broadcloth of his shoulders. While they were still playing that game in which they were long practised, the old man appeared from his long sleep in the parlour. He announced himself at the kitchen door with a short dry cough, as if to deride their soft exchanges, then he stepped forward to welcome his friend.

"Come courtin again?" he said.

"How could I stay away?"

"How indeed," said Aunt Elizabeth with a smile and a toss of her head.

Bawbie the maid, half-in and half-out of the kitchen, giggled to see that they who were so old could be so foolish.

Aunt Elizabeth, knowing so well what would be in a young girl's mind, ordered her sharply about, to make the tea

Then Mr. Elphinstone brought a parcel from the car – maybe a packet of Gunpowder hyson, or a jar of china ginger or a bottle of brandy, for he knew the things his friends liked and he loved to pleasure them. They could give and take presents with the generosity that is as much in the taking as in the giving. *Here my friends,* Mr. Elphinstone's manner said, *is something rich and strange. I bought it for you on the hot mysterious plains of India, down the yellow rivers of China; like magic, hey presto,*

from the golden slopes of France. Smelling the dry fragrance of the tea; biting into the hot translucent ginger,
sipping the imperial wine; their manner said; *It's good.
It warms the cockles of your heart. You've made a miracle.
Women with gay bandanas round their heads sang in the
gardens of India as they picked those leaves. Junks with their
high fantastic sails weighed slowly down the rivers of China
bringing their ginger to the sea. The grapes ripened on the
golden slopes of France to make this royal liquor.* Stephen,
seeing the fantastic little comedy for the first time,
thought *What a fuss they make about a pound of tea.* But
when he looked again and again he saw that it warmed
them. *Dammit,* he said to himself, *there's true friendship in
which they play a game where each gives what he can so that
they may all enjoy it together. They are an alliance of powers in
which none makes any reservation. With such friends a man
might dare all the shadows that haunt the bounds of life.*

As the sun went blazing like a phoenix to its death
beyond the hills, the three old people sat in the arbour
by the garden wall among the smell of the flowers and
the gentle airs of summer. A small table between them
bore the tea, or a bottle and glasses. The old man
smoked his briar pipe, Mr. Elphinstone enjoyed a fine
cigar and Aunt Elizabeth kept her arms folded in the lap
of her black silk gown. They talked, or listened to Mr.
Elphinstone talking, for there was no end to his observations upon this curious world. Sometimes Stephen
joined them and they welcomed him and let him talk as
one of themselves. But he noticed that they drew closer
together when he left and there was a new ring of delight in the laughter with which they explored the inex-
haustible bawdries of the world. Then Stephen felt his
bones go weak with a dreadful loneliness, for he knew
then that he had no friends of his own age who were as
dear to him as the old people were to each other. At
such times he knew that it must be a dreadful thing to
die alone. He summoned up the remembrance of those
he had thought his friends – his father, his brother and

Jane. But none of them, not even Jane whom he had thought he loved, could warm him against the cold of his loneliness. There was a bar between them, more than the miles to London or Avignon. Or was it that they existed for him no longer? Standing then under the laburnum trees and hearing the voices from the arbour at the other side of the garden, the very marrow in his bones cried for his mother. He saw her walk past him, dappled with the green and gold that fell from the trees. He sickened to be a small child who could take her hand and run down to the pools with her. If only she could have spoken a word to him, or touched him once with a warm consoling hand. But she died again upon the invisible air and he was still alone.

Then Mr. Elphinstone brought Susan and Kennedy to the farm and Stephen suddenly found that he had friends. Susan was twenty-three and ripe to be married; Kennedy was thirty-one and ripe to marry her. They were agreed on everything except the date. In nothing at all were they notable to look at, except that they were alive. Her dark hair and her grey eyes shone; her rather plain face was brown with the sun; she walked with a spring in her step, as if walking were no effort at all. She wore her clothes carelessly so that they might have been part of her instead of charms superimposed with a deal of thought. In everything she gave the impression of being a lively person comfortably at home in the world. He had little to his name but a pair of most intelligent eyes that gave you an unexpected look of order out of the surrounding confusion, for he was one of those who seem as if they had just been blown about by a high wind. He was a university lecturer in political history. The two treated their devotion to each other as the best joke in a wholly amusing world. They were like no other people of his own generation that Stephen had ever met.

"Talk," said the old man, "they would talk the hind legs off a brass monkey." They had only to notice some-

thing that took their fancy and off they would go in an
endless argument. The problem of whether dogs can
think, the amenities of birth control, the necessity for
communism – anything was enough to start them off on
a philosophic excursion during which they undermined
the bases of all morality. There were few illusions, such
as the superior wisdom of the old and the glory of em-
pires, that they did not laugh at; and nothing at all
which they did not dare to talk about as if the most
recondite mysteries of the world were all part of the
morning's news.

Stephen did not like it at first. He was unaccus-
tomed to conversation as an art and he hated it when it
was used to attack the things he had been taught to
honour. Such as the sanctity of business.

"But dash it all," Stephen said, "that's socialism."
But that didn't shock Kennedy or Susan at all. They
attacked the whole basis of Stephen's life thus far. They
made fun of his career. They ridiculed his successes as a
salesman. Too much work, they said, left the senses too
dull for artful conversation.

"But look at your father," Stephen said to Susan.
"He's made a lot of money and he's quite intelligent."

"My father, "said Susan, "has not done an honest
day's work since he was twenty-two. I admire him immensely. In fact I think he's the cleverest person I ever
met. He made all his money by playing off honest hard-
working people like you against each other: they did the
work and he took the profits. And as soon as he had
made about three times as much as I could ever spend
for him he retired to pass the rest of his life in conversation and a graceful mild intoxication. He may have been
a business man but I'm sure he was never tired out by
business in his life."

"If you're a socialist you must think there's something far wrong with that way of making money."

"My dear," Susan replied. "It's a long time now
since I realised I was living on my father's immoral

earnings. But I prefer his way to yours. He knew the system that allowed him to make money: and he fooled it to the tune of a hundred thousand pounds; you don't know it's stupid and you go on allowing yourself to be fooled by it; and I'm quite sure you'd die for it if you were ever asked to."

"Yes," said Stephen, "but I might get control of it. I might make a million pounds. I might have houses and estates and yachts and be consulted by statesman and have power over people like you who only sit about and talk."

"And would you enjoy them?" Susan asked.

"Why shouldn't I?"

"Because you have been so busy being an honest working man that you wouldn't have had time to learn the art of enjoying."

"That's nonsense," said Stephen.

"On the contrary it's plainest sense."

"Well I never thought you had to learn how to have a good time."

"My dear," said Susan, "Don't be so naive. You know perfectly well that you can't even get drunk successfully until you've learned how much you can take without the ultimate disaster."

"But that is the end of all morality," said Stephen.

"In business there can be no morality," said Kennedy; "as soon as you allow competition, any rules that restrict it do nothing more than give a premium to those who break them. I am of the school that believes the Red Cross should be bombed in war, freely, on each side. There can't be rules in war. Nothing that is immoral, since it is stupid, can have a morality of its own. We who are wise men will amuse ourselves with the wonder that is in the world and with the mysteries that are a man."

It was evening and they were down by the river. The westering sun came down the water to them like a riven flame. The slim young silver birches were touched with the delicate rose of life in the warm light. Away on

the other side of the river a heron stood motionless
above a silent pool. When they held their peace they
could hear their hearts beat in the quiet. Stephen, lying
on his back and watching the midges dance on the air
above him, forgot to argue with Kennedy; and Kennedy, happy to have argued, was content to be still. The
girl sang an old song so low and sweetly that the music
seemed to come from far away across the evening. Then
Stephen felt that the wonder of the world was growing in
him. It was less the things that Susan and Kennedy said
than the way they said them that quickened him. He
had been brought up to think that some things were
right and that everything else must be false. To do your
job; to honour your school; to be true to your flag; to
get on – those had been unquestioned truths. But he
heard them questioned, not by undesirables like socialists
or manifest cranks with long hair, but by people who
seemed if anything more accomplished than himself, and
backed by Mr. Elphinstone's hundred thousand pounds.

At first he asked himself *What is the truth when they've
done with it?* But now the resentment had passed away
and he felt a delicious new freedom growing on him as
the coolness of the evening grew upon the warm air. He
had been put upon by catchwords; now he saw them to
be something less than eternal wisdom; he himself had
seen them for what they were and they could never be
his master again. It was a glorious new freedom that
made him feel the world was his to be made his pleasure.
Because Susan and Kennedy had shown him the way to
freedom he loved them.

The next few days were dowie with the mist that
sometimes comes at the very sill of harvest. The world
was enclosed by intangible grey walls, there was no life
on the laden air and every ear of corn was bowed with a
load of moisture. They were dull fretting days, for they
came between the men and the harvest. The old man
walked about the yard in a grim silence.

On the night of the third day the mist passed into a

drizzling rain from the sea. Lying in bed in the big attic
room Stephen listened to the drops striking the window
panes monotonously. As he listened there passed before
his mind the succession of weary days and years he had
spent at his trade – all of them irrevocable and all of
them wasted. He could see the hundreds, the thousands
like himself, little men with little black bags running all
over England on tremendous errands about scented
soap and candy while the nightingales were singing un-
heard in the high woods and the rivers maintained their
quiet traffic under the stars. Then *Who cares a damn for
nightingales?* he said to himself with an impatient laugh.
Leave them to the poets. But he could not leave them, for
he saw Mr. Jeremy Elphinstone and the old man and
Aunt Elizabeth talking under the sunset in the garden.
He saw them so clearly that he might have leaned forward and touched their hands and ever so clearly he
heard them tell their bawdy tales and deride the stupid
world at their ease. Then it seemed to him that Mr.
Elphinstone was a most immoral but how delightful bird
stepping across the green and mocking at all who
thought and did as they were told. He was an old immoral nightingale singing of the freedom of the high
woods under the sovereign light of the moon, and that
moon was reason. "For we have no guide in this world
but reason," Jeremy had said, adding a little drop of
water to his whisky (it was Old Pulteney with the taste of
juniper in it, at least that was what he always maintained)
"and the man of feeling is the world's fool without it.
Not, my friend, that I despise the instincts. I've played
many a fine game with them in my day. But, if I may
change the metaphor, when you build your house let
reason be the architect so that the instincts may be fitly
articulated each to each."

Stephen remembering said to himself *And what
have I ever had to do with reason. I have been the world's fool.
I have run about England with my little bag hot dusty and
discouraged to the point of despair, and all because I thought*

that there was no other way that a man might live. But mean-
time Elphinstone and the old man have been drinking under the
shade of the laburnum trees and shaping their world after their
own will and taking their pleasure wherever they could find it.
They are free and I have been a slave.

Listening to the rain, and thinking of the weary
days and years he longed almost beyond bearing for his
life to turn to wonder.

Next day the mist passed away and shook the ears
of corn free from the clinging rain. Susan and Kennedy
drove to Hillhead just after breakfast. "We've come to
take you to the high hills," Susan cried to Stephen,
throwing her arms round his neck and kissing him on
the lips. There was a delicious excitement in her manner, a touch of ecstasy at the return of the sun and the
lively wind. It enchanted her kiss and passed into
Stephen and carried him away with it. Laughing and
making foolish jokes, they went down through the aftermath of the hay in the Lady Park, rowed themselves over
the river in the little Hillhead boat and then walked
across the pastures towards the hills. All that afternoon
they stravaiged along like children, only far more light
hearted than children could ever be. The paths led
them upwards through the fields of harvest, from the
haughs where nature herself seemed to have become a
husbandman, so rich were the crops, up to the high
windswept farms where the treaty between man and
nature was jealously guarded on either side. Then at last
they came out on the waste, among the tough wiry grass
eaten down by the sheep, and the protestant whins and
the aromatic sweet herbs, at the margin of the high hills,
the hunting ground of the winds. So by noon they won
to the summit of the first hill and there they lay down to
rest. When they had got their breath they ate the little
food they had brought with them. Then Susan and
Kennedy curled up beside each other and went to sleep.
Looking down from the top of the hill Stephen fell into a
kind of trance in which all his powers seemed to be

engaged in making some great decision. Nothing of the debate reached the consciousness of his mind but for the space of two hours there was a rapt communion between him and the farm and at the end of that time the decision came into his mind. *There are many ways of living for many kinds of people, and I will find the life that is best for me.*

When Susan and Kennedy woke it was half past three and they wanted their tea. Especially Kennedy, for when Stephen teased him about being an old wife, he roared out in rage, crying, "Old wife be damned. Afternoon tea is the corner stone of civilisation. I must have tea. I will have tea. Gunpowder hyson or the grocer's one and sixpenny – I don't care what so long as it is hot and sweet."

"Away with you," said Stephen, pushing him down the hillside, but Susan took his arm and pleaded with him. "For heaven's sake, Stephen, find him tea or he will do something desperate." Then she whispered, "That's the worst of philosophers."

Kennedy let them laugh; he had more important things to think about. He stood on the top of a high stone searching the hillside for a sign of tea. "Silent upon a peak in Darien," said Susan pointing to him silhouetted against a cloudless heaven. "Stout Cortez – with Hovis," said Stephen, putting his arm round her waist and recapturing the delicious excitement of her kiss. But not silent for long. Kennedy gave a sudden shout; and, waving his arm to follow, he ran pell mell down the hill. Susan and Stephen followed him, hand in hand, laughing.

After half an hour of headlong descent they came to a small farmhouse at the beginning of the arable land. The low buildings were whitewashed and shone in the sun. They were clean and bare, in harmony with the land about them; for the grass in the fields though sweet was thin, and the cornstalks stood so few out of the flinty earth that a man with time to spare might have counted them. The fertility of the little farm was so thin as to be almost transparent, like a harvest scene painted upon the wind.

"By god," said Kennedy, "It's heroic. Here is civilisation maintained valiantly on the rim of the desert. These acres were never meant to grow corn: this garden was never meant to bear the tame domestic flowers. But somebody has put his will upon them, and, lo, here is our cup of tea at four o'clock. Who shall say that there is not something sublime in man?"

He knocked at the back door of the house and a middle aged woman came out, beating her floury hands together.

"We are hungry for tea and scones," said Kennedy taking off his cap, gallantly.

"Well now, think o' that," the woman said, giving him a long searching look out of her keen grey eyes.

"I've been thinking about it for the last hour," Kennedy replied.

"Thinkin's cheap," said the woman, rolling her hands in her floury apron. She showed no sign of taking a hint.

"So is tea," said Kennedy, "and scones."

The woman laughed. "I'm nae a restaurant."

"Then," said Kennedy, putting on his cap again, "That's that."

"O wait ye," said the woman. "What are ye? Gentry or plain gaun-about bodies?"

Kennedy looked quickly round him, then went closer to the woman and whispered, "We are a circus and we've left our elephants round the corner."

The woman nodded. "I kent it. Mad. Ye'd better come in and hae your teas. They'll cost ye one and threepence each."

"With scones?"

"As mony as ye can eat."

Kennedy turned to Susan and Stephen. "Come on in," he said.

Sitting on a hard form by the kitchen window, they

ate a massive tea, of fat scones warm from the girdle, spread with butter and syrup. The wind pursued them in through the open window and the house was as bare within as without. Great stone flags covered the floor. The walls were ochred a deep brown, turning to black where they were stained by the smoke from the low peat fire. A plain wooden sideboard scrubbed to the quick of the wood filled one side of the room and bore a diversity of plates cleaned and polished to the bone. Two hard wooden chairs stood one on each side of the fire and there were a few other chairs that had not even arms in the name of comfort. On the long high shelf opposite the fire a number of curious things had gathered throughout the years – a deliriously coloured tobacco jar, an old fashioned salt-cellar, a bright brass berry-pan, a stuffed fish and a fiddle. There was hardly anything else in the room.

"A bittie bare," the woman said as she rested her arm along the stone above the fireplace. She was a grand figure hammered into living steel by the wind on the flinty acres. "But this is a bare toun in a hungry country."

"Why don't you go further down to the fat lands in the haughs?" Stephen asked.

She waved away the suggestion. "I couldna bide doon there. I would miss the wind for company."

"Is that all you have to speak to up here?" Susan asked.

"It's enough. O I've a man – but what's a man whan ye've sleepit wi him for thirty year – he's just your ain image but nae sae unchancy. Noo the wind – ye never ken what it'll be daein next."

"But how do you live off these bare acres?" Stephen asked. "There can't be much money in this kind of farming."

"Money. I've hardly seen it for thirty year. We've nae money but we hae meat and drink and a place o' our ain and we daena ca the King our maister. Mind you, there hae been times whan I'd hae gaen't a' for a turkey carpet wi roses on't."

When they rose to go, "Three and ninepence," she said. "That'll be a surprise for the grocer. He kens ilka penny I hae tae spend and this extra'll mak him think I've come intae a fortune." But when Stephen refused the change out of his five shillings she laughed at him, saying, "I daena tak charity frae a Lendrum loon and if ye'd been a real Brewster ye'd hae had mair sense than offer me't."

"Ye ken me," said Stephen.

"Wha wouldna ken a Brewster. There's been mony a fine speak round this fireside about your grandfather in his prime. Sic a man he was. The deil micht hae been his brither. But there's nane like him noo. The men gang toddlin tae their ain beds at half past ten and a woman like me that has some life in her maun lie and listen tae the wind. There's your change, my lad. Ye've something better tae offer a woman than money."

They waved to her as they walked down the stony farm road towards the west, the sun going before them in his autumnal glory.

"You should stay," they teased Stephen; and, though he laughed at them, something stirred in his blood, a memory perhaps of the lives of his ancestors who had made such a speak in the countryside and had so often kept away from the song of the lonely wind. He squared his shoulders and hoped that he looked a Brewster of the old free blood.

So they came to the inn at Lendrum.

Though the Lendrum Arms was old it had not improved with age. In fact it was little more than a public house, but it was distinguished in two things, a little back garden and a landlord who was worthy of a better age.

When he had cleared the spittoons and stuffed owls into the corner of the back parlour, Kennedy sat down on the sofa by the open window and called for whisky. Jemima Bauchlefeet, the serving maid, brought him three nips and a jug of water. Kennedy just looked at the whisky, and then he said, "Jemima, bring the master."

"Eh?" said Jemima, scratching her hip as an aid to understanding.

"You heard what I said, my dear," Kennedy replied.

"O aye, "said Jemima with an uncertain smile full of uncertain teeth.

She brought Mr. Castell. He was a shrivelled man with lively brown eyes and very tight trousers on his very thin legs. He carried a bottle carefully in his two hands. "Not a word, Mr. Kennedy," he said, "I'm sorry that it should hae happened." Taking up the glasses one by one he threw the whisky into the garden saying, "Wash. Naething but wash. I agree wi ye: patent still whisky's naething but petrol." Then he laid the other bottle on the table. "Now there's the stuff that'll dae your heart guid. Straight frae Speyside and pure as the mountain dew. Eh me. There is not many of us that know the difference between a blend and a good malt whisky nowadays – the commercial travellers hae killed the taste o' the countryside."

"Just leave the bottle," Kennedy said. "If it's good we'll be here for a while."

It was uncommon good. Not that Stephen liked it very much, for he had been brought up on the poor blended stuff that the English drink with their soda. But what a noble heat it engendered in the blood; what a divine ease it fathered. After the third glass Stephen made a long speech elaborately flowered with compliments in which he declared his undying friendship for Kennedy and Susan. He had never attempted public speaking before and his first essay was so successful that he was unwilling to make an end of it. Words came unbidden, nouns and adjectives sprang into happy conjunction with the inevitability of the mating stars.

After the fourth glass the speech became a kind of blank
verse with a lyrical cadence which so moved Kennedy
that he went to the harmonium in the corner and impro-
vised an accompaniment to it in the vox humana. Susan
lay on the sofa and watched them through a golden mist.
The world had never seen anything half so kind as the
smile she gave them. "O Susan, my dear," Stephen said
over and over again, "the world is very very beautiful."
"Very, very beautiful," she replied softly in a singing
voice. "Ah you know," said Stephen, greatly moved by
her understanding. In fact he was so moved that he
went over and, raising her to her feet, kissed her on the
lips to their great enjoyment; enjoyment so deep and so
mystical that it had to be repeated over and over again.
Then Stephen went and shook hands with Kennedy and
so praised his sweet-heart's kindness to him that Kennedy took a new love for her and went over and kissed
her too. That seemed to Stephen the most beautiful
thing in all the world. He put his arms round their
shoulders and called down blessings on their heads. As
Kennedy said, it was a sacramental moment. Then
suddenly and for no apparent reason they all three fell
to laughing, until the water stood in their eyes and their
very bones were sore. They rolled on the sofa; they lay
against the wall; they were riven and shattered by laughter far beyond their control. Then Jemima Bauchlefeet
opened the door and shouted, "Your suppers is ready in
the kitchen," as if she thought they and the whole world
had gone mad.

Ham and eggs, eaten in Mrs. Castell's kitchen
under Jemima's disapproving eyes, brought them a little
nearer to the earth. Their feet regained the solid
ground; but their heads remained in heaven. A delicious haze invested everything that happened thereafter
with a quaint inconsequence. Things happened but
seemed to have no relation to each other. People came
and went for no reason whatsoever. Conversations of
tremendous importance began suddenly and as sud-

denly ended in laughter. Susan retired to sleep in Mrs. Castell's bed and Stephen and Kennedy went to the bar where they found the same inconsequential order of events. The little room with sawdust on the floor was full of people with curious faces, people who didn't say anything much but managed to be almost intolerably funny. Then they found a friend whom Kennedy introduced to Stephen as Uncle George. He was a large blue man with several chins and a tiny mouth through which he seemed to be always drinking whisky or blowing out smoke. Every now and then he went into ecstasies of what might have been laughter but which sounded more like a very bad squeak. He had had a great deal to do with horses and women, the first professionally and the second as a diversion. Stephen loved him very much and told him so, frequently. As the evening wore on they became highly confidential and went for several short walks in the garden to admire the sunset. Soon it was ten and well after closing time, so Mr. Castell decided to lock the front door and close the bar. Being good citizens, the company made no objections and all carried their drinks into the little back parlour where Kennedy began to play the harmonium. Everybody wanted to sing and they demanded tunes as diverse as 'The Muckin o' Geordie's Byre', and 'The Oregon Trail'. Kennedy settled the whole matter by playing the Hundredth Psalm and the whole company, including Uncle George, joined in with varying degrees of drunken unction. There was a lot of singing that night, including a beautiful rendering of 'The Bonnie Wells o' Wearie' by the village policeman, about midnight. At two o'clock the company decided to go home.

It was then that Kennedy, who may have been slightly affected by the drink he had taken, demanded a horse to carry him to Hillhead. Now that was easy. Uncle George had a horse in the stable. Then, said Kennedy, lend me the horse. "It's yours," said Uncle George. So they went out into the yard under the great red harvest moon. The horse, an old Clydesdale mare, was brought from the stable and Kennedy was hoisted on to her back. Then Susan came down all flushed and sleepy in the moonlight, like a young man's dream. She was placed on the horse and swayed there with her arms clasped round Kennedy. They cried for Stephen next; but he did not answer and after a bit they found him in the parlour trying to feed one of Mr. Castell's stuffed owls with parsley. Since he refused to be parted from the owl, they allowed him to take it with him, so he too was placed on the horse with his arm round Susan to steady him. They were ready to go, when somebody said that Susan's head, being bare, would be cold. A great cry for a hat got up and the village constable in an access of gallantry gave her his helmet. Then Uncle George hit the horse across the quarters with his bare hand, crying, "G up"; the whole party cheered, and the horse moved slowly down the yard into the open road.

She was a patient mare; long accustomed to the plough and with no mind at all to wildness. She bore her burden gently through the woods where the owls were scandalised by drunken snatches and cries of vague delight. All went very well till they turned into the cornyard at Hillhead. Then the mare, frightened at a shadow, broke her even pace and Stephen, losing his balance, slipped over her quarters into a heap of straw. Susan and Kennedy noticed nothing of his misfortune, and continued into the close. Stephen had fallen lightly and the straw was soft. It was grateful to his body, tired with an excess of pleasure. Sleep came over him. But just before his eyes closed he looked up and saw the old Clydesdale mare moving round the corner of the close with Susan and Kennedy and the policeman's helmet fantastically silhouetted against the moon.

"Good night," he said to the quiet world; and settling the stuffed owl in the crook of his arm, he fell asleep.

By the next day at dinner time the evening's adventure had become the speak of the countryside. What the good and godly said about Susan would hardly bear repeating and many heads were shaken over young Stephen Lees. "Jist his grandfather ower again. Drink and women: women and drink. It's aye been the same story at Hillheid and it'll aye be the same. It's in the Brewster bluid."

But old John Dorum the merchant at the cross-roads, a tough old man who had drunk the great days of debauchery into their grave, said, "I heard about ye, Stephen. Man, it was a grand ploy. The publican's owl and the policeman's helmet. Eh man, o man, there hasna been the like in Lendrum since your grandfather penned a flock of sheep in the kirk. But that was thirty years ago and we've grown unco sober since. There's nae fun in Lendrum noo-a-days. The auld men are deid or deein and the young men are frightened; aye man, feared o' their ain shadows, and their wives, and the tongue o' the woman across the road. Ach tchach. And it wasna the drinking that made sic a steer in the aulden days. We werena sic careless deevils because we drank. We drank sic a lot because we were sic careless deevils. Weel, they're a carefu lot we fathered, and there'll be plenty that'll look askance at ye the day. But nae me. Na, nae me. Here, jist ye step in ahint the treacle bar-rel."

This was a great barrel about eight feet high that had stood in a discreet corner of the shop for genera-tions. At one time it had undoubtedly held treacle but for a long time it had only been a screen for John Dorum's obligements. Behind it there was room for a small table and two chairs. Waving Stephen to one of the chairs, John Dorum brought two bottles and two glasses and sat down opposite him.

"Well," he said holding up his glass of beer, "this is hopin that ye'll bide lang in Lendrum. Eh man, o man, the things ye bring tae mind."

They toasted each other. Then Stephen sat back to

listen to the old gentleman.

"That barrel there," John Dorum said, "used tae hae treacle in't, but there hasna been a drop for fifty year and I'll tell ye the reason why. It was about Martinmas term time, on a Thursday mornin, and your grandfather and Auld Mains and Low the horsedealer were haein a quiet dram ahint the treacle barrel. They'd been there for a while, in fact it was mornin nae langer but weel gaen in the afternoon whan in cam Birks, a maist unpleasant man. Ye'll no mind o' Birks, he was a sniffin sneezin body and a stickit minister forbye. It was nae wonder he stickit, for ministers was men in thae days and Birks had nae head for naething, specially for a dram. Bein the naesty body that he was, Birks soon keekit round the back of the treacle barrel and discovered the three lads at their dram. 'Aye, aye,' says he shakin his head, 'so this is the wye ye waste your substance and ruin your immortal souls.' 'Souls be damned,' says Auld Mains, 'come and hae a dram like a dacent Christian.' 'Never,' says Birkie haudin up his hand and half turnin away his face as if the very suggestion had a bad stink, which was just like him; but your grandfather just poured out a good half tumblerfu o' the spirit and slippit it intae Birks' hand. 'Well, since you're sae kind,' says Birks (meaning now that I'm sure o' getting it for naething) 'I canna but drink it.' And drink it he did. After the first glass he had tae lean against the treacle barrel, and, as the afternoon wore on, he slippit further and further doon till in the gloamin he was sitting on the ground wi his head against the cock. Then naebody minds what happened after that, except that everybody left and I gaed ben intae the backshop for my tea.

"Whan I cam back intae the shop again, I put my foot on something sticky. Then I heard a groan. Dammit man, my hair stood on its ends for I thocht there had been murder dune and I was steppin in the bluid. But whan I crackit a match I saw that the bluid was black; that reassured me; for though I kent the men o' Len-

drum were a gie black lot in thae days I kent they werena black tae the very bluid. Then 'God be here,' I said
tae mysel, 'it's treacle'. So I lichtit the lamp and lookit in
ahin the treacle barrel and, o man, I'll never forget what
I saw there. Puir auld Birks sittin on the ground wi his
heid against the barrel. The cock o' the barrel was lippin
the top o' his collar, and, the tap bein full on, a thick run
o' sweet black treacle was seepin doon atween his collar
and his naked skin. Man, Stephen, I tell ye it was runnin
richt doon atween him and his clothes and tricklin oot at
the legs o' his trousers. The best part o' fifty gallons o'
my best cow treacle. Eh but he was a sticky customer I
tell ye and it was a sticky business gettin him hame.
As for the treacle, he took maist o't wi him, that cost him
a pretty penny I tell ye. But it wasna all wasted. His wife
saw tae that. For she just gaed him ae look then she
boiled him, claes and a', and fed the kye on the water
that cam aff o' him. Eh, Stephen man, they were great
days." The old gentleman sucked in his beer with rather
melancholy appreciation. Then he looked up and said
in a whisper, "Aye, Birks peyed up for the treacle that
was lost, but sometime just ye ask your grandfather wha's
hand it was that turned the tap."

Stephen stopped a dozen times to laugh on the
road home. Memories of the night in Lendrum blended
with the story that old John Dorum had told him, and
together they filled him with a reckless delight. "By
god," he said to himself, "once I get started there'll be
no stopping me."

The world grew very wide for Stephen in those
amazing days, for Susan and Kennedy could circle the
earth in a ring of words.

"And why not?" Kennedy said. "The world is my
parish and the whole of life is the text of my sermon."

"Including the policeman's helmet," Stephen suggested.

"You think to come from the sublime to the ridiculous. But you're wrong. The fact that Susan got drunk

114

and wore a policeman's helmet is neither ridiculous nor sublime. It is just another aspect of the truth about the human race, that there is an infinite variety among their actions that cannot be judged by arbitrary rules."

"Then what rules...?"

"Judge not that ye may not be judged. And what good are judgments anyway? Unless to provide an excuse for not doing the things that you're afraid to do. If you want moral laws, I tell you there are only two that can be honoured by an intelligent man – the first is: Cultivate your own garden; and the second is, Allow your neighbour to cultivate his. All the others have been invented by the puritans for the governing of fools. And let me add that my garden is nothing less than the whole world and as much of eternity as I can compass with my own mind. If any man tries to deny my right to enjoy the garden then I'll clout him on the nose. Let us all three go and drink some wine."

When they had each eaten steak with fried onions and were halfway through the third bottle of Nuits St. Georges, Stephen looked round the dining room with great contentment. Outside there was evening, the hard afterglow of the windswept northern town. The three tall windows of the room, so tall that they seemed to reach from earth to heaven, looked out on the Castlegate where the houses might have been cut solid from unrelenting granite. A little wind, a snell wind from the sea, was throwing up handfuls of dust and making the newsboys shiver at their stance beneath the statue of the Duke. It was bright and cold and clean and just a little inhuman. But inside the room – how different. The three tall windows enclosed the softness of evening and content. Over by the grill where the cinders glowed in a lowe of heat the chef was busy with his mysteries.

Looking at the rosy face of the chef far away in the shadows by the fire, at the waiters moving about quietly in the friendly room, at Susan and Kennedy across the white tablecloth and at the bottle of wine dying a so

pleasant death, Stephen felt blessed by a great ease. And
then he sighed. "It will be hard to leave all this."

"But you won't leave it," Susan leant over and
touched his arm. Her grey eyes were soft and eloquent.

"I must," Stephen said; and the words made it all
the harder to think of going away.

"You're twenty-five and your own master," said
Kennedy.

"And there was never a better time to get living
your own life," said Susan.

"But what is it?" Stephen asked. "God knows. I
don't."

"Then you're blind," said Susan. "For this is it
before you. This and all you have been doing in the past
few weeks."

Stephen ground a bit of bread to crumbs on the
tablecloth.

"I can't deny it. I've been thinking a lot about all
this. It would be fine to retire from the silly business of
selling scented soap when there's too many people
selling it already. I'd like fine to live at Hillhead and be
a country gentleman and shoot a bit and fish and work
when I felt like it. At least I wouldn't be doing any harm
and I might be doing myself some good."

He looked rather shyly at Susan for encourage-
ment but she only replied, "If that happened there
would be only only one thing to say."

"What?"

"R.I.P., poor Stephen," she said and shook her
head sadly.

"But why do you say that?" he asked in surprise.

"Because there would soon be an end of Hillhead
and yourself too."

"You mean I couldn't make a living that way?
Well, my grandfather manages along easy enough and
he doesn't look as if he ever lost much sleep over his
affairs."

"But he knows his trade."

"And I could learn."

"You think that would be easy?"

"Well, where my grandfather is so comfortable, I could surely manage."

Then Kennedy, who had been listening to them, interrupted to ask, "But are you sure your grandfather is so comfortable?"

Stephen looked surprised. "I never thought anything else. There is no want of anything about the place. We live well enough and there's no scarcity of money. If you asked me I should say the old man was very well off."

"Yes," said Kennedy, "but if I told you that the old man probably hasn't a hundred pounds in the world beyond what's sunk in the farm and that every penny he spends has to be planned for and worked for months before he spends it, and that the man who comes after him in Hillhead will have a ten times harder job than he has – what would you say?"

Stephen looked hard at Kennedy but never thought to doubt the truth of what he had said. All his impressions of the old man, built up through the last few weeks were now completely upset. The idea of a comfortable old gentleman with a few thousand in bonds, of the careless old sinner living heartily on the goodness of his land without care or conscience; that idea was manifestly false. The ease and the peace and the plenty, which he saw, or thought he saw, in the old man's life had all been put there by himself. He had sentimentalised the old man because he did not know enough. It was a pretty idea but it was a wrong one. It fell away from Stephen's mind, leaving the vision of the old man standing alone and unbuttressed to the four winds of fortune, keeping his world intact by the power of his martyring spirit. The new vision of the old man so thrilled him that he smote the table with his hand.

"By god, I would say that it would be ten times more splendid to be the man who came after him."

"Do you mean it?" Kennedy asked.

"Yes."

"O Stephen," Susan cried, "I love you." Then she leaned over the table and kissed him.

The chef winked to the head waiter and threw a point steak on the grill. He would have been the last man to deny that life was full of wonder.

They finished the bottle and ordered up another one. When it too was empty they left the restaurant and walked home to dear Dunelm in old Aberdeen. As they went down through College Bounds the world swayed gently and when they came to the Kirkyard gate the harvest moon hung low between the Cathedral towers. Nearby the river sang upon the weir. The dead men made no sound at all.

"Soon we will all be dead too," said Kennedy.

"Yes," said Stephen with his eyes fixed upon the antics of the drunken moon, "but we'll do great things before then."

Susan kissed him again. "I love you, Stephen, because you mean it."

"By the Lord God, I mean it," said Stephen, solemnly.

And when he woke up the next morning he still meant it.

CHAPTER SEVEN

The Ruined Harvest

THE NEARNESS of the harvest brought a new excitement into life at Hillhead, for the bravest season of the year was at hand. It had been an ideal summer, of which the like had not been seen for twenty years. Day after day bloomed bright and warm; night after night declined into cool dews and livening rain. "It'll never last," the old man had said when they were cutting the hay, but every morning the Ben had stood up clear and fair along the Howe. "It'll never last," he said when they were leading the hay; but the improvident glories of each new day reproved his evening's caution. And now, as he ordered the binder to be dragged out of its shed and the cloths to be carried down from the loft, he almost believed that one more harvest might be saved.

For hours he would stand under the triumphant weathercock at the gable end, looking up the golden Howe to the Ben. Seeing him there with his hat well down over his eyes and the smoke curling slowly up from his briar pipe, Stephen said to himself, *Damn me for a fool, that I thought him an old done man. I was blind then, for all I saw was bone grown brittle and joints grown stiff and the old skin that has dried and wrinkled. But a man is more than skin and bones. He has a fine pride that makes the blood go singing round his heart.*

As he stood there under the weathercock at the gable end, the old man had a lot to be proud of. There were ninety acres of oats and barley ripened for the harvest. The fine dry wind came up the Howe from the sea and tossed the light gold heads of the oats like bells till they rang the husky changes of the harvest. Silent, the barley hung its million beards as the wind ran in a

darker tide of gold across the shining sea. The year's
passion was spent. The almighty thrust of life that had
sent the spears of grass through the sides of the warm
earth, that had given unnumbered breathing forms to
the heat of the engendering sun, that had come at last to
the flower of its perfection, was now withdrawing upon
itself, its work all done. For weeks and months a man
might have stood in the fields and felt himself lifted up
by the passion of the earth surging towards ripeness.
But now in the afternoon's more tempered heat he
might stand in the peace of the world's fulfilment. Listening he might hear the snap of a broom pod opening
on the bright burnished seed, and the dry sound of the
rustling corn, the loveliest song of the maternal earth.
Like the earth, but greater in the freedom of his
thought, the old man stood, all passion spent, and reckoned up his harvest.

"Just look at him," Stephen said to Kennedy as
they lay together under a beech tree, waiting for the
work to begin, "he's rounded, whole, complete and
satisfied. He's sure of himself and the world he lives in."

"Yes," Kennedy said, "but why?"

"Because he belongs to an old tradition, to the pre-
war world where everything was fixed and definite."

"I wonder," said Kennedy. "You know, I think a
man like your grandfather makes his own time and his
own order. The world has always been a bit of a wilderness, but a man, if he was strong enough, could make his
own golden age as he went along. And I'm sure that, if
the world were falling in a shower of small stones upon
his shoulders, the old man would still go on his usual
way, planning his harvests and damning the weather for
its inconstancy."

"Well," said Stephen with a sigh, "it's a brave sight
but it seems more than mortal to me."

"Away," said Kennedy, "to hear you a body would
think you'd been brought up on the parish."

"Maybe we all are," Stephen replied, "for these are

degenerate days."

They didn't have much time to think of the degeneracy of the age. Harvest came on them all at once. As soon as the dew was off the crops the two binders were started among the oats. Round and round the field they went, cutting their even swathes and throwing off the sheaves all neatly gathered and bound. It was a brave sight in the windy afternoon. The horses, three to each machine, strained at their collars as they breasted the rise of the land; their iron hooves bit into the soft ground and their long tails streamed out behind them. High up on the binder seat the driver waved his whip and called out to them, urging them against the drag of the hill. The binding needle flashed in the sun; then the sheaf was swept on to the ground. The other men worked steadily behind, building the sheaves into stooks in even rows like tents along the field. Round and round in the sun and the wind till the many operations of hand and brain and muscle and pinion were settled into the steady rhythm of harvest. Stephen gloried in the work; he dared it to tire him; and when the first field of twenty acres was cut, stooked and ready for the cornyard he felt as proud as if he had been God himself. He grudged the nights that must come; and the rest that the horses must have and the dew that must fall. He wanted to go on without let or hindrance to the harvest home and the crown of the farmer's year. For a kind of glory had now possessed him.

Next day they were to begin on the big thirty-acre park of oats behind the steading. In the evening the old man and Stephen took a last look at it. The night was very still and warm. The world was so quiet that Stephen felt the corn, the wave upon wave of golden heads bowed with their ripeness, was waiting for the lovely death of its harvest. But the old man was uneasy.

"Ower warm and ower still," he said. "I dinna like it. There's thunder in the air."

Stephen laughed at him. The old man said noth-

121

ing. They went in to bed.

The thunder wakened Stephen about midnight. It was so near that it shook the old house and the lightning preceded it in a fearful illumination. Peal after peal threatened the old house with destruction. The sound came down from the heaven in mighty blows and it seemed that no work of mortal man could stand against it. Stephen cowered in bed, crushed down by the storm's immensity: but the steady defiance of the house assured him. He rose and went over to the window. The lightning was so near that it had no shape; no dragons of fire, no writhing serpent shot across the sky; but great sheets of light swept up the river valley. It was an intense white light that rent the dark with a sudden illumination, showing up distant trees and stones and the pools in the river as clear as if a strong beam had been thrown on them at a three-yards distance. It was terrible in its unreality: first the darkness, black night filled with mighty unseen forces; then the dreadful light suddenly creating an intense world out of nothing; then the as-sudden passing of that world in the annihilating riot of the thunder. Stephen, watching the storm, passed through a swift series of emotions. He was frightened; then he was thrilled with a splendid terror; then the terror went out of him and he was possessed by the might of the storm. He was swept up by and carried away into the unearthly glories of the upper air. After the thunder came the rain, not falling with the gentle and livening persistence that brings fertility to the earth, but pouring out as from the sluice gates of heaven. As the lightning failed and the thunder died away from the sea, it came down heavy and dull, like the death of the storm. When Stephen looked out of his window next morning his heart almost failed him. Disaster had fallen on the harvest and all the fields of proud corn were in ruins.

For the first time since he went to Hillhead Stephen dressed unwillingly to go out to meet the morn-

ing. That was ungrateful, for there had never been a
more sweet and gentle day to greet him. Utter peace
and beatitude had followed the storm. The sun was
delicately veiled but not obscured by a translucent mist
that fined away from a milky white into the palest blue of
the sky. The grass, newly washed by the rain, shone with
the last green growth of the year. Every flower had a
jewel in her ear and the little rain pattered down from
the trees as the light wind shook the laden branches.
The air was deliciously sweet and new to the senses and
all the foolish birds were singing. The land was so delicate of colour, so soft and milky, so unlike the dusty
world of autumn, that it might have been a new world
coming to life upon the morning air. But Stephen had
no time for those sweet seductions. He went slowly
round to the cornfield and looked at the ruin which the
storm had made. Where there had been wave upon
wave of proud heads there was now a twisted mass of
muddy straw. The stalks had been broken, then the ears
had been battered into the earth. Some parts were laid
flat as if a roller had passed over them. Others were
twisted all ways, first knotted into a sodden mass and
then pounded down by the weight of the rain. Here and
there a few heads stood erect, supported by the mass
that had been laid all round them, brave and forlorn like
the ring of knights around the King at Flodden.
Stephen looked over the field for a long time, in a mood
of empty desolation. Then he turned angry at the stupidity of the ruin.

"Damn you," he said to the young smiling day,
"what the hell do you care."

"Dinna worry yoursel, laddie," the old man said,
coming up behind him. "If it's nae ae thing it's anither.
When ye've been a farmer as long as me ye'll ken that
the bite's never safe till it's intae yer mouth. This'll mean
a hard hairst and a sma barn, but we might as well hae
our breakfasts. Misfortune and a teem belly are cauld
companions."

The men were in a different temper when they met in the harvest field again. The fun had gone out of the game. They rhythm was spoiled. Work was now a hard darg against the collar. As the binders could not cut the laid corn the reaper had to take their place. But the reaper, while it cut the corn, did not gather and bind it; so the gathering and binding had to be done by hand. That was back-breaking work, the more because most of the corn was so twisted that it would not make a tidy sheaf. The men had to tear the matted stuff apart and gather it in with a band in any way they could. The result was a big untidy wisp that scunnered them, for they liked a tidy harvest. A hundred times a day they cursed that hour of rain.

Some parts of the corn were so twisted that not even the reaper could do anything with them. They had to be cut out with the scythe. Now the scythe has cut many a good harvest and it has a pleasant rhythm if the muscles are in tune. But there could be no rhythm in those ruined acres. The laid stuff had to be hacked out with the scythe, work as hard to the spirit as to the back. But the scything was nothing to the gathering and bind-ing. That was Stephen's job and it nearly broke his heart. He had to rive and pull to get enough detached from the tangled mass to make a sheaf, and it was no sheaf when done was, for the straw was all heads and tails and it would have taken a clever man to say which was the right end up. Worse than that, the thistles were plentiful in the laid patches and every time Stephen pushed the ends of the band into the sheaf to secure it, the jags bit deep into his finger tips. During the first hour or so he was always stopping to dig them out but that was a waste of valuable time, so he had to bear with them, and after the second day he was able to treat them with something like indifference.

They were grim days, for the beatitude that had followed the storm did not last beyond its morning. Sullen grey skies hung low down. Clouds ever blown up

from the sea in a louring procession would hang motionless for a time, as if supported upon the hills and the
horizon, and shut out the valley from the living light.
Stirred up by the cold wind they would as sullenly de-
part, but always more came up from the sea to take their
place. All the grimness of the cold North East, that had
been so gaily masked by the grace of summer, now rose
up like a grey presence from the sodden earth. The
ground was wet and dead; the wind killing in its insis-
tent damp cold. Together the wet and the cold possessed the ruined harvest fields like the savage spirit of
the countryside, inimical to man. All the men at Hillhead felt it. Even Willum grew silent and worked on
dourly in a kind of dumb protest against fate, for there
was no genial warmth to breed his lazy stories now that
the sun was obscured. The taste had gone out of the
harvest; they had only one thought, to get it over and
done with.

But there were two of them to whom adversity was
a challenge which they accepted with a grimness equal to
that of the season. Tam and the old man went into the
business of saving what was left of the harvest with a kind
of pride in matching themselves against ill fortune that
thrilled Stephen to the marrow. They did not lose a moment of working time, more than the weather demanded. It might be nine or ten in the morning before
the reaper could be started, but from that moment they
drove the men and horses as hard as they could go, till
night came or evening brought the chill rain from the
sea. As the oats had to be gathered and bound after the
reaper, it was never possible to stook all that had been
cut during the day. So Stephen and Tam went out in
the morning to make up the leeway. Morning after
morning it was the same. They were faced with an acre
or two of the unwieldy sheaves now soaked with the rain.
The mornings were cold but not as cold as the drops that
lodged in every ear of corn. Tam and Stephen wore
oilskin coats and leggings but no covering could have

protected them from the showers that fell on their faces and trickled down their shivering bodies from every sheaf as they lifted it under their arm to stook it. They became soaked no less than the sheaves and soon the water was oozing from their boots. They had reached the depths of misery

As each day broke cold and sullen, and as no living wind blew out of the west to dry the grain, it became more and more certain that the harvest would be a failure. But in measure as their affairs grew hopeless the old man and Tam seemed to take savage delight in saving what they could.

"There would hae been ten quarters tae the acre afore the storm," the old man said casually, "now it willna thrash five – and that'll be puir and blauded. Two hunder pound lost in a shower o' rain, Stephen. And the minister's gettin ready for the harvest thanksgiving. He was round yesterday, hopin that our generosity could be relied on as usual. Well, laddie, I suppose we can gae him straw tae his heart's content, but the Kirk, I've noticed, is keener on the grain."

Stephen was near angry with him because he could make a joke, however grim, about his misfortune. It was not a joke to him; nor to Tam. They were bitter, angry men as they slashed and pulled and drove the harvest on till their minds were tired and their bodies were sore.

"Why do you bother?" Stephen asked Tam, as they stood in the cartshed looking at the rain that swept across the drookit fields. "Give it up as a bad job. It isn't your harvest. You won't be the loser."

Tam replied with a touch of anger in his voice. "It is my hairst. The auld man maybe planned it, but I made the ground a' through the winter and spring; I sowed the seed; and I've watched it growin twenty times a day; and it's my hairst though I winna gather the profit nor bear the loss. There's a year o' my work in that parks and if a man isna tae care for his work what is there left for him to care for? But if I could get a chance

126

tae bear the profit I'd willingly tak a chance tae bear the loss."

"Are you another socialist?" Stephen asked.

Tam shook his head. "I'm nae naething. I'm a man that has been born on the land and I want tae live by the land. But it's a thin living the land has for ony o' us the day and it's likely tae be worse afore it's better. There's naething but trouble. Bad weather and bad prices are bringin the best men doon." He stopped; then he added in a worried voice, "They say Leas has signed his trust deed yesterday. He was in a bad way, then the storm finished him. Anither seven and sixpence in the pound."

"What about it? The inefficient must always go to the wall," Stephen replied. "It's an economic law."

"A bad law when a hard-workin man like Leas has tae fail because o' a run o' bad luck. He had tae buy his place when the laird sold up the estate. He hadna enough money so he had tae raise it on a bond. What wi the fall in prices the place isna worth a third o' what he had tae pay for't. Worse than that, he hasna been makin enough tae pay the interest on the bond. Of course he's been drinkin a bit tae try and forget about his troubles, and that never did a man ony good when he was in the hands o' the banks. The storm has finished him. If he'd had a good hairst he might hae been able tae carry on till the better times. But now the creditors willna wait. He's signed his trust deed and that's the end o' him. Och, but it's a dreary thing for a man o' fifty-five tae be out in the market without a penny."

"It's the way of the world," Stephen said.

"Then it's a damned poor way, that's what I'm comin tae think. Here's me that for five and twenty year hae been slavin and scrapin tae get enough tae start a place o' my ain. But what chance hae I that ken naething o' business, o' buyin and sellin and markets, whan men that hae been a' their lives at the game daena ken the way tae mak a livin. There was a time when hard work was enough. A ploughman like mysel could save and save till he got into a croft. Still slavin and slavin he could get a better place, until at the end o' his days he had a two or three pair fairm and his wife had a Sunday gown. There was some purpose in a man's work in thae days.

"But there's little purpose noo. Hard work's nae enough. Ye need tae hae a business brain. O, there's plenty o' good farmers in the countryside. There's plenty o' men like your grandfather that can fatten the best o' cattle and raise the best o' corn; but there's nae mony men that can mak a profit by it. Times are changin, but we daena ken the way tae change wi them. We're needin men that can teach us the ways o' business; if we only had them, we could easy raise the kye and the corn.

"It's the banks and the speculators and the booms and the slumps and a' that gamblin wi men and money by financiers that couldna tell the difference atween a midse and an endrig – that's what's playin the devil wi the countryside. It's nae fair, man, it's nae fair. We've enough to thole wi the weather and the pests without haein tae worry about whether the crops'll be worth onything at all when we've won them hame."

Tam and Stephen looked out from the cartshed across the sodden field where the rain was still falling unabated. A grey hopelessness settled over their spirits, for they felt themselves caught in a net of unjust circumstances. Then Stephen remembered the grand words that Kennedy had used about the glory of being a man and there came back to him something of the power which he had felt in the long glories of the summer.

"But damn it," said Stephen, "why do we put up with it? This is our country. If we're to work for it we have a right to demand a fair reward."

"Fine words," said Tam. "But ye'll speak a damned lang time about rights afore ye get them."

Then damn it," Stephen cried. "If speaking won't

get you anything, you must take what you want."

Tam laughed rather sadly. "There's naebody in this countryside that has guts enough tae tak onything but what they get. They'll run wi their hats tae the government and say thank ye for a kind word. But they're a' livin in the past. And they're scared o' change. A' they can dae is cry out about injustices and be starved tae death like rabbits in the snaw."

Stephen, because he could see no way out of the difficulties of the farmers, and because those difficulties were raising a problem for him that he was not yet ready to meet, grew angry with Tam's persistence.

"But you can't blame the farmers for that. It's their own affair and if they prefer to starve by their old ways, they've surely every right to."

"No," Tam said slowly. "I'll be damned if they have. The laan's the men's livin as well as the farmer's, and when the farmers suffer the men suffer tae. But why should the farmer grow poorer, because he willna change, and mak the ploughman poorer wi him; when a' the time the butchers and the dealers and the bankers are gettin richer and richer."

"That's the way it happens," Stephen said; but there was no comfort in the words for, in spite of himself, he had a sense of the world's confusion destroying the fair security of Hillhead; as the wanton rain had destroyed the harvest.

"Then it's a michty poor way," Tam said. "Whan I look round the countryside I see enough for a'body, master and man, gin it was measured out. But the farmers hae nae thocht and nae measure except the days o' ease and plenty in the time o' their fathers. Still I wouldna blame them ower much. They've been God Almichty in their places sae lang that they canna believe their heaven is changin oot o' a' their knowledge. They can only be squeezed tae death and cry on governments. We're squeezed tae, but we needna cry, for naebody'll listen."

"But if you cry loud enough surely you'll get justice."

Tam cried, "Ach," impatiently: then he added, "It's nae justice we want, it's men tae lead us. My god, if only your grandfather had been twenty-seven instead o' seventy-seven."

But the times were thirty years too late for his grandfather to lead them. They spoke about Leas at the supper table that night.

"Poor James," said Aunt Elizabeth. "He'll have nothing now and that'll be hard for him; because although he never had very much he was accustomed to having a little. And he was such a genteel body. Even when he fell down drunk he fell down quiet. But now I'm afraid he's down for good and he'll never get up again drunk nor sober."

"Couldn't his friends have got together and saved him?" Stephen asked.

"What way could they save him that couldn't save themselves?" the old man replied, giving Stephen a grim look.

Stephen flushed, for he had been put in his place - but Aunt Elizabeth came to his aid.

"These are cold times," she said. "I think we should all have a little of Mr. Elphinstone's cherry brandy."

The brandy warmed them against the cold winds of misfortune and they talked of more pleasant things, of the gay young trees in St James' Park when the spring comes and of Bond Street, fantastic as a fairy tale at five o'clock on a winter afternoon.

"When you are old, my dear," said Aunt Elizabeth, "it does you good to turn over the bits your memory has saved from the world."

But Stephen, listening to her husky voice recalling so easily and with so little regret the pleasures of her life, felt that she had saved everything. She was very rich, like an old empress, and she ruled over a great empire with memory as her minister. There was something about her that warmed Stephen; she made no demands on him, but offered for his enjoyment the things that she had enjoyed so fully. She was all kindness to her friends and gratitude that she had been allowed a term of this so diverting life.

When she had gone to bed the old man cocked an eye at the closing door and said with open admiration, "She's a great spirit. There never was a woman got sae much fun out o' sae much trouble – and a' the trouble was o' her ain makin."

"That seems to be a mark of the Brewsters," Stephen said with a laugh.

The old man gave him a long look under his thick eyebrows. "Aye? Then ye should get plenty o' fun out o' what I'm gaun tae tell ye."

He sat forward with his hands on his knees. "I ken fine what ye meant when ye spoke about Leas at supper-time. Ye thocht I micht hae steppit up and saved him. Well, I couldna. I owe the bank three hunder pound and I'll owe it as much again wi this bad hairst."

The words were so incredible that Stephen could not take them at their full value.

"But the stock on the farm and the crops – they must be worth a fortune," he said.

"Fifteen hunder at the outside and fallin every day wi the fall in prices. Another year or two as bad as this and where'll the Brewsters be? Where Leas is the day."

"What'll happen then?" Stephen asked, now struck desolate at the thought of such ruin.

The old man laughed. "Och, laddie, daena worry yoursel. The money'll last my time, and I'll outlast your Aunt Elizabeth. There'll be nane to worry about what comes after. Whatever happens there'll be enough tae bury me in my ain grave, and aince I'm out o' sicht I'll be forgotten, though the more I die in debt the langer I'll be kept in mind."

He knocked out his pipe and prepared to go to

bed. Stephen looked at him, thinking that he was pre-
tending a carelessness that he did not really feel. But
there was small sign of emotion about the old man.

By the Lord, Stephen said to himself, *he's too tough for
any circumstances to break him.*

But when he thought of the future of Hillhead,
when the Brewsters would sow no harvests there nor
lead the ring of hospitality about their table, he grew
very sad; and he swore there must not be an end to such
a long story.

Stephen spent the next few days in savage hopelessness, made all the more savage by the vile weather.
Every morning was the same – rain that cleared off
slowly through a trailing mist to a bright blink of sun at
twelve. But just when the corn was drying at the mid
afternoon the clouds descended over the Ben and by
four o' clock the mist had come down and brought back
the rain. There was now no hope that the battered crops
would rise again; they would soon be so spoiled that
they would not pay the cost of cutting them; and even
those that had been cut and stooked in good weather
before the storm were being rotted by the inveterate
rain. The water was eating into the dry ears, while the
grass was growing up through the bottom of the sheaves.
There was little that the men could do but suffer the
broken time and watch the slow destruction of so much
good. Stephen fretted for action; he wanted to throw
his body against the monstrous iniquity that had defiled
the countryside; but action was denied him so that he
had to stay at home and think upon his troubles. Then it
seemed to him the little wrong of the weather was all
part of the greater wrong that was oppressing the countryside. There was John George trailing about in the
ruins of his glory, cadging free drinks from his tenants;
there was Leas a broken man thrown out into the market
without a penny in his pocket, there was Willum encum-
bered by his many children and their bastards, without
any hope of ease or comfort till the end of his days;

there was Tam met with the frustration of the hopes that had kept him working for five and twenty years; and there was Hillhead and all the splendid living it had stood for through two hundred years threatened with a miserable end. So many things with so much good in them were being squeezed to death by circumstances that they did not understand and did not dare to control. What could he, Stephen, do but lay a wreath upon the grave of beauty and go his own way. So much he would decide; but as soon as he had made that decision, his mood suddenly changed, and he felt a passionate desire to fight the dark, creeping despair.

It was then that he got a letter from Clarkson, the sales manager of the company. It was a rather pompous exercise in business English. But that was excusable, for it offered Stephen the post of assistant sales manager at six hundred pounds a year. If he accepted the offer, and Mr. Clarkson let it be inferred that there could be no doubt about his decision, he would be expected to start work at the beginning of October, as they were planning a big campaign in the North of England. Several small companies had too great a share of that market and were due to be put in their proper place, where they could be the more easily absorbed by the combine which Stephen and Mr. Clarkson had the honour to serve. The selling campaign which was intended to work their undoing would be a most important one; and, since Stephen had special knowledge of the North of England, he would be given a big share of the work. That would mean a lot of responsibility, and, of course, a good deal of hard slogging; but, if the campaign were successful, the rewards would be in proportion. Mr. Clarkson then hoped that he was completely renewed in health and that his reply would be received immediately, along with the probable date of his return.

Stephen read the letter at the parlour fire after breakfast; and, giving a disgusted look at the weather which was working itself up to new heights of viciousness behind a north wind, he sat down to write his acceptance.

He found it difficult to get the words down on paper. He stuck in the middle of the second sentence, and when he came to himself he realised that he had been staring out at the window for the best part of half an hour. Giving himself an impatient shake, he returned his attention to the paper; but now he found that something prevented him from writing. He rolled the paper into a ball, took a new sheet and began again; but there was a kind of fever working in him. His fingers tingled so much that he had to throw down the pen. Then he rose and went over to the window, walked round the room, sat down, got up again and finally went out for a walk to settle the confusion of his mind.

He took the road by which he had gone with Susan and Kennedy to the hills – down the Lady Park, across the ferry and through the fields by Lendrum. As he walked along, with his head down against the wind and the rain, he tried to compose his reply to Clarkson. *Of course*, he said to himself. *Here I'm offered all that I've been working for: and it's only the beginning. Clarkson will become a director soon, in five years maybe, and they'll need a sales manager. And there's Jane.*

Then he realised how seldom he had thought about her since he left London. They had written each other twice: she to tell him about the people who had stayed with them at Avignon: he to tell her – but what could he tell Jane about the life at Hillhead. She had become a little unreal for him during the past two months: now she became real again only when he thought about his job. He strove to get the matter clear in his head. If he went back to London in October he would have a small room in the company's new office off the Strand. There would be travellers to organise, advertising to plan, interminable discussions with Clarkson, memoranda, reports, statistics and charts. He would probably join a good club, one of the more business ones. He would be certain of a place in the office cricket team. He would play golf for business reasons. Then he would marry Jane. They would have a flat in one of the vast new service blocks, with steel furniture and a cocktail cabinet. They would go to Avignon, or Monte Carlo, or Invernessshire with the rest of the Dorman crowd. They would entertain worth while people. They would make excellent contacts, and Jane would see that they got the best advantage from them. Then, as the company grew, which it certainly would, there might be subsidiaries, with nice directorships. In fact there were no limits to what might be – no limits but his power to shape his fortune. And he was sure that, if he cared, he could do as well as any man.

Almost Stephen convinced himself that it would be the best of all possible actions to accept the job at once. Then he remembered what Kennedy had said about the men with the little black bags. The image revolted him and then made him laugh. He tried to forget it, but he could not get Susan and Kennedy out of his mind. He heard them at their talk, snaring his senses with a ring of words. Their voices, like the sirens, cried him away from duty to wander for ever among enchanted meadows of thought in the boundless freedom of this mind. And o but freedom was a lovely thing. If he went back to London he would be tied for ever: once he committed himself to the company he would never win free. He would be one of the Dorman crowd; a good crowd who would give him everything that money could buy except freedom. He would be their man. He might go to Avignon; he might go to Monte Carlo; but wherever he went he would be one of the Dorman crowd. They would shape his future for him; he would be a glorified little man with a glorified black bag. *No, by god,* he said to himself, *I want to be free. I want to live in my own way, to make my own mistakes and have all the glory of my own success. I want to go away and see the world. There's the blue sea beyond those hills, and across the sea there are many strange lands. The world's full of names, but where there are names there must be people. I could see Russia and the Steppes that go on and on for a thousand miles, or a thousand years. I could climb the great mountains, sail on the great seas, travel eastward into the deserts where silence has become eternal. Down there is the blue sea, and beyond the sea there are small white towns set on the precipitous shores. "Row me out to Desenzano." How does it run – "O Venusta Sirmio." I could talk to bearded men from the hills, like brigands out of a masquerade. I could make love to women under the vines: women with the hot passions of the engendering sun. Great God, I've never kissed a woman who did not know where she would stop before she began – and I knew it too. I'll find gold in the hills; pearls in the sea. I'll talk, and drink with strangers; I'll find out the remotest secrets of the Earth and stand alone upon the last cliff that looks out upon the furthest ocean: then in the end of my days I'll come home to my own country, to die and be joined to my own people. I'll not be afraid of the Everlasting Dark, for I will have had a good life, and the whole world will end when I close my eyes.*

Ach, but that's nonsense, he said, shaking his senses free from their dream. *That was all very well in the time of Queen Elizabeth, but I'm no Raleigh.* Again Kennedy came into his mind *And I'm not a man with a little bag. The world's work must be done, and I will do it.* But he heard Kennedy asking, "Is the work worth while?" Well, was it? The company was a big one: it would be larger still. It was splendidly equipped. It could beat its rivals. It might even control the market. But he knew the means by which that end would be attained – the plotting, the bribing, the lies so thinly disguised as business ethics; the lies more cleverly disguised as advertising; the financial operations, the manoeuvres on the Stock Exchange, the relentless wear and tear of human powers to achieve – what would it achieve? Would the work be any better? Would civilisation bloom fairer? Would men sleep more easily in their beds when they had swallowed his patent medicines? Would children grow more beautiful and laughter be more careless in the little brick

towns of England? He asked himself: and he heard
Kennedy answering a total "No"; and he knew that
Kennedy was right. *O hell,* he said to himself, *I wish I had
never come here. Then there wouldn't have been any questions.*

As he climbed up the hills above Lendrum the
equal motion and the effort brought some order out of
his confusion. The issues then became clear to him. His
habit of mind, well disciplined at school and business,
drove him towards the safe course. Let him accept the
offer that he had worked for and take the safe low road
to fortune. An insurgent instinct pulled him to freedom.
Let him go wide across the unknown seas and find the
dangerous high road to adventure. Reason played the
weak judge to the counsel of his instincts. Now it drew
out the virtues of one course; now the virtues of the
other; and would not come to judgment. As the debate
went on, the cause of safety began to lose. The events of
the past two months had made such a deep impression
on Stephen. They had filled him with so many exultations, attacked him with so much despair, so deepened
and enlarged his life, that London and business seemed
small and tedious, like childhood seen from the first
freedom of a man's life. *Maybe I'm not the same man,*
Stephen said to himself, *and if I went back I would be a
stranger.*

But it's madness, madness, he said; and he set himself, resolutely, to think of the differences that the pro-
motion would make in his life. Responsibility – he would
welcome it, the chance to make plans and see them
through to success or failure. Authority – he would like
like that too. Jane – but his mind shied away from the
thought of her. It would be a life of steady effort, of
good money, or reasonable amusement. Then he won to
the top of the hill, and stood looking down on the lower
world. Up there, away from the sight of harvest, the
uncertain day had its own swift glories. The wind had
rent the banks of cloud, and the sun was sweeping the
land with slanting shafts of light. Here was shadow:

there the light; and, in between, the light and shadow
blended. All to the west stood the mountain tops in the
lessening cones of light. Showers of rain swept down the
valleys into the rays of the sun; and the meeting of the
rain and the sun's light produced a misty whiteness, like
an ethereal steam from the conjunction of two so pure
and lively elements. Down by Lendrum where the valley
widened, the cloud shadows rolled across the haughs,
now darkening the pale drowned fields; now obscuring
the reflected lights from farm windows. And eastward,
over the high ridge of the land, through a channel cut by
the ice in a prehistoric age, there was a line where the
horizon darkened to a deeper blue, the sea. The hills
and the wind and the rain and far away the sea with the
sun behind and beyond them all – these elemental things
played havoc with the young man's mind. Their magnificence challenged him.

  By god, he thought, *I could do it. I came here, and took
my place at the harvest. I can work. I am strong. And for once
in a lifetime I'll be reckless. I'll say 'no' to them; and when
that's said, then I'll be free.*

  He sat on the top of the hill for a long time, thinking of ways and means. He had saved some money, and
he had some good speculations on the Stock Exchange.
At the moment he might be able to collect £600, which
would take him far across the world. At the worst he
need not starve. Coming down the hill again he stopped
and had tea with the woman at the little farm. When he
came away, he thought *They've nothing: and yet they
manage to live; and by god that woman's more alive than most
of the people I know in London. If she and her man can do it,
then so can I.*

  So thinking, he returned to Hillhead in the evening. But he put off making a decision till the morning.
When Aunt Elizabeth had gone to bed, he told the old
man about the letter.

  "I've been offered a new job, assistant to the sales
manager, and they want me to start as soon as possible."

138

"Man, man," his grandfather said, pleased like, "a good job?"

"Six hundred, and prospects."

"Six hundred and you're only twenty-five. I never made more even in the best days o' the War. Ye'll be a millionaire afore you're fifty."

There was open admiration in the old man's voice, but Stephen was not quite sure that there wasn't a touch of mockery as well.

"And so ye'll be leavin," the old man went on, leaning back in his chair and giving Stephen a look that seemed to take him all in, from the day he was born. But it was not unfriendly.

Stephen nodded. "I'll be sorry."

"Aye," said the old man, "and so will your Aunt Elizabeth. Listenin tae the twa o' ye I've come tae ken London and the great folk as weel as the back o' my hand. Nae that she hadna tel't me plenty afore: but now you've kind o' brought my acquaintance wi society up tae date."

That took the feet from Stephen, and he didn't know what to say.

Then the old man laughed. "And I'll be sorry tae. Ye've been fine company; and I will say that I never sae much enjoyed the sicht o' anybody playin at bein a fairmer. But a young man has tae gang his ain gate and ye mustna miss your market. I've nae doubt but ye'll be a big success; and I'm only sorry I'll nae be here tae see ye; for I've seen mony strange things in this world, but a Brewster wi siller tae spare would beat them a'. Weel, weel, never mind that; your Auntie Mary will be proud o' ye. O aye, it'll be a proud day for Mary, and, laddie, there's been little about the Brewsters that she's ever been proud o'."

Then Stephen was sure that the old man was laughing at him, and making a fool of his career. As the old man's ridicule was the one thing he could not bear, he hurried to explain himself.

"But I haven't made up my mind to accept yet."

The old man held up his hands. "God almichty: ye'd be mad tae think twice about takin six hunder pounds a year. Sic like offers daena come twice in the life o' ony man. And if your Auntie Mary was tae hear o't she'd ding the hoose about your lugs. Whan a body's offered six hunder pound a year, that's nae the time for thinkin. Laddie, laddie, ye should never think about money. Ye should tak it wi baith your hands." He stopped, with a dry look, then added, "– and spend it afore ye lose it."

Stephen felt the ground cut away from under his feet. The old man had undermined his newly found resolution. It was very discouraging. The first person to whom he had as much as hinted his desire for freedom, had laughed at him, and told him not to miss his market. Because that person was the old man, whom he admired above all others, the resolution went out of him, leaving him blank and resigned.

"If I go," he said, "I should go on Saturday."

"Three days." The old man reckoned. "Nae lang o' ye left, but lang enough tae hae a party. We'll see ye awa in style, for dammit, we may never see ye again."

Then the old man went to bed, leaving Stephen alone to the confusion of this thoughts. *O Hell,* he said to himself, striking his fist on the mantelpiece, *why can't I think the same for an hour on end.*

Like a wise man he wasted no more time but went to bed. Next afternoon, in a fever of irresolution, he sought counsel from the superior wits of Mr. Jeremy Elphinstone.

"You ask my advice," said Mr. Elphinstone, who was tying up his Michaelmas Daisies in the garden, "Well, I won't give you it. But if you will sit down in the arbour with me, I will be delighted to make a few observations on life in general and on business in particular. First of all, however, tell me, what do you think of Michaelmas Daisies?"

"I can't say I've ever thought about them at all."

"Pity," said Mr. Elphinstone, "for I've been thinking about them for quite ten minutes and I've come to the conclusion that there never was a duller flower with a pleasanter name. Or is it pleasant? There is something very stupid about the daisy's plain humility. It is a form of perversion I have never been able to understand."

They sat down in the arbour and Mr. Elphinstone lit one of his excellent cigars while he listened to Stephen's story.

"Now," he said, "I will make the few observations which I promised you. But first let me draw your attention to the Cathedral clock."

Stephen looked across the garden to the twin spires of St. Machar which rose above the ancient trees.

"I can't see it," he said.

"That is the beauty of Dunelm." He blew out a little cloud or rich smoke. "It is hidden from the whole world, even from time. And that is a valuable matter as your powers diminish but your appetites remain. Now touching this question of your career. I'm not going to make up your mind for you; because it has been my golden rule to gamble only for (though never with) myself. But as I see the world of business, there are only two kinds of people in it: those who try to make money by their own work, and those who make money by the work of the others. The first may do well enough, among the petty cash: they may even collect a fifty thousand or so, by stern application to business and a liberal interpretation of their moral code as occasion demands, although at no time do they risk serious disagreement with their conscience. The second, my boy, and I'm proud to think that I'm one of them, they have no moral code, except that to be found out is downright stupidity. Since the system under which we live – a very foolish one, I grant you, is based on the principles of smash and grab, they develop the system as near its logical conclusion as they can go. They do not delude

themselves with phrases like the 'Greatest good of the
greatest number,' or 'Service not self', though they're not
averse to using those phrases to delude their victims.
They make large sums of money with the greatest ease.
While the good, honest industrious creatures are working hard and creating wealth, they sit above them, and
make plans for relieving them of that wealth when it is
made. I can assure you we are successful. If I were a
young man entering a business career I should have no
difficulty choosing which side to be on. In a system of
smash and grab I would be a fool to join those who
handicap their smashing and grabbing by very foolish
ideals called "rules of the game". I should join myself to
the pirates and become wealthy while I was still able to
enjoy the diversions offered by this deplorable world."

"I see," said Stephen.

"You don't," said Mr. Elphinstone. "But I'll tell
you. Unfortunately for your success in the greater world
of business, you belong to that part of the world which
has a constitutional fondness for the rules of the game.
You have enough intelligence to see that the system of
smash and grab is a stupid one, for all except the small
minority, the pirates; but you have neither the supreme
selfishness, nor the logical mind, which will enable you to
make the most of its essential stupidity. So, in the
greater world of business you are bound to be one of the
exploited, and that, I should imagine, would be a intolerable thought to a man of your spirit."

"Then what?"

"I am coming to that, all in my own good time. As
I see you, there is something of the leader of causes in
you. You have a kind of commonsense, which you may
have inherited from your grandfather, but you have also
a touch of the crusader which you have got from god
knows where. I can see you as an intellectual socialist,
organising the vast masses of the proletariat who want
nothing more intellectual than a little more tinned
salmon but who may be used to bring about a more

142

reasonable world, if they don't realise what they're doing. Yet I don't think your destiny lies that way. You would get too soon tired of telling the tale that must be told, and I fear that you must work with something more lasting than people."

"Not the Church," said Stephen, alarmed.

"Let the dead past bury its dead," said Mr. Elphinstone, reassuringly. "No. I'll tell you what I mean. You have come from a race of farmers who have lived for the everlasting heritage of the people, I mean the land. It is in your blood, and some day you'll go back to it. You will be best when you are dealing with living things, and not with the amoral excursions of business. My boy, you belong to an older order, and you have the kind of brain that might be the breeding place of a new one that would do more credit to the intelligence of humanity."

Stephen jumped up. "I don't want to go back. I'm sick of the whole damned business, but what else is there for me."

Mr. Elphinstone looked at him benevolently.

"You mean, what are you to do for money?"

Stephen said "Yes".

Mr. Elphinstone nodded. "In a society where money is made a substitute for God, and is certainly more powerful than the original, money, or the lack of it, gets an undue importance. But let me assure you of this. The existence of Poor Law – another of the ingenious dodges by which we pirates delude our victims, for we take all their money and then say, 'But of course, poor fellows, we sympathise with your misfortunes and would not see you starve' – by this pleasant though most inadequate device, you may be certain that at no time will you ever really starve to death. Besides, should you find yourself in reduced circumstances, you will find that our system always gives opportunities to men of more than average intelligence. For, as soon as your intelligence rises above the average, then you can use the average for your own ends. You are a fairly intelligent man; with practice your intelligence may develop prodigiously: therefore I say you have the world before you. There is no need to be afraid. The world is there waiting and you can make it your crust of bread or your oyster as you will. You must make your own choice; but, for my own part, I'd have no difficulty. There is an unexpectedness about oysters. You never know what you'll find inside them."

Stephen poked the grass with his stick, saying, "I wish I were as sure as you are. I'm afraid I wasn't born to take risks. Remember we are country people, and country people are cautious. It's all right to say I should make the world my oyster, but I might get broken in trying to open it."

"You are indeed cautious," said Mr. Elphinstone, "and caution has its uses, provided it is used at the beginning and not the middle of the enterprise. But anent this matter of being broken, let me tell you a story."

"Please do," Stephen said, accepting the inevitable gracefully.

"I believe," Mr. Elphinstone continued, "that you share my regard for your Aunt Elizabeth."

"Indeed I do," Stephen said. "I think she is the splendidest old lady that ever lived."

"How admirable to find a young man who has a due regard for his seniors. Well now, do you find it possible to think of any circumstances that would find her lacking that dignity with which she regards the world."

"None at all, unless death."

"Even in death: for in death even the meanest acquire a dignity from their total indifference to all mortal cares. But let us return to Mistress Davies, a woman of incomparable dignity and unconquerable spirit, the mistress of herself and of her world. Now I will tell you the story her life."

"She was, as you know, your grandfather's only sister. The Brewsters had always been remarkable in

144

their zest for life, remarkable even in the North East where that zest was only too often self-destroying. The sons of your great-grandfather were hearty, very hearty. They were the rallying points of devilry, the roots and rise of riot. It would take me till sunset to tell you the stories about their adventures that I have collected here and there from old men who knew them in their early prime: but it must be enough to say that no young men were more shot at by angry fathers and none were more spoken about in a countryside where most people danced skillfully on the very brink of perdition. John, George and James were a roistering trinity: and young Elizabeth was in no way behind them. Not, my dear boy, that she drank or followed wanton courses, but in her early years, from seventeen to twenty, she was the very soul of mischief. O, very adventurous, in climbing a hayrick in a high wind, or riding the minister's pony, bare-backed into the Kirk during service, or drinking a tumblerful of her father's brandy. She had also an adventurousness of another kind. She was interested in men; and, being very beautiful in a dark-browed teasing way, she found it very easy to make their acquaintance. Her researches into human nature took her into many dangerous corners of the Lendrum woods, but her native wits were always able to deliver her in time, though I should imagine she had little to spare. She was empirical in everything; bold far beyond the mark of caution; and a Brewster always. It makes me sad to think that I was born just fifteen years too late for her.

"In her twenty-second year she surprised everyone by marrying Mr. Davies, the butler at Lendrum House. He was nearly twenty years her senior, and a Welshman as well – the latter an impediment that the country could not understand (or, for that matter, forgive); but there must have been a touch of wonder about the man who had such intimate contact with the great. Anyway, she married him, and went to live in the butler's house at Lendrum.

"It was not in the nature of Elizabeth to be happy as a butler's wife. Paul, for all I can discover, was an amiable fellow with great dignity but no devil at all, and in those days Elizabeth found the devil a most agreeable fellow. She wanted the devil in men rather than the men themselves, and Paul was disappointing to say the least of it. In the first year of their marriage she bore a child, a daughter, but the delivery was a difficult one, and there would be no more. Elizabeth had nothing to look forward to but another thirty years of Paul, then widowhood on a quite inadequate pension. That might have been all right for a woman of a tamer spirit. It was an insult to Elizabeth. The long dull days in the butler's cottage in the woods fretted her nerves. She drank a good deal, and since she drank alone, the brandy filled her mind with dreadful fancies. She would suspect that Paul was carrying on with the housemaids. When he came home, she accused him of wanton lusts and furtive infidelities, and, as he denied the accusations furiously, the scenes ended with dishes flying, and all sorts of violence. So they worked up to the first crisis of their married life. And this is how it actually happened, to the scandal and delight of the countryside.

"One afternoon Mistress Davies had had an even longer communion with the brandy bottle that was her custom, with the result that her suspicions of her husband grew to intolerable power. So vividly did her imagination show him carrying on with the housemaid, that she could bear inaction no longer, but ran half-demented up to the the Big House. She stormed into the kitchen, a half-drunken fury, demanding Paul. At that moment he was serving dinner to his master and a company of distinguished guests, who included the Lord Lieutenant of the County, his Grace the Duke of Dyce. Paul was in the act of pouring some wine for his Grace, when a great clatter got up at the service door, and Elizabeth slew into the room. She wasn't what that wellbred, though very dull, company could have expected, with her clothes half torn from her shoulders by the footman who had tried to hold her, and her eyes staring with the drink and the fury of her imagination. It was a situation they must have read about, and I'm sure they wondered just which of their host's women was come to denounce him, and they must have been mightily intrigued to see how their hostess would conduct herself. But to their surprise and disappointment it was the butler on whom she threw herself with all the fury of her nails and her tongue. Whatever delightful anticipations he may have roused in the minds of the party, she must have been a dreadful apparition to Paul. Taken completely at a disadvantage, he could do nothing to defend himself and went down before the fury of her attack.

"Having thus disposed of her husband Elizabeth treated the company to the rough edge of her tongue – a most accomplished tongue, even in those days, and then in supreme defiance, began to undress before them. Skirts and petticoats, torn off by her angry hands, flew round the heads of His Majesty's Lord Lieutenant and the Commandant of Militia. A pair of stays hit the Bishop of Aberdeen and Orkney where he had most need of them; and, had not George John and the footmen removed her, there's no doubt that she would have scandalised both Church and State by her splendid nakedness. Fortunately, they were able to bear her away in time, she managed to take the tablecloth and the second best china with her. The ruin was final and complete. Only a fool or a man of no imagination (which is the same thing) would have asked Elizabeth Brewster to waste her youth as a butler's wife. Paul had been that fool, and she had made a riotous end to the buttling. They left for London at the end of the month."

Mr. Elphinstone puffed out smoke at a bewildered ladybird, then continued "Their subsequent relations were not happy. That is the certain epitaph on any marriage between a woman of spirit and a man of no imagination. Paul and Elizabeth took places, sometimes together, sometimes separately. The excitement of life in London, even fifty years ago, and the stimulus of varied company kept Elizabeth off the bottle and in high spirits; but London (ah, that London of hansom cabs and long drives through the conniving dark) offered her many adventures, too many for her husband's peace of mind. It was now he that became jealous, and stimulated his imagination with brandy. Those were jealous days. Infidelity had not yet become a social grace. Paul, imagining who knows what orgies on the Richmond Road, grew more tortured and more drunken, till Elizabeth was forced to make up her mind whether she would behave or leave him altogether. Just when she was trying to make up her mind, an uncle of Paul's died and left him the lease of a public house in Chelsea. They moved in at once, settled down in a respectable flat in the King's Road, and for a little time seemed tolerably happy.

"Alas Paul had now acquired a taste for drink, and became his best customer. Elizabeth drank to be even with him. The result was lively, and very ineresting for their neighbours in the King's Road. You see they used to quarrel in their drink and in the heat of anger Elizabeth used to throw furniture, not at Paul as a smaller woman might have done, but right through the window into the street. If she wanted to draw attention to her grievances, she could heve found no means more effective. Chelsea was a dignified place in those days, How remarkable then, as the householders were taking their walk of an evening, to hear a crash of breaking glass and to see a frying pan, a small chair or an item of unmentionable domesticity come dirding into the street from a third floor window. Only the fact that she was Elizabeth Brewster, with an inviolable dignity when sober, kept her out of jail. She was bound over to keep the peace, but the license was withdrawn; and, once more, they found themselves on the market.

It was not easy to find a situation; but at last Paul

was appointed caretaker of a large Anglical church in the Midlands. Elizabeth had not enjoyed being married to a butler: still less did she approve of verging. She soon found amusement. The clergy in those days were a thirstier type; and did not take a final farewell of carnal delights till old age had left them no alternative. The verger's cottage soon became popular among the junior clergy of the diocese, and more than one of them went to service in a state of most unholy unction. The Church of England is broadminded, but that the verger should run a shebeen within the very precincts of a Parish Church was more than even the latitudinarianism of the broadest Anglican would cover. Paul and Elizabeth once more left at the end of the month and went on their travels again.

"Elizabeth would now have been about thirty-seven, and her daughter was almost fifteen. The child could not have had a very agreeable life, certainly not one likely to dispose her to happiness. She was, I believe, fretful and spoilt, for her mother and father not only adored her but each spoilt her to spite the other. Somehow they had managed to give her lessons in singing and dancing, and at the age of sixteen she went on the stage. Her parents saw nothing of her for the next seven years.

"A great deal happened to Elizabeth in that time. When they left the Cathedral, she and Paul had a little money with which they opened a cooked meat shop in a back street in Hull. Now there is little that can be said in favour of Hull. But there could be no debate about the natives' fondness for cooked meats. They supported Elizabeth in fair numbers, and with a keen regard for the last ha'penny. Alas, though they were making a little money, they did not keep it. Paul had now declined in a stupid habitual drunkenness. After three years he had his first bout of delirium: in another two years he had his second; in eighteen months he died in an asylum. She gave him an excellent funeral, and sold the business. Then, my boy, what did the new, but by no means disconsolate widow do? She went to Paris with the proceeds, and did not return till she had spent the last penny. She was now about forty-five, alone in the world and penniless. She had not been home for more than twenty years.

"Back in London she met her old friends, and through them heard that her daughter was very ill. The child had been most unfortunate. Though she sang and danced prettily enough, she had not the amplitude which made such a valuable substitute for talent in those late Victorian days. Her engagements had never taken her into anything better than the cheapest music halls; and she had married an actor no more successful than herself. She had borne him two children within eighteen months, to the ruin of whatever charm she ever had; and he, finding that she gave him nothing but tedious obligations, had skipped the country. She and her children, left without money, had existed on charity for some months, till she had caught pneumonia and had been taken to hospital. The children, one three, the other eighteen months, were in the poorhouse. She was dead before Elizabeth reached the hospital.

"Through all her ups-and-downs, Elizabeth had never allowed her people to think that all was not well with her; but now she had to ask your grandfather to send her money to bury her daughter and redeem her grandchildren. It is unlikely that your grandfather had any money to spare – he never had – but he sent all that Elizabeth asked for, and she was able to bury her daughter as fitted a Brewster's child. Then she took the babies from the poorhouse, and started to make a home for them.

"It was to Leeds that she went, and for an excellent reason. Some people think that London is the place to hide in. They are wrong, for too many go to London at some time in their lives. But no one ever goes to a town like Leeds of his own free will and if, by some bad chance, they have to go, they leave as soon as possible. If ever you want to hide your shame from all your friends, go to the Midlands. There you will never be found, not even at the Judgment Day.

"As I was saying it was to Leeds that Elizabeth Brewster took her grandchildren; and it was there that she found work in a restaurant, as a waitress. The hours in the restaurant were long; the floors were cruel to feet in cheap shoes; and the wages by no means generous. When her day was finished there she had to go home to the attic where she boarded with a widow of melancholy and sanctimonious habits. There the children were waiting for her, an evening's work to begin on. So, from week to week, from year to year; while she passed through fifty on to fifty-five; each year the children needed more; each year she grew less able to provide it. Whatever she may have done wrong by Paul, she most nobly atoned for through a dozen weary years. Sometimes, I believe, they were reduced to a few shillings. Her furniture knew its way to the pawnbroker by itself; but she never gave in and she had always her black silk gown. The gown must have been a symbol; it witnessed that she had once been Miss Brewster of Hillhead; it was the last outward sign of her pride that no misfortune could destroy.

"The boys went to work when they left school and by the time she came to sixty it must have seemed that an easier time was coming to her, for they were not wholly unkind to her. But of course the War broke out and they both found themselves in the Army without quite knowing how they got there. The elder boy was killed in France in 1916: the younger one died in Palestine two years later. Elizabeth was once more alone.

"Her next state was the most remarkable in all her curious life, for she became housekeeper to a clergyman in Glasgow. He was only a Baptist or a Congregationalist or something of that sort, yet he was undoubtedly a pious man with an unimpeachable position, just a little further from God than the Established Church. Eliza-

beth kept house for him for three years, with the aid of a
bottle which she hid judiciously, out of the public eye. It
was a return to glory for her. She got a new black silk.
The gold-rimmed glasses appeared on her splendid
bosom; and she took her holidays at Hillhead with the
dignity of her age now flowering upon her. When your
grandmother died she deserted the clergyman, and
returned to Hillhead, where in peace and a tranquil
mind, she became the great lady that we are so proud to
serve."

Mr. Elphinstone threw away his cigar with a sigh,
for the action put a period to one more pleasure
snatched from eternity.

"Now that, my boy, is a notable story, and very well
told, I believe. It is also a curious study in human values.
And what does it prove? If it must prove something."

He looked at Stephen, but the young man did not
reply.

"It proves," Mr. Elphinstone continued, "that there
was something in Elizabeth greater than anything she
did. Though she often had little, yet she was never
broken. Let us now go in and drink tea."

At Hillhead they were preparing to say goodbye to
Stephen. It was Friday morning; he was due to leave
next day; and the farewell party had been called for that
night. After breakfast Stephen decided that he would
send a telegram to Clarkson, accepting the job and
telling him that he would be at the office on Monday
morning. But his grandfather proposed that they
should take a walk round the farm, and Stephen had not
the heart to refuse him. So they made the round of the
fields. As if he wished to give Stephen something of
Hillhead to take away with him, the old man kept recalling the making of the farm. He drew the lines of his
beloved drains across the fields, told of the great labour
that had gone to win them from the wilderness, and
evoked the memory of his fathers in a way that made
Stephen proud again to have sprung from such a line.

As always their walk took them to the mound at the head of Brewster's Dyke. There they sat, for a long time, looking down to the house across the fields, in silence. It seemed to Stephen that he had seldom been happier, for the old man had talked so easily to him, and now, in silence, had accepted him into his dearest friendship. The old man sighed.

"Ye'll be awa the morn, and dammit man, I'll miss ye, even though only tae laugh at ye. It's a pity ye didna come sooner, for I could hae made a man and a farmer o' ye."

Stephen gripped the stone bench, caught up by a rise of emotion.

"D'ye mean that?" he asked.

The old man rose. "Ten year ago. Five year ago. But it's ower late noo. A'thing's ower late. We'll gang intae our denner."

"But..." Stephen began. Then he stopped. He rose and followed his grandfather in silence.

He talked to Aunt Elizabeth after dinner, when the old man had gone to his sleep. Though it was a raw day she asked him to take her for a round of the garden and, as they were stepping slowly over the green; she leaning on her stick, and he giving her his arm she spoke about his departure.

"The house will be very quiet tomorrow night when you're away," she said. "It's a very old house, but it doesn't seem right that there should be only old people in it. As long as I can remember there has always been something beginning in it: this is the first time there has been nothing but an end. When you came back it was so different. It warmed your grandfather and me to have a young Brewster sitting at the table with us."

"Did I fit in? Was I a real Brewster?" Stephen asked eagerly.

"Like your grandfather fifty years ago, only quieter."

"A Brewster diluted thin?" Stephen suggested with a laugh.

"No," Aunt Elizabeth replied, rather sadly, "A Brewster tamed."

Stephen looked away, over the good land that his people had made.

"That's my tragedy."

Aunt Elizabeth shook his arm, laughing and said. "No, no, no my dear. A Brewster's never tamed until he's dead."

When he had drunk afternoon tea with the old people, Stephen walked over to Lendrum to send his telegram. He had intended to go the short way, across the river and through the fields, but he changed his mind and went by the woods instead. Going along the path by the old trees, he remembered how he had come that way from London. *A lot has happened to me since then,* he said to himself. He thought of how he had gloried in the work that the Brewsters had made, how the old people had welcomed him, as if to home, how he had worked in the fields, how Susan and Kennedy and Mr. Elphinstone had invited him into delightful new worlds, how Tam had shown him the evil that had fallen on the countryside, and how he had had so many and such deep experiences. Once more his mind swung towards freedom. *O hell,* he said to himself. *Why am I creeping into a safe job, as if I was any loon without a shirt to my name. There's my grandfather – he never played for safety. He has little money: he may soon have less; but he is not afraid. There is Aunt Elizabeth – she has had little but misfortune. Yet she's like Cleopatra in the autumn of her glory. And here am I, that have had advantages they never had, rabbiting into a nice safe burrow – lord god, it won't bear thinking on.*

Looking over the water he saw the Kirk of Lendrum, and once more he felt a challenge as from the dead men in their graves. And looking back he saw the pale uncertain sun on the fields which his fathers had made. A sudden illumination came into his mind. "Like

154

your grandfather fifty years ago," Aunt Elizabeth had said. By god he was. He was a Brewster, and wherever he went he would have his fathers at this right hand. Not dead, for their work lived; and he was part of their work, and they lived in him. Wherever he went he would have their virtue behind him; and whatever he did he must never shame them. *Lord God,* he cried, *now I can never be poor; and though all the living desert me, I will never be alone, for I travel with a company of the glorious dead.*

He turned and walked quickly towards Lendrum, to send his telegram.

The party was assembled by the time he got home. Mr. Elphinstone was there all rosy and clean and mildly speculative of eye. Susan and Kennedy had hurried back from Glasgow, where they had been investigating the gradual decay of the unemployed. And the old man was there, but silent. Aunt Elizabeth was handing out drinks from the sideboard.

"Well, my jolly adventurer, so you're going," said Kennedy.

"Back to the flesh pots," said Susan with a kind smile.

Mr. Elphinstone sniffed his sherry, sighed happily, and turned an eye on Stephen. "Well, here's long life, prosperity and – is it goodbye?"

"No," said Stephen, "not goodbye."

"Ye'll come again," Aunt Elizabeth said, kindly.

But Stephen cried, "No, my dear, no. I'm not going. I'm staying, whether you want me or no."

He stood facing them, with his eyes shining; and they looked at him, unable to believe his words.

But the old man just rose, saying, "Daft and damned; but its God's will, so we'd better hae our supper." Taking Susan's arm he led her into the room where the meal was prepared. Stephen followed with Aunt Elizabeth, and they were completely happy.

CHAPTER EIGHT

The Blessed Machine

AND NOW, Stephen said to himself, *I'm free.*

As soon as he had said it, which was twenty times a day, he wondered if he had made a fool of himself. Happily his friends left him in no doubt that they thought him very wise. Kennedy and Susan were unbounded in their delight at his gesture to fortune. Mr. Elphinstone took the decision as a compliment to himself and at the same time regarded it with a benevolent amusement subtly gilded with admiration. Aunt Elizabeth just said, "You'll be much happier. No Brewster was ever meant to be an office boy."

But Stephen was not so sure of his grandfather's opinion. "It needs a bit o' a hero tae dae a thing like that – a bit o' a hero or maybe a bit o' a fool," the old man said as if discussing something that had happened on the moon. Then he walked away leaving Stephen to wonder what he really thought. It was just a little disappointing. Stephen shrugged his shoulders and said to himself *The old man's like that; so infernally detached.* But he could not shrug off the detachment. It stayed with him; and by reflecting something of the greater world's indifference, brought his view of himself out of the rosy romantic glow into the colder light of reason. *Ach,* he said to himself with a laugh, *I've been thinking the whole world from the Equator to the Poles must be excited because I've given up my job: like a little boy that walks up the aisle of the kirk and thinks all the congregation are looking at his new Sunday suit. But there's none of them cares a damn though I throw myself in the river.*

Then he felt he was indeed free to come and go in

the world, but there was something desolate behind the sense of freedom.

And now because of that desolation and because he had cut himself away from his former life, Hillhead became all the dearer to him. There was now no barrier between him and his love of it. When he sat on Brewster's Knowe, looking over the fields of stooks that were ready for the leading home, he did not need to feel that he was untrue to his career or to any loyalties beyond the hills. For his future lay wherever he cared to make it. And since the future was too vast to think about, and since he was not yet able to stand alone upon a point of time, one man alone in an indifferent world, he had to find a shoulder to support him. Then the spirits of his fathers rose up at his need from the fields that they had made and stood at his right hand. *This is our work*, they said to him, *the work of six generations. We are dead; our bones are yellow in the Lendrum clay; but there is the harvest that we planned a hundred years ago and you are the son that we dreamed of when we took our young wives to bed.* Stephen's blood grew warm when he felt the spirits of the dead men rising out of the harvest fields. He was comforted, made strong by their invisible presence and by the beauty of the work that they had done. And more clearly than ever before, he saw the generations breaking in the wastes where life began, each caring for its inheritance and adding something to it and handing it on to the pious hands that came after them. Generation after generation had come up in a green spring, had flowered and ripened into harvest and then had been gathered away leaving the land richer than they had found it; generation after generation until now Stephen walked in their fields. But not alone; for they walked with him. They were as real to him as if they had come up from the river in their broad Scots bonnets, grave old men with bearded faces; and they strengthened him with the wisdom of those who have lived so long that they can laugh at fortune. Stephen had never found such majesty

157

in the living world and never a power that so warmed and exalted him; so, as he was a man who had a need to worship something greater than himself, the grave old men became his gods and their fields his heaven.

Soon the present claimed all his powers. The weather, having exhausted its wantonness, cleared into the benign calm of autumn. The sun came out all day and dried the sodden land, drawing up a mist of steam that veiled the moon. Then a bone dry wind blew in from the sea and finished the healing work till the ripened corn shook free from the destroying water and the sweet rustle of harvest ran through the countryside. The sun brought a new power to man and beast. Tam and Stephen felt a spring in their step again as they walked down through the stubble at six in the morning. The wind had driven the narking thoughts from their brains. The deadening sense of frustration had been removed. Nothing stood between them and the harvest. They worked from six in the morning till the fall of night and finally, as if by a miracle, the last bout was cut, the last sheaf stooked.

"Now man," Tam said, "there's just ae step tae winter."

Though the phrase was meant to mark Tam's satisfaction with so much hard work done, the words remained in Stephen's mind, like the sound of a bad omen; for, in spite of the fair face of autumn, there were signs that eternal winter was settling on Hillhead and on the countryside.

"Aye," said Jimmy Mutch, the old stone breaker, resting on his hammer to give Stephen the benefit of his long experience, a favour he delighted to bestow on any who would listen, "aye man, folk are jist dwinin awa. I can mind when there used tae be six workin smiths in Lendrum, now there's only two. Joiners and masons and ditchers and dykers used tae be sae common they ran aboot among your feet like mice in a girnal. Nowadays there's hardly a man that kens the difference

atween a mortice and a mortar board. A' deid. A' deid.
I've buried them a'. I've howkit the graves for them.
Aye, ye micht say I've buried the best o' this country-
side."

The antique scarecrow shook his whisker at
Stephen. His pipe, loosely held by his few remaining
teeth, shook with a motion of its own long after the head
was still.

"I bury them far faster than they're born. Mind ye,
I've dune what I could tae even things up, but it's little a
man can do wi ae wife – a dozen loons and lassies at the
best; and the young men, ach, they've lost the knack o
gettin bairns. O it's bad bad, man; and nae trade for the
doctor means nae trade for me. Aye, they're hard times
for the tradesmen when the likes o' me's forced ontae
the roads for a livin. Ach, they're a fushionless lot that's
left; they haena even the hert tae dee."

He returned to his stonebreaking, delighted at
having expressed himself so well.

Aye, hard times, Stephen thought to himself as he
went home, *hard times when even the gravedigger complains
that he's idle. But dammit we're not all dying off without a
struggle. There's Tam...* Then he remembered how bitterly Tam had spoken in the cartshed, of his ambitions
that were becoming impossible to attain. Even Tam, a
man who would work from dawn to dark, who would ask
no ease or comfort as long as he had strength in his
body, even **he** was daunted and discouraged and tortured by frustration. The days had gone by when work
was enough. The woman at the croft on the hill had
never a penny to rub against another. Her world was
bare without and within. She had courage. But what
did she get from all those virtues? A bare girnal and
weary bones. Stephen looked over the countryside
where the fields were full of the tangled harvest now
reduced again to order, It was warm and rich and
smiling in the autumn sun. There were peace and
plenty, the work of unnumbered generations. But for

the latest generation there were care and suffering and slow death of hope starved out by forces they could neither control, nor understand. Again Stephen saw the generations of men who had carried their burdens along the green ways of Lendrum, each with his care made sweet by faith in a future rich beyond imagining. And this was the future – care and suffering and the slow death of hope. *By God,* Stephen swore, *such a great story must have a better end.*

Every day it became more urgent that Hillhead should be saved from the shame that threatened it; every day it became clearer to Stephen where his duty lay.

He asked Kennedy what was wrong and Kennedy gave an answer at once as was his habit on any subject under the sun.

"The breakdown of the system, my boy. The dead hand of capitalism gripping everybody in a rigor mortis. Antiquated ideas in a changing world."

"O lord," Stephen replied, "I've heard all that before. Now I want some body who'll reduce it to cows and turnips."

Kennedy thought for a bit then he said, "I know the man for you. Young Strathmuir, so called to distinguish him from his father Old Strathmuir. He's a tremendous man who is daft on machinery and organisation and all that. His ideal is to be a midwife to the future. If you like, I'll take you down to see him. All you need with an enthusiast like Strathmuir is a will to listen."

Young Strathmuir welcomed them with the eagerness of a prophet who had far too few disciples and immediately took them for a tour of his farm. The experience was a notable one.

He was a most impressive person, thirty years old, six feet high and as broad as a barn door. He had been a footballer and he still had the aspect of a forward looking for trouble in the loose. Not that there was any brutality in his manner but he had a kind of eagerness in conversation and he threw himself on any new fact determined to make the most of it. When he had thoroughly exhausted it and the person who had brought it to his notice, he cast aside the remains of it and passed on to something new. Within five minutes he had got all the essential facts about Stephen's life and was ready to take his visitors round the farm.

As the prophet of a mechanical age, Young Strathmuir had no time for walking. They must go the round in his car. That was something new for Stephen, accustomed the leisurely tours with his grandfather. The car seemed to have no speed between five and fifty miles an hour and the accommodation roads between the fields were deeply rutted by the farm carts, but Young Strathmuir drove on with no regard for the car or the comfort of his passengers. He took them through the pasture, through the stubble, into the potatoes, across the turnips, everywhere that a car would go and along the ruins of roads for which no car was ever intended.

All the time he explained his methods to them.

"Farming hereabouts is a religion," he said, "and everything's fixed like Christmas. You do what your father did before you and hope for the best. Well, it maybe worked all right before the war, but it's like some other religions, it doesn't pay a dividend any longer."

"But I've a lot of sympathy with the old ways," Stephen replied, for the young man's open contempt for tradition annoyed him. "I'd rather look at a pair of horse than a tractor," he added.

"Maybe," Young Strath replied, "But they're a damnable waste of time and labour. I've something better to spend my time on than hoiterin, day in, day out, at the stilts of a plough, and so has any man wi any intelligence."

"So what do you do?" Stephen asked.

"I spend my time thinkin out better ways o' doin things, ways that'll pay dividends wi half the labour instead o' spendin my labour on ways that canna pay."

"Now that," said Kennedy, "is the road to civilisation."

"But does it pay?" Stephen asked as if he didn't believe it could.

"I'm losin less than my neighbours and payin my men more."

"Yes, but aren't you doing that by employing fewer men?"

Young Strath pointed to a field of potatoes that seemed to stretch away to the very horizon. "There's a hunder and twenty acre o' tatties there. I've another two hunder acre on the other side. And I've eighty down the road. That's four hunder acre. I can handle them because I have tractors. Wi horses I wouldna dare plant a quarter o' that in case of a wet season at the lifting. Now there's a mighty lot of work for men as well as machines in four hunder acre o' tatties."

"Yes," said Stephen, "but if you didn't grow potatoes you would just grow something else."

"Aye corn or grass to feed cattle on. But there's little work in corn and less in grass. Now tatties, they need a lot o' cultivatin. They have tae be cleaned. They have tae be lifted. Man, at liftin time I need a squad of sixty men and women for weeks. That's casual labour for half the countryside. After they're lifted they need tae be dressed. That's more labour. I've machines for dressin tatties and elevators for loadin them, a'thing that saves labour, but they need men tae run them. And I may tell ye this, I give work tae twice the men that ever worked here afore and the work's nae half as hard."

"That's just rationalisation," Stephen said.

"Call it what you like," Young Strath replied. "It's only common sense. And it's the only way."

Stephen saw clear enough that it was not the way of his forefathers.

They had stopped at the side of a fifty acre park where two men were cutting the last of the corn. What they saw there was different from the traditional harvest scene. Instead of teams of three Clydesdales straining against the weight of the binders while the drivers cried them on, two Fordson tractors were driving remorselessly round and round the diminishing square of corn. Stephen was fascinated. He watched the tractors go on and on, tireless engines doing their drivers' will with no sense of effort or limitation. Monotonous in their well disciplined power, they mesmerised him. *But how ugly compared to the harvest at Hillhead,* he said to himself. *For at Hillhead the men and the horses make a noble partnership. They throw the weight of their bodies and the strength of their spirits against the yoke. They fight together for the harvest: Here it is mowed down by a relentless machine.*

"It takes the romance out of harvest," he said to Kennedy.

"On the contrary," Kennedy replied, "it has brought in a romance of a higher order. For what does the losing partnership of the man and the horse represent but the losing effort to counter mortal weakness. The man with the horse is fighting against the forces of nature; the man with the tractor has turned those forces against themselves." He pointed to the corn field. "There go the conquerors. They have tamed the laws of nature. She is their slave. They have won the greatest victory that man has ever won – they've conquered fatigue."

"I don't know much about that," Young Strath said with a laugh, "but I do know they're doing my work in a third of the time."

Kennedy and he sat in the car and admired the wonders of man's invention but Stephen did not join them. He had been so deeply influenced by the life at Hillhead that this revolutionary farm seemed to him a sacrilege. It was blasphemy against all that he had so newly come to worship. Besides he was too newly escaped from what he thought of as the machine to admire what seemed to him just one more aspect of it. *Ach,* he said to himself, *those tractors are the work of the devil. They were invented by men with the little black bags. It can never be through them that we'll save Hillhead.*

So he kept on telling himself, till he began to have a real dislike of the monstrous farm. He would let himself look at nothing; for he knew that, if he looked, he would hate whatever he saw. His humour grew so strong that even Young Strath noticed it; and in a short time all conversation came to an end. Stephen and Kennedy said, "Thank you," and went away.

"Well," said Kennedy on the way home, "you're a fine one."

"I'm sorry," Stephen replied looking straight in front of him, while his emotions drove him into a passionate speech.

"It's clever, but it's all wrong. I don't care though the machines can do three times or three hunder times as much work as men and horses. They'll ruin country life. If they were going to make anybody any happier I wouldn't mind their ugliness. I wouldn't mind the oil and the dirt. But I don't believe the men who were driving them were any happier than they would have been if they had been swinging a scythe. And I know what I'm speaking about. I've gone down to the fields and matched my own muscles against the work to be done and it is like being drunk with the joy of living. There's something sacramental about working in the fields with your own two hands."

As Kennedy's car rattled along the road to Old Aberdeen Stephen sat looking through the dusty windscreen into a golden age where figs grew upon thorns watered by the holy sweat from the labourers' brow.

Kennedy said nothing, but when they joined Susan and Mr. Elphinstone in the drawing room at Dunelm, he told them about Stephen's discovery.

"Reactionary," Susan cried in derision.

Stephen stood at bay against their laughter.

"What do you want," he cried, defending himself.

"You do your best to get me to throw up business and then when I do it you call me a reactionary. What's the difference between mechanical cosmetics and mechanical farming? Tell me. Tell me.

"Ach, you damned intellectuals, you make me sick."

"Well now," said Mr. Elphinstone, setting down his glass of port, "I can appreciate your sentiment though I deprecate the expression of it. And I can also see that you have fallen into error. You're confusing the machine with the pitiable methods by which the workers of the machine gather its fruits. The machines are wholly good in themselves, for if they are intelligently used they set man free from the degrading business of labour."

Stephen jumped up crying, "I refuse to admit any degradation; I'd starve sooner than believe it."

"Then you're likely to starve pretty soon," Kennedy said, "for now that we've provided the farmer with machines to save his labour, you surely don't think we're going to pay him a good living to do without them."

"But you can't do without the farmer," Stephen said.

Kennedy only laughed. "Are you sure? If the present farmers won't use the lovely machines that we've made to ease their labour then we'll soon find men who will use them."

"But where?" Stephen demanded.

"Young Strath – and he isn't a solitary instance. There are plenty more. I grant you they're scattered – one here, one there; but they'll increase and the rest will have to follow them – or get out of the game."

"How beautiful," Stephen said bitterly.

"The beauty of the inevitable," Kennedy replied.

"But is it inevitable?"

"Nothing more so. It is inevitable and just. When machines are invented to make life easier it is only a fool that will refuse to use them because they are something new."

"And to be a fool," said Mr. Elphinstone, "is the sin."

"But the past," Stephen said. "What about it? Is it to be thrown away because somebody has invented a petrol engine? Aren't traditions worth anything?"

"Ah traditions," said Mr. Elphinstone getting ready to lay down the law. Traditions as far as I can see them – and I can see further than most people – may be divided into two classes – those that are in the nature of eternal laws and those that are merely opportune. Take the tradition that a farmer must care for his land and keep it in good heart. That is a tradition which, for the sake of the land, must endure as long as we live by the land. It is to be honoured for ever. But the tradition that a farmer must plough with horses is different. That was a good tradition until something was discovered that would plough more efficiently than the horse. As soon as the tractor appeared that tradition was no longer worthy of honour; and in a few years I should imagine it will be immoral to use the horse since it is wasteful and therefore foolish. So when one worships the past, as I observe you do, it is well to distinguish between what is still valid in this present day, and what has merely the charm of the out of date."

"Supposing you're right," Stephen replied, still angry and confused, "what better are we going to be with the machines. Strath says he can make money. But why. Because most farmers are, as you would say, out of date. But if all farmers used machines and speeded up production, would their last state be any better than their present one?"

"That," Mr. Elphinstone replied, I am unable to say. Unless they reorganise the financial system in which they work, they are unlikely to be any better. But I am able to say this – the men who use the machines will be able to survive longer than those who don't. In fact, they may survive until they have put society on a more intelligent basis, whereby it will yield them a fair return for their labour."

Stephen sat down with a weary gesture. "You'd argue me out of anything," he said and felt sore with his friends because they could not, or would not, see that the old ways were sacred.

But as he was leaving to go home Susan walked with him to the garden gate, "You're over the head in sentiment but it suits you well and I love you for it." Then she said goodnight and ran back into the house.

Her words brought the touch of pleasure back to Stephen's troubled spirits. The feeling that someone understood him made it less urgent to maintain his faith against all reason.

The very next day that faith was attacked from the quarter in which Stephen expected nothing but agreement.

At dinner time he spoke to Tam about his visit to Strathmuir, in the hope that Tam would despise the tractors. But Tam's reactions were disappointing.

"A tractor's nae a horse: that's true. It's nae bonny and maybe you couldna get fond o't. But dammit man, they'd be michty beasts in a backward season. Come years when ye're behind wi the work ye could tak advantage o' ilkae fine day and rive on wi the plough or the binder. And man," he continued with wonder and envy in his voice, "what labour and sair banes we would hae saved this hairst if we'd had one o' them."

Stephen turned on him in surprise.

"But ye don't mean tae say that you would like one here, at Hillhead."

Tam replied cautiously as his habit was, "I wouldna say that. But sometimes I've just wondered what we could dae wi it, if a body was tae find it sittin in the close some mornin." Then a kind of excitement began to break through his caution. "Ye see Hillhead has aye been first in this pairt o' the countryside; the foreman in a' connected wi the laan. And that's what it should be.

Yet I've sometimes thought we're maybe standin still. Och it's nae that I want the tractors; the likin for horse has been bred in me; but, man, I would dae onything that would help Hillhead tae keeps its place."

"That's just pride," Stephen replied because he was disappointed and felt in a way betrayed.

"It may be," Tam replied and the words came out with a power of feeling behind them, "but it's mair than that. I'm nae thinkin o' Hillhead alane. I'm thinkin o' mysel. The less money there is for the fairmer the less there is for me; and whan I see your grandfather losin his ain livin I see him losin mine tae. It's a fine thing tae stand by the auld customs. But what are they worth tae us if we grow poorer and poorer. I wouldna say a word tae the auld man: he's aye been decent tae me. But there's times when I've heard o' things that are happenin doon in Angus and far awa in Fife and I've fretted like a dog that's tied tae a post when it sees the rest o' the dogs chasin a fine fat hare. I'm nae an auld man Stephen; I've a wife that I'd like tae keep in comfort and young bairns that I'd like tae see dae weel in the world; and it's hard tae bide here thinkin that I'm lettin my chance gae by me. And what **is** change anyway? There's aye been changes. I've heard my grandfather say that his father damned the binders ower hill and dale because they put an end tae scythin; but we're pleased enough wi the binders the day. Maybe my loons'll be as fond o tractors as I am o' the horse, maybe: and dammit but I'd like tae be able tae start them. Life's harder nowadays: if ye want tae mak onything ye've tae be in at the beginnin. But the thing's begun and whaur am I – drivin my horse like my father afore me."

He knocked out his pipe impatiently and thrust his hands into his pockets. There was something tense in his attitude, a sense of strain and of frustration, as if he saw something that he could not get at.

O hell Stephen said to himself, *this is too difficult.*

Then Tam pulled his bonnet down over his eyes

and picked up the hay fork, ready for the afternoon's work.

"Tractors are maybe richt, or maybe wrang. But I'd risk onything rather than be starved tae death in a place where once we were a' sae proud."

Stephen set off feeling that the white heat of his passion for the old days had been somewhat subdued. His arguments with Mr. Elphinstone and Tam had left him battered; like a bit of iron beaten on the anvil.

An encounter with the old man changed it completely.

In a shady corner of the yard there stood an old pump, a picturesque but decayed contraption. This was the oldest memorial about Hillhead, for the well had been dug by the first Brewster and the second had enclosed it with a low wall shaped like a horseshoe. For many years all the water used in the steading had been pumped from the well and many a young man, set to filling the cistern in the evening, had stood within the low wall looking wistfully down the glen to the woods where the Lendrum maids were walking two and two, while he stayed chained there to the tiresome labour. But the old man, who had suffered that intolerable discipline in the years when he was too fond of wandering, installed a gravitation supply from a spring on the high land behind the steading, as soon as he became master of Hillhead. Then the gate in the horseshoe wall was blocked up and the pump was allowed to moulder slowly into ruin. This antiquity had become very dear to Stephen, for the hands of the men and women he worshipped had once made smooth the rusty handle and their feet had worn the flags that covered the deep resounding well. Through it he seemed to get in touch with his fathers. And now it had become so dear to him that he wanted to see it in use again.

Taking courage he put the idea to the old man.

Now the old man had lived a long time and had seen many foolish things, some of them his own doing.

He had small opinion of the human race and not for many years had he been surprised at their works. But the proposal to open the old well really set him back.

"And what would ye dae that for?" he asked, when the power of words came back to him.

Stephen flushed, already feeling by-ordinary foolish, but he replied, bravely enough, "Because it was made by your grandfather's father."

The old man nodded. "It was that. But he's deid noo. Besides it wasna a good place for a well, bein' aneath the midden. Nae doubt he thocht he was clever but I did better."

"All right," said Stephen, for something to say, "just wait till somebody does the same to you."

The old man laughed, "Ho, just lat them try."

Stephen went out to the garden with a flea in his ear. Almost he hated the old man. But after a bit he laughed and felt better, And with that laughter went a lot of foolish sentiment about his fathers.

Then one afternoon he found his grandfather sitting in the parlour with the farm books spread out before him on the table. He would have withdrawn but the old man stopped him.

"You're a business man, aren't ye? I never was good at figures and I some doubt thae figures are nae very good for me." He held up a sheet of paper. "This would be what they call a profit and loss account, but it looks take me as if there was mair loss than profit in't." He threw down the paper with a short laugh and then looked at Stephen with a smile in the corner of his eye. "Eh laddie," he said, "if only figures were cattle how I could fatten them up."

Stephen was strangely touched. He laughed, as the old man intended him to laugh; he was proud that the old man should confide in him; but he was sad that the need for such a confidence should have arisen. It was the first time the old man had admitted that circumstances were beyond his powers.

"Can I help you?" Stephen asked; and he offered not only of his knowledge but himself.

The old man laughed. "Naebody could help me but God; and I'm damned sure he's nae carin. I wouldna, if I was God and he was me. But ye've been trained tae business, so cast your eyen across thae papers and see if they'll mak sense."

He rose and gave his seat to Stephen.

"I'll awa and see the nowt," he said. "That's something I can understand. Guid luck tae ye, laddie: and if ye find a thousan I owerlooked, daena be shy tae tell me."

He picked up his staff, pulled his hat down over his eyes and walked off to the pastures.

The books did not make pleasant reading. Not that Stephen was able to understand all the entries or even the greater part of them; for the old man's book keeping, like everything else about him, was highly individual. All transactions were entered in the same column, both incomings and outgoings, while some entries, such as payments for seed corn or receipts for debts long overdue, were supplemented by character sketches of the persons involved and general reflections on the morality of the countryside. No one but the old man himself could have found his way through the confusion of debits, credits and folklore that made up the books, but after an hour or two one thing became very evident – that he was spending far more than he made. In three years a bank balance of just over one thousand pounds had become an overdraft of seven hundred. As far as Stephen could understand the counterfoils of the chequebooks, the old man's expenses were still running on in the style of his most prosperous days. On the other side it seemed that the receipts from the sale of cattle and the like were decreasing. And if they had fallen in good years what would happen now that the harvest was a failure? At last Stephen pushed the books away from him with a sigh. The old man's affairs were in a worse state than he had suspected and they would soon be past all mending.

"Well," the old man said when he came back, "I daena see much sign o' comfort on your face."

"There's less in the books," Stephen replied. "But I can't tell you where the money's gone."

"Where the Brewsters' money has aye gone – down our throats. Well, well, there'll soon be an end o't."

"Unless we can stop the loss," Stephen replied, "and we might stop it if we could trace the money."

The old man laughed, rather pleased with himself, "Man, man, so the books beat ye, eh? I daena wonder for they beat me tae and it was me that wrote them. Well, tae tell ye the truth I only keepit them for the look o' the thing and for a diversion on the winter nichts."

"But it's serious now," Stephen said, "and what we want is a detailed account of what everything cost you and what you got when you sold it. We've got to cost everything that happens on the farm and when we've done that we'll know where the money's gone."

The old man settled himself in his chair. "I doubt this is going to hurt me more than it'll please you. But ca on. What's nae in the books or me we'll mak up."

They spent days on the job while Stephen asked questions and the old man told him the answers. Every expense, every bargain was enquired into and entered in the sheets of paper that grew into tedious bundles on the parlour table. At first the old man could hardly be bothered to remember, or when he did remember remembered too much, so that he went off into long monologues of recollection; but he soon took a fancy to the inquisition. That touch of the theatrical which had put the bloom on his adventures as a young man made him see the examination as a game. Before the end he had taken charge of the enquiry and was enjoying it immensely.

"My, Stephen," he said, "I'll be sorry when this is finished. There's a kind o' pleasure in cuttin up my business. It's like bein' at my ain funeral, and that's a thing I've often wanted tae see, if only tae hear whether my auldest and dearest friends would say the things about me that I've said about sae mony o' them on like enjoyable occasions."

And when Stephen had finished the examination and had made an abstract of the result the old man read it through with grim satisfaction.

"It's aye been my habit tae be thorough; and this time I've done't wi a vengeance; for, if this be true, there's naething I dae about this place that maks a penny; and nae a beast that isna ower the lugs in debt tae me."

He folded up the sheet of paper and placed it in his breast pocket.

"I think I'd better sleep on't, though it's the last sleep I ever hae," he said. Then he settled himself in his armchair by the fire, drew his handkerchief over his face and fell asleep. The dangerous tide in his affairs might wait his own convenience.

Two days later while they were sitting on Brewster's Knowe he announced his decision. "It doesna pay tae work the laan," he said to Stephen, "so we'll need tae put it down tae grass. Jock and Sam will be leavin at the Term – O, I'm sure they'll be, for they'll likely both be expectin bairns here and there – and we'll not get anybody in their place. That'll save a hunder pound in wages; and if I sell the two pair o' horse, that'll be three hunder pound in the bank tae keep them quiet. That's the only thing for an auld man, Stephen, tae put his laan in grass and sit back in his seat and dwine awa intae his grave. It's a good thing the auld Brewsters are nae here tae see this day."

The touch of bitterness behind the old man's resignation made the defeat an intolerable shame to Stephen.

"But surely there's some way to keep the land in cultivation and the men in their places? The Brewsters aren't going out like this after two hundred years?"

But his grandfather replied, as if the matter were already signed and sealed beyond all question, "A poor end, maybe, but it'll last my time and that's a' I need care for. If there hadna been that damned war and the damneder fools that fought in't, there might hae been a different story tae tell. Forty years ago I would hae made plans tae last till the end o' time, but a' the plannin in the world'll never keep the Brewsters in Hillhead, for them that should hae come after me are in their graves. They didna think o' me when they ran for glory; now I've nane tae think o'; so I'll gather about me the gear o' comfort and tak my ease till the end o' my days."

He rose to go home but Stephen remained on Brewster's Knowe, thinking of all that had taken place since he came to Hillhead. Gradually his thoughts formed themselves into a pattern and that pattern drew towards a conclusion from which there was no escape. First of all he realised that Hillhead was the most powerful thing in his life. Since he had come back to it, new and splendid powers had been born in him. From the noble thing that his own people had made, he had won courage to take from life whatever he might desire. And most strong of all, he had had a vision that had given a new meaning to the world. For he was not just Stephen Lees, one among the millions of the world. He was a Brewster and the generations of Brewsters had been in labour to make him; the man and the farm were one and were the farm away the man must lose the secret of his virtue. Then more than ever before the thought of the Brewsters losing Hillhead became personal to Stephen. If the farm passed into other hands, then the Brewsters that were left would be without a home. There would be no place of which they could say, *This is ours and we have made it.* They would be expatriate; for although they might claim this and that country as their own and wave its flags and die in its battles, no man can love a whole wide country and the many millions that live there. Such patriotism is a vague and sentimental thing. The true patriot is the man whose roots are in some small corner of the earth where his fathers have added to its beauty and enriched it with their work. The man who has some such place to love is like a tree whose roots are deep in native earth; the man without is drift-wood blown about the world. So might the Brewsters be scattered and lost from each other for ever; and old men with their bonnets and the grave bearded faces would walk their fields disconsolate that no living child of theirs was left in the only land that they had ever known or loved. Every instinct in Stephen's body cried out that the Brewsters must remain, for there could be no future without the enduring virtue of the past.

That was not all. Stephen remembered how Tam had cried out against the frustration of all that he had planned for. There was more to be thought about than the comfort of the masters. Their servants' living had to be saved. All over the country land might be going down to grass while men were being turned away workless to stand at the corners of the towns. But surely there was wealth enough in all those fertile fields to keep them where they belonged. Surely there was a way. Surely.

Stephen looked over the countryside and smote his fist on the hard stone seat. *"You've been a proud land,"* he said, *and we've been proud people that made you; and, by the Lord God, we'll be proud again, the two of us. If the old ways have failed us, then we'll find new ones; and when we've found them we'll have money again and full houses and children walking the old forgotten roads to school. For if we can't make a world to the pattern of our dreams, then we had better die; and we need not die unhappy if that world is founded truly on our bones.*

So Stephen climbed down from Brewster's Knowe and went to see the one man in that countryside who could show him the way to save Hillhead.

Strathmuir.

Young Strath was naturally a little suspicious of Stephen, for he had not forgotten their first interview, but as soon as he saw that Stephen had really come to learn he told him everything he could. His conversation was a miraculous draught of hope, for he would not admit that there was any problem too difficult to solve. Indeed he welcomed difficulties because they gave him a chance to exercise his ingenious mind. He was afraid of no experiment, for his physical courage had somehow communicated itself to his mind, and gave him a freedom with ideas that was most uncommon in the country-side where ideas, unless they were old, were considered of the Devil.

When Stephen confessed to him that he was afraid he was too old to learn farming, Young Strath laughed. "Ye needna worry. Good farmers are cheap. Ye can buy them at twenty tae the shilling – or a shilling in the £. There's something more needed nowadays. I'm not a farmer: I'm an engineer. My job is to plan. It's the day o' the expert and my line's production. In the colleges there's all kinds o' experts in the chemistry o' the soil, and the feedin of cattle, in milk and eggs and everything ye can think o'. They tell me what's best to do in their own line and I fit all they tell me into a plan as far as this place is concerned – a plan, mind ye, that'll pay my men a decent wage and leave me a decent profit at the end o' the day. Lord man, if ye've the will to learn from them that know, and the head tae make plans and carry them through, there's naething tae hinder ye bein' a farmer."

That Young Strath was a new type of farmer was shown by the fact that he spent far more time in his office than in his fields. Now Stephen knew that if he had gone for advice to any contemporary of his grand-father, the farmer would have taken him into the fields and, while leaning on a dyke between the turnips and the corn, would have delivered himself slowly and with many digressions of an individual essay in experience, tradition, folklore and prejudice. To illustrate his argu-ments he would have pulled a head of corn or a stem of potatoes and by the way he handled those creatures would have witnessed to a certain spiritual affinity with them, as if there were a virtue in the touch of them. But Young Strath handled time charts and production sheets. Everything was costed down to the time it took the grieve to look at the sky in the morning and foretell the weather for the day. Farming, to Young Strath, was more than a traditional art. It was a business and efficiency was the test. And business and efficiency were things that Stephen both knew and understood.

"But do the men like it?" Stephen asked, wondering how a sound traditionalist like Willum would adapt himself to such a system.

"Them that don't like it, hate it, and them that do like it are michty keen," Young Strath replied. "Come on out and I'll show ye."

It was late in the evening, gone ten o'clock, when they went out into the yard. The mirk of the night was settling over the Howe and a thin moon was rising beyond the hills, a moon so thin and with so fine an edge of light that she merely made the falling dark grow darker. All the singing birds had long gone home to their nests and the voice of an owl hoo-hooing in the treetop was like the voice of an uneasy dream. But the farm men had not yet gone to bed. Across the yard a shaft of brightness shone out of the tractor shed door and Stephen heard the intermittent tap of a hammer mingled with the snore of a forge.

When they went into the shed they found three men deeply engaged in the innards of a tractor. On another farm they might have been in the stable, polishing their harness or plaiting straw decorations: here they were rubbing the grease from the intimate details of their machines, or fitting together small components that looked absurdly delicate between their spatulate fingers.

They looked up and nodded casually to Young Strath.

"What's wrong wi her?" he asked, pointing to the dismembered tractor.

"O naething," one of the men replied, "we're just cleaning her up."

Young Strath looked at his watch. "Half past ten. Time ye were hame tae your wives."

"Aye, aye," the man replied: but he went on with his work. Nor did the others pay any more attention. They did not intend that the master should come so easily between them and their pleasures.

Stephen was fascinated by the incident. There was a touch of the fantastic about the great shed. Beneath the ring of white light the men went on absorbed in their pleasant labour; and in the far back parts of the shed, tractors and wagons and strange machines of Young Strath's own invention stood in the gloom like monsters of a future dimly apprehended. Outside there were still the moon climbing over the long ridge of the hills and the brown owls in the treetops and the wild geese gabbling down the Howe like uneasy and unearthly spirits.

"But how beautifully it fits together," Stephen said in surprise. "And there can't be anything wrong if the men are happy."

Young Strath laughed. "This is nae the first time I've had tae send them hame tae their wives – though that's maybe a small service since they've a' too many bairns already."

Such incidents removed all Stephen's distrust of Strathmuir's ways; and his own understanding of those ways gave him confidence to turn to the planning of Hillhead. He went into the matter fully with Young Strath and together they calculated that by selling the two pairs of horses and buying a tractor the land might still be kept in cultivation, one of the young horsemen might be retained, the loss on the corn crops reduced, and even a few pounds of profit made on them.

That was not all. They considered the feeding of cattle that was the old man's greatest art. It had been his pride and the pride of his fathers to breed and fatten only the best, and to send the finished beasts to market

178

in the very bloom of perfection. And because he was a master of that art, the old man had always got the top prices in the market. But Young Strath proved by figures that admitted no question that the bloom cost more than it brought in, that it swallowed up the whole of the profit.

"It may be a pity but it's true that ye canna mak money by fattenin the best. Buy cheap, fatten quickly and sell as soon as the beasts can face the market – then ye'll maybe come hame wi a pound in your pocket. Only a rich man can afford tae feed the fancy stuff; if a poor man tries it he'll soon be in the market himsel."

And the old man had admitted, "There's hardly a beast about the place that's nae ower the lugs in debt tae me."

So Stephen and Young Strath made plans whereby the old man would buy the good cheap commercial cattle in the markets of the south and feed them to the point where they would yield a profit, but not a penny further.

There were other and more dreadful things planned for him. Like all proud farmers of the older type he had a profound dislike of hens and pigs and all such small deer that scrounge a living round a farm toun. He tolerated them because they ate up the scraps and in theory made a pound of pin money for the women. But he was certain, far more certain than he was of heaven, that the beasts were parasites, that did not pay their way. But Young Strath had proof, proof in figures upon paper and money in the bank, that hens and pigs and such creatures could do more than pay their way. They could even make good the losses on the lordly cattle. "Fifteen shillings net on every pig we feed. Two hundred and fifty pounds on five hundred fed in a year. Not a fortune and maybe not very much for the labour; but it's good money in our hands; and I'm damned if I can see that money made in ham's worth less than money made in brisket."

So they planned that Hillhead might feed a

hundred pigs a year; and after the pigs there would be the hens; and after the hens whatever might yield a profit at the moment. For, Young Strath said, "The only secret in farming now's to catch your market. Fashions change from day to day and ye've got to adapt your production to them. The men that can adapt themsel's survive: the men that canna adapt themsel's go down. That's always been the way and as far as I can see it'll always be."

"We'll survive," said Stephen and he meant it, for he knew that given a chance he could save Hillhead.

But the chance was the difficulty. He hardly dared think of what his grandfather might say if he knew of the plans that were being made behind his back.

Stephen had another problem standing between him and the future: the past was refusing to let him alone. Clarkson had of course been annoyed when he refused the job offered to him and his annoyance had passed through several stages from incredulous protest to dignified remonstrance and finally into an angry consignment to the Devil. His father had gone sky high with indignation and horror. His Calvinist mind, well-founded in the faith that business success being the greatest sign of spiritual grace the offer of a large salary is a mark of heaven's divinest favour, was as outraged as a church father at the sight of the wantonings of the pagan flesh. His spirit trembled for what might befall his boy, for he had been so long apprenticed to business and he was so enthralled by its divinity, that he was sure the man who flouted it and dared to refuse its favours would in inevitably be destroyed. He knew well enough what was the cause of all the trouble. The arch-fiend, his cynical, swearing, drunken father-in-law, had got at the boy, to debauch his morals and squander his money. In his more frantic moments he had visions of the old man and the young one holding fearful orgies in the town and chasing the loose women of the streets with shouts of incontinent desire. Much thinking made his fears more real to him, till he often believed that they were facts, and whenever he met Clarkson, or any of his superiors in the company, he tried to avoid them as if some dreadful shame had fallen upon him. At last in desperation he wrote to Jane.

Jane, however, did not need any call to arms. She was fully aware of all that was happening, more fully aware than Mr Lees; but, being far, far wiser, she was biding the time for action.

During the summer Stephen and she had written very seldom to each other for they were not the kind that need to be always expressing their love at the length of seven pages. Their letters at any time had been infrequent and confined to matters of fact such as dates for dinners and invitations to dances. Therefore she was not in the least alarmed to hear only twice from Stephen in two months; but she was alarmed by the tone of his letters, for she noticed a touch of what she called idealism in them, a tiresome quality of which she understood very little and which she disliked very much. She was alarmed, because the plans which she had made for Stephen and herself did not admit the luxury of ideals and she feared that Stephen might not be able to withstand them without her. When she heard that Stephen had refused the job she saw that her fears had been justified and that she must act quickly if she was to save the game. But she was careful, for she knew that a young man in a high state of idealism was a dangerous young man indeed. So she did not write to him, or try to influence him in any way. Instead she made up to her father and made him promise that if she could get Stephen back to the company a place would still be found for him. As Mr. Dorman loved his daughter, since even he had to love somebody, he consented. Then, having made that secure, Jane considered the best way to deal with Stephen himself. She went to her best dressmaker, ordered herself a lot of new clothes and, as soon as they were ready, wrote to Stephen telling him that she would be north to see him in a few days' time.

That gave Stephen a great deal to think about and forced him to an issue that had been for a long time at the back of his mind.

His affair with Jane had begun two years before when he had met her at a dance held by the company's office stamp staff. Before then he had pursued several young women with considerable success but none of the affairs had outlasted the parties' quick and mutual disillusionment. Jane, however, had been different from the others. She had realised the importance of a young man's career and had done everything she could to help him. There had been invitations to her home to meet her father in a social way; and, although that way did not differ very much from his ordinary habit, for Mr. Dorman could never get far away from his business schemes, it gave Stephen considerable prestige in the company and marked him out as a very fortunate young man.

They had been proud of conducting a thoroughly intelligent and commonsense affair, an affair combining the minimum of sentiment with the maximum of intelligence, with some inevitable passion thrown in. It had not been very exciting, a touch of glory was missing from it, but they were both agreed that glory had no place in the modern world, and they had been well enough contented. They had conceived a well-ordered love to fit well-ordered lives, a love calculated and controlled, a matter of convenience. But now Stephen was forced to think about that love in relation to the new life he had found at Hillhead. Then he saw that he had grown out of the well-ordered life of London; he had found the touch of glory; and that glory demanded a like magnificence in his love for Jane. He longed for that magnificence and he battered himself into excesses of passion by forcing himself to think about her. But thinking was not enough; the excesses passed leaving him empty and dissatisfied. Sometimes he wanted never to see Jane again. At other times he swore that his own new glory would kindle the like in her and that they would share the new magnificence together. So alternating between despair and hope he waited for her.

Jane arrived when they were leading the corn from the Little Park. Willum who was building the rick saw her long red car come up the Hillhead road and, "Man Stephen," he cried, "look at the cairridge comin tae see ye, a' red and shining like a fiery serpent. Eh, if only I had ane like that instead o' a wife and thirteen bairns, what a time I would hae among the dames. Lord man, I'd be worn awa tae a shadow in a week. Dammit man aye."

Then, as the car came near enough for him to see Jane as well, he opened his mouth and forgot to shut it, for her elegance so dazzled him that he knelt on the rick in a state of suspended animation till she had gone out of sight around a corner.

Coming slowly out of the trance, he kind of whispered to Stephen. "Did ye see what I say saw, man? Eh lord, lord, if she's sic a treat we her claes on, whatever would she be when she's naked?"

Stephen quickly threw up the last few sheaves from the bottom of his car; and, telling Willum to unyoke the horse, ran round to the house to welcome Jane.

Whatever he may have feared would happen when Jane met the old people the scene in the parlour was totally unexpected. For, instead of running in to take command of a difficult situation, he found Jane and the old people being charming to each other while he himself was suddenly overcome with embarrassment at the sight of his sweetheart. He was so embarrassed that he could hardly find the words with which to welcome her but the others saved his face with the very perfection of good breeding, until he asked to be excused in order to make himself presentable.

When Stephen had gone out, the old man became gay as he always did at the sight of a pretty girl. His eyes took on a sparkle. He was all admiration and wit and small kind courtesies. Aunt Elizabeth was like a benevolent queen, magnificent in her bearing, most generous in her welcome. Together they made much of their visitor as if she was somebody they were very glad to honour, and who, Aunt Elizabeth's manner subtly implied, was indeed greatly honoured thereby. Jane had not missed that implication for she was less brilliant, less decided than at her arrival. There was even a touch of humility that was entirely new to her manner.

And no wonder. As she had driven up the Hillhead road that grew more and more rutted as it neared the houses, it seemed to her that she was going to the back of the world. With some contempt and a great deal of amusement, she noticed the impression she had made on Willum and she expected to make no less an impression when she drove into the close. Hillhead was not the sort of thing she was accustomed to, except at a distance, to make town more desirable. When she stopped her car at the kitchen door, the old grey house seemed very dingy and deplorably close to the midden. The wind had blown a lot of straw about the kitchen door and there had been hens, many, many hens. Looking at her car, seven hundred pounds worth of machinery and chromium plating, and then seeing herself in her mind's eye, a most elegant vision in oatmeal tweeds, she felt a creature from another and brighter world. And the wonder in Bawbie's round eyes as she came running from the milkhouse in her bare arms assured her that the job before her would not be a difficult one.

But as she sat in the parlour she began to feel just a little overdressed beside Aunt Elizabeth in her black silk gown; and at the same time uncomfortably naked before the old man with the glinting blue eyes. However, nothing could upset Jane for very long; she recovered her assurance; but she treated Aunt Elizabeth and Mr. Brewster with a respect she seldom showed to anything under a hundred thousand pounds.

It had been her intention to speak to them very

pointedly about the mess that Stephen was making of his career, but she found it difficult to make an opening.

"Will ye smoke a cigarette?" The old man asked, handing her a box from the mantelpiece.

"A glass of sherry, my dear," said Aunt Elizabeth giving her a dram of Mr. Elphinstone's best.

Jane took both the sherry and the cigarette, for she had no choice; and, as both of them were very strong, they made it more difficult still to turn the conversation the way she wanted it.

But after Aunt Elizabeth had gone to see about the dinner, the old man remarked, "Aye, ye'll be missing Stephen. He's sae obligin. I'm sure a lassie like you could twist him any way she wanted."

Suspecting that he was making fun of her, Jane made a direct attack.

"I hope so," she said. "I didn't come all this way to look at the scenery."

"To take him back?" the old man asked.

"Yes. Before he makes a complete fool of himself, or lets other people do it for him."

She looked at the old man, prepared to match the hardest look he might give her, but he just patted her arm kindly and said, "God gae wi ye, lassie, and I hope ye'll maybe hae words that I hadna; and if ye haena the words ye hae the clothes. If that braw gown doesna speak sense tae him naething will; for there hasna been the like o' it in Lendrum since the Laird spent a' his money and the fine ladies come nae mair."

"He's got to see sense," Jane said for she couldn't think of anything better, having the feeling that she was walking along a dark pavement in which there may be open trapdoors.

"You speak what's nae doubt in your mind," the old man said. "What does he want tae gae wanderin through the world for at his age, whan he should be settlin doon and makin a place for himsel and marrying a lassie that'll help him on. A lassie like you that kens what's good for him and'll see that he does it whether he wants to or not. That's what a Brewster needs. And that's what we've never gotten – yet."

The old man had become so gentle and so earnest in his manner that Jane felt a sudden elation. He was on her side after all. She warmed to him; and when he sighed and said, "We'll miss him for we're auld folk here, and lonely," she pitied him because she saw that he loved the boy. And because she respected him and pitied him, and because he had broken down any restraint there might have been between them, she spoke her most inward thoughts.

"I want him too. Very much. If only he cared he could do great things; and he must care, for he and I between us would be invincible."

"And would that be all?"

"What more could there be?"

"Bairns maybe tae keep the power when you are tired o't."

"Yes," she said, "children too. Anything he wants, if only he'll come back where he belongs."

Then Aunt Elizabeth came in to call them to dinner.

They rose to go through. As the old man stood aside so that Jane might go before him, he put his arm round her shoulder and said, "Speak tae him, lassie, as ye've spoken tae me; and, mind, my heart gaes wi ye."

They ate dinner in the little front room where a crowd of Michaelmas daisies stood in a tall stone jar on the sideboard and the last deep blue flowers of the clematis swung in the light wind beyond the window panes. As the room faced direct to the noonday sun they were suffused with light around the little square table and the white hair on the old man's head shone softly like an aureole above a pagan saint. Opposite each other, Jane and Stephen stole privy looks at each other when they thought they were unobserved. He saw her lovelier than ever; more than ever as if her deliberate will informed her smallest action. She could only see the harm that country life had done him; for he had lost his London air: in his khaki shirt and old tweed jacket he looked like any yokel; or, what was manifestly worse, like the people that go hiking into Metroland. But neither was allowed too much time to think upon the other, for Aunt Elizabeth was in her glory that day. Sitting at the bottom of the table with the soup tureen before her, she was indeed a noble lady. Her black gown had taken on a yet more splendid lustre; there was a touch of the imperial about her gold pince-nez that lay across her bosom like an order of chivalry; and in her conversation there was a serene command of all about the table that not even Jane could resist or even think to.

They talked about life in London; and Jane, not unwilling to impress the old lady, mentioned that she had been staying with the Manifolds in Gloucestershire.

Aunt Elizabeth nodded. "Manifold Park is a charming place though perhaps a little better upstairs than below. And how did you leave Sir James and his lady?"

"You read the Bystander?"

Aunt Elizabeth shook her head with a smile.

"O, quite well," Jane replied.

Then her surprise becoming too much for her, Jane asked, "You know the Manifolds?"

"Too well," aunt Elizabeth replied. "I was their second chambermaid for a year."

"O," Jane said, and then ate a deal of soup.

The old man laughed. "Forgive her, lassie, she has nae sense o' shame; never had and never will."

"It's quite all right," Jane said, and then ate some more soup.

Aunt Elizabeth talked on in an even, kindly but very authoritative voice about the Season and the Highland Games and the many activities of the gentry, not as if they mattered very much but with just the amount of interest proper in a hostess who talks the language that her guest will understand. But, if she did so with the idea of putting Jane at ease, she failed; for although Jane had no illusions about the gentry as individuals, there was something about their order which she did respect and which, with Stephen's help, she was determined to share. So it annoyed her to hear one who, by her own unashamed confession had been a chambermaid, speak about them in that disinterested way as if they had been the Albert Memorial or Brighton Pier. At the same time she had an uneasy feeling that the old woman was sizing her up and contrasting her with some curious standards of her own, standards that Jane wanted to despise but could not, since she had no idea of what they might be. She found the old woman's manner impenetrable. There was no hostility in it, for hostility was a thing she could have sensed at once and understood. It was, she began to suspect, no emotion at all; behind the urbane front there was perhaps nothing but indifference; or at most the kindly tolerance an old woman might have for a child that was none of her own. Jane was not accustomed to being treated as a child. It was the greatest insult of all. And she hated Aunt Elizabeth for it. Very bitterly she noticed how the old woman leaned over and put her hand on Stephen's arm whenever she said something to him.

Then in her anger Jane said to herself; *There at least she's vulnerable, and there I'll make her admit that I am more than child. For I'll take him from her this very day.*

The meal came to an end with Aunt Elizabeth still in complete command.

The old man left the table with a little bow to Jane, saying, "I maun awa tae sleep now for I'm like a bairn. Bide till teatime for my sake, won't ye."

As Jane watched him go slowly out of the room she said to herself, *There's one of you that can't stand against me.* Then she turned to deal with Aunt Elizabeth.

For a moment the two women faced each other across Stephen; but once more Aunt Elizabeth refused the attack by denying that there could be any.

"Now, my dear," she said to Jane, "take Stephen out to the garden or down to the wood and make him realise all that he is giving up. For anyone must be mad who would wave away London for this quiet place unless they were old and making ready to die."

Very gently but very firmly she drove them before her into the garden and stood framed in the open door like an old goddess at the door of her temple. Stephen looked back at her with affection brightening his eyes; but it was hardly love that made Jane turn away so quickly. It was an overpowering sense of relief to be out in the open again; and a fierce delight in the victory that she was about to gain.

Stephen and Jane walked slowly over the fields to Brewster's Knowe and there sat down within a ring of high broom bushes that grew beside the old stone seat.

Stephen's thoughts and feelings were still in almost complete confusion for the sight of Jane made her unbearably desirable, but there was some impediment within himself that held him back and threw his emotions into disorder in their swift flight to Jane. He wanted to make love to her, to tumble her in the grass, to rouse her passions with his own so that they might lose themselves in each other and all the troubles of his mind be resolved in the dark heat of love. Once within the ring of the broom where the dry pods were snapping open on the burnished seed, he took her into his arms and kissed her desperately, as if the world would have ended with the kiss. She replied to his ardour, lying back in his arms with her eyes closed and her tousled hair upon her face. But her mind was not on the business and Stephen knew it, for his ardour spent itself like waves on a sandy shore; and when she pushed him away he sat up with a sigh to listen to all that he feared she was going to say.

Jane made out a good case for his returning to London at once. She omitted no argument of his own advantage or her's, and she came as near to pleading as was in her nature. Feeling caught within the ring of broom, Stephen rose and walked over to the old stone seat where she joined him, and they sat there together, looking down across the autumn. Still she argued with him, offering him, as it were, all the cities of the world, but when she looked to him for his answer he shook his head. "I can't go back."

"But why?" she demanded. "Because of the old man, your grandfather?"

"Yes, partly that," he agreed.

"But if he didn't want you to stay? What then?"

"I think he wants me."

She told him what the old man had said to her in the parlour.

"And now what?" she asked.

Stephen looked beaten for a moment and Jane felt a slight thrill of triumph; but a new thought came into his mind, and he said with a new and strong conviction – "Even then I would stay because I must".

"Even though you're not wanted."

"Even though I'm not wanted."

"And even though I would refuse to stay here with you."

The weakness of desire ran through Stephen's bones, and he turned away from the question. "Don't let's speak about that," he said, gripping his arm. "It won't bear thinking about."

"But you've got to think about it. And you've got to choose."

"Then if I must make that choice I'll still bide here."

"But Stephen," she pleaded, "think what you're doing. Think of the plans we made and the things we could do if you would come back with me. O my dear, think before you throw everything away for some ideal that won't last the year out."

Stephen replied, "I have thought, for days on end,

but there's only one conclusion... I *MUST* stay."

"If you do, you'll betray everything you've believed in."

"And if I don't stay, I'll betray everything I've come to believe in the last few months."

She laughed, but not very happily. "You're speaking as if you'd been converted."

He too laughed, but "Maybe I am," he said. Then, "O my dear, can't you see that something extraordinary has happened to me since I came here. I'm not the same man that left London. I have been living differently and thinking about new things since I came here and the days have grown up like a wall between my past and me. The roots of my life are here and it is here that I must stay."

"And the past?"

"That's beyond the wall and cut off from me, maybe for ever."

Jane shook her head. "but what is the wall? I don't understand."

Then he told her a little of all that had happened to him, of the land of his fathers and of the vision of the generations resting their hands upon his shoulder and crying to him to finish what they had begun.

"But Stephen, Stephen," she cried, both pitying his madness and impatient with it, "you're doing all this because of people who are dead."

"No, not for the dead but for myself and for others who have to live by the land. Look," he said, pointing across the Howe, "there's good country – rich enough to support its people in comfort. But there is little comfort in their houses and no money in their pockets, because they have fallen behind the times, because their old ideas can't deal with the modern world. But I understand the ways of the modern world and I can help to change the old ideas of the countryside."

"But why? What has it to do with you?"

"Because – because it seems to be my duty to stay."

"Duty. Duty. What have you or I to do with duty. We've only one duty, to ourselves, to get as much as we can out of the world as long as we're alive. Our only duty is to do what we want to do."

"There's more to do than duty," Stephen said after a moment's thought. "It's maybe not duty at all that's keeping me. I want to stay. The troubles of the country-side are a challenge to me and more than anything else I want to accept that challenge; for I know that, given the goodwill of the men concerned, I could put an end to the troubles. O my god, Jane, it is intolerable to the dignity of men and the memory of my fathers that we should be gripped to death by circumstances and yet make no fight to bend them to our will."

"God help you," Jane said, "because nobody else will. How do you think your neighbours will take your plans to reform them? Not with any good will unless human nature is changed completely. O my dear, if you stay here with any idea of leading a crusade, you'll only be laughed at and your only reward will be failure."

"Even then I must stay. Because here I am some-thing. In London I was nothing. It's not my place. It has no meaning to me nor I to it. But here I am in the place that I grew out of. Every field, every tree, every turn of the road means something to me. I'm in my own place. In London I'm only one among ten million who have nothing in common but hunger. Here I'm among people that have the same traditions and speak the same language as myself. And it's a matter of life and death to me to live inside that tradition, because I am made that way."

"Well, it'll be a fine life," Jane said. "You'll maybe have your tradition but you won't have much more. What has your grandfather got out of his tradition. No money. No influence. No control over his own life even. Nothing that makes it worth while living. Do you think that's going to be enough for you?"

"No. Not by a hundred times enough. But those

of us who are young, we will make a better world."

Jane sighed. "Then we'd better say goodbye."

"But Jane," he cried –

"It's no use, " she said. "The world you speak about and the world I live in are two different places and there's no road between them. For my world is real and the good things it offers to the people who are clever enough to take them are real too. But your world is a dream and it's only reward is disillusion. So, my dear, goodbye."

She rose to go.

But Stephen could not bear the thought of parting, for the step that she took away from him dissolved the very marrow in his bones.

"You can't go. You mustn't go." He cried. "I love you. O, my dear, I love you."

He pulled her down on the seat beside him again and kissed her desperately as if to assure himself that she was still there.

"My dear, my dear," he said. "I would do anything to keep you. Anything. Anything."

"Then you'll come with me," she whispered.

Instead of replying he kissed her again; and she, thinking to make sure of him, tempted him with a yet greater glory.

"If you'll only come back to London everything we ever planned is ours for the taking. I didn't tell you this before. I wanted to keep it as a last surprise for you. But I will tell you now. When we were at Avignon we were not there for pleasure only. Father had conferences with some French business men and the result was an agreement whereby our company is to take over a part of the French business."

"What is it?" Stephen asked with some eagerness.

"A high explosive. Something more powerful than any on the market. The most powerful thing in the world. My dear, think of it. The company as it is will be twenty times as much in a few years. Governments will come to us with unlimited money. They will give anything we like to ask for our patent. Our shares that are thirty shillings just now will be worth as many pounds. My dear, if you will take your chance now, this very minute, you can have anything you ask for in ten years."

She stood up before him holding out her hands to him and between her hands lay fortune.

For a moment there was a flush of glory on Stephen's face as he saw the magnificence that might be his. But the vision of power faded and its place was taken by the fields still covered with the harvest.

A high explosive.

"O my god, never, never," he said. "Explosives to make war, and kill, and destroy. To spread desolation over fields like this and kill good, innocent people like my friends. My work's to build not to destroy. It would be better for me to die than go with you."

"But Stephen," she pleaded with him, dismayed at his reaction. "My dear, war has nothing to do with us. We don't make war. We too will build. And if we don't, then others will, and they will be the masters and we will have to do what they tell us."

"No, no. I could not have the responsibility of making the explosives that people might use to destroy the very things I value most."

"But the responsibility would not be on you. It would be on the governments that used the explosive in war. It is no concern of ours what they may do with the explosive we make. Our responsibility ends when we make it."

"If only I could believe that," Stephen replied. "If only I could believe it. But I can't. There isn't such a thing as a divided responsibility in matters like this. If one man died as the result of the explosives we made, all of us would be to blame. I can't do it, Jane. I can't."

Jane made a gesture of defeat. "Then I'm finished, for you've changed. I don't know you any longer and my plans and my words are wasted on you."

Stephen signed. "It's the wall between us. I belong to my people and I have responsibilities to them. You belong to yourself and you have no interests to think of but your own. You could not live in my world for you would be false to yourself; and I could not live in your world for I would be a stranger there. So – "

"So that is the end of the story," Jane said. "It's a poor end to so many wonderful things."

Stephen took her hand, driven to her by a wave of desire and sorrow.

"My dear, how I wish I had never come home – then I could have gone on in the way we planned. But be patient with me. Don't let me say goodbye today, never to see each other again. Be patient with me and wait for me a little, for the dream in my head may be a false dream and some day I may find that it has betrayed me."

But Jane shook her head.

"No, no, my dear. You have said too much today; and, whatever I may have misunderstood, there is one thing that I have understood too well. I can see not the wall you spoke about but a weakness in yourself. You dream and you believe in your dreams. Wherever you are, your dreams will go with you and will divide your mind between the thing you have to do and the thing you would like to. But a man with a divided mind and a weakened will is no use in the world where I belong. In my world there is only one chance and ten thousand who are waiting for it; but only one man out of the ten thousand can take that chance and he is the man with the single mind and the strongest will. Once I thought you might be that man; now I can see you never will; and so, my dear, and for the last time, goodbye.

"Now will you see me to my car."

They walked down to the steading in silence.

Stephen asked if she would drink a cup of tea with Aunt Elizabeth and the old man but she refused.

"No, no. I must get back to London at once."

Without another word she stepped into her car and drove away, leaving Stephen alone in the close. As he listened to the sound of the engine diminishing away in the distance, it seemed to him the last voice from a world that he would never see again.

There were others who listened to that sound, with no particular feelings of regret.

"That would be a car," Aunt Elizabeth said to the old man.

"Aye," he replied, "I some thought she would be leavin without ony tea."

Then Stephen came in.

"Aye, so she didna take ye wi her," the old man said.

Stephen shook his head, for he was empty of words.

Aunt Elizabeth put her hand kindly on his arm, "But she'll maybe come again."

The old man gave a short laugh and said, "Na, na; Nae as lang as I'm here, I doubt. She tell't me a lot that she'll nae like tae mind on. When ye're young it doesna pay tae be sorry for a puir auld man that's never been sorry for himsel. Sit ye doon, laddie, and drink a cup o' tea. Ye'll see a lot o' ferlies yet afore the world's ended."

So Stephen, left alone with the old people, drank his tea and tried not to think about Jane. But however he might smile he feared that his heart was broken.

CHAPTER NINE

Harvest Home

STEPHEN'S HEARTBREAK lasted for three days; but
once his body got accustomed to the thought that it
would never lie close to Jane, he felt a curious sense of
relief that first of all shocked and then delighted him. It
shocked him that his great pain could come so quickly to
an end; then it delighted him to realise that he was
indeed free of his lost years, free to go on with the new
work that lay all round him. That the work would not be
easy he knew quite well, but he felt enough strength in
his bones and vigour in his mind to move the eternal
hills of God, yes, even to make the old man see with his
reforming eyes. But it was not yet time for that tremendous onset. The rest of the harvest still had to be
brought home.

Even now he dared to try the old man's temper
with a hint of change. He had been to Strathmuir to see
how his new friend led home the harvest. There he
found no carts creaking their slow way to the cornyard
with their loads of sheaves. Instead two threshing mills
stood out in the fields; and the corn was being fed to
them straight from the stooks. Down the rows of stooks
men were forking the sheaves on to tractor wagons and
lorries, then the loads were driven to the side of the mill.
There the sheaves were forked up aloft, where the feed-
ers caught them and cut their bands and fed them into
the drum. The drum sang in hollow gusts of sound,
rising and falling in the wind as it stripped the ears from
the straw. The mills devoured the harvest at one end.
The straw fell on to the moving elevator belt that carried
it high into the air then dropped it into a heap which
three men were fashioning into a great rectangular rick,

like an antique cottage. At the other end the corn ran
out in a shining stream of polished grain and it in turn
passed through elevators to a cart. As soon as one cart
was full a tractor pulled it home and another was put in
its place. So the work went on steadily through the day
and for the next day and the day after till the fields were
bare of harvest and the long labour of the year was
ended.

To Stephen it seemed that it was ended far too
soon and in altogether too summary a way, for he was
the old man's grandson and he believed that a cornyard
well-filled with tidy ricks was the farmer's glory.

"And what's the point of rushing it through like
that?" he asked Young Strath.

"It saves time, it saves labour and it saves corn. Ye
can see for yourself the time and the labour it saves –
there's nae ricks to build. As for the saving of corn –
think of the shaking the stuff must suffer in the ordinary
way o' doing. Ye fork it from the cart on to the rick.
That loses ye some more. In the rick the rats get at it,
and the amount ye lose there depends on the number of
rats and the time they get to eat it. Then ye fork it from
the rick on to the mill and again there's something lost.
If ye hairst corn when it's dead ripe and winter it in
ricks, I reckon you'll lose a bag tae the acre. On my
hundred and sixty acres that's eighty quarters and at
twenty-five shillings that's a hundred pounds. That's not
so much on a place like this that grows ten or eleven
quarters to the acre; but on poorer land that grows five
or six the quarters that are lost probably mean all the difference between a profit and a loss."

"How many quarters will Hillhead grow?" asked
Stephen.

"Eight, maybe, or even as much as ten in the best o'
years."

"And there's eighty acres of corn, say forty quarters
lost. That's fifty pounds."

"It's a big price to pay for doing as your fathers

did."

"Too big," Stephen said and he went home with a great resolution in his mind.

He thought he stated the case very clearly to the old man as they sat on the dyke of the cornyard waiting for the dew to rise, but the old man's reply was just as clear.

"Laddie, laddie," he said, "Ye come tae me wi that and think it's a new story. Man, farmers hard up for ready money hae been threshing out o' the stook since ever there were threshing mills. Awa wi ye, man, I've never selt green corn and I never will. The stuff maun sit in the rick and thole its winter and harden and dry intae meal that'll mak your belly glad. Ye'd thrash out o' the stook would ye? Nae in my time. For if I hadna a full cornyard I might as well nae hae a hairst. Where would be the pleasure if I couldna gang tae the cornyard in a winter mornin and see the ricks standin snod and warm aneath the thatch and be able tae count up the quarters and figure out the straw? Awa man wi your fancy notions; ye'd tak the pleasure frae the farmer's trade. It may be a better way than mine, but the auld ways'll serve my turn and when I'm deid ye can please yoursel – but not till then."

"But look here," Stephen began –

He could have saved his trouble, the old man had turned away and was on his way to the stable.

Stephen turned a little glum. If that was a foretaste of how the old man would look at changes, the job was going to be even harder than he thought.

Now October was running on towards its close and the frosts of winter brought glorious harvest weather. Every morning the dry east wind came up the river from the sea and dried the dew and set the sheaves rustling with a song of ripeness. Tam and Willum built the ricks in the cornyard while Jock and Sam and Stephen and a man called Leslie drove the carts. The Merry Widow, a neighbour and dear friend of the old man, forked the sheaves in the fields, helped by Tam's wife and Willum's and sometimes by Kennedy and Susan. All day long the old man directed the building in the cornyard or stepped down to the fields to see how the Merry Widow was getting along. Not a moment was lost except the hours when the horses must be fed and rested; and in their eagerness to make the most of the good weather they worked late into the night, till the colour died out in the west and the evening star came out in the quiet sky and the great red harvest moon came up above the hills.

They drew close to each other in those golden days, for the harvest was a friendly labour. Throughout the year they had worked each at many diverse jobs: now all the activities of the farm had been drawn together in the consummation of the year's long plan, and every man and woman had a place in the last brave labour. Since all their work was directed to the one end, and they could see that end take lovely shape in the cornyard, each willingly took his place in the appointed plan and worked in harmony with his neighbour. They had only one thought, that the work would go on and the harvest be made safe against the winter. Two hundred harvests had been gathered on Hillhead; two hundred times the Brewsters and their people had swung themselves into the rhythm of the season. So now again they gave themselves to the rhythm gladly and found a new strength thereby. As the cornyard filled and the stooks in the fields diminished, the labour became a rite; there was a heartening pleasure in it. Blessed by the sun and gladdened by the wind, they felt a deep content with their labour, as if, after much wandering, they had found again the old gods that haunt the margins of the cornfields.

Like the jolliest of all the gods, the Merry Widow filled the season with her laughter. She might well have been the genius of harvest herself, the Mother Ceres of a very rustic mythology. She was a woman of forty-five whose splendid physique, though hardened by work in

the fields, had always been kept round and rosy with
pleasure. She looked like what she was – a pagan in the
old true sense of the word. But she had no morality
except that life was sacred. No matter what misfortune
came her way she met it with a dauntless heart and
burned it away with laughter. She was a round woman
with a round sunburned face – round firm breasts, and
quarters like a young blood mare. The sight of her
drove Willum into ecstasies of regret for his lost youth.
The old man was her greatest friend.

She was not precisely a widow for she had never
been married, but she had shared her cottage in the
woods with many lovers and to most of them she had
borne children. Some of the fathers paid her a little
money, but only now and then; for they were so many
and she was far too busy to keep trace of them. What
little she did get that way was quite inadequate to live on,
so she did casual labour about the countryside. She
washed and cleaned. She baked. She gathered potatoes.
She worked in the harvest fields. She went round with
the threshing mills. She even hoed turnips and spread
manure in the Spring. She was willing to do anything,
for no labour could tire her and at the end of the longest
day her laughter was still ringing across the dusty fields
in delight at some outrageous bawdry.

Kennedy admired her tremendously and forked
the sheaves along with her whenever he could get out to
Hillhead. One at each side of the cart they pitched up
the sheaves with beautiful easy movements of their forks
and all they time they kept up tremendous arguments
while the mare tossed her head uneasily and the man on
the cart added an uncertain obbligato of grunts and
curses as he plunged about on uncertain footing.

"Now that," said Mr. Elphinstone as he watched
them one evening, "is to my mind a most delightful
scene. It has the spirit of the Golden Age."

The load had gone home to the farmyard and
Kennedy and the Merry Widow were walking towards

them over the stubble. She was a free and hearty figure as she strode along with her fork over her shoulder and her free arm swinging bare from the shoulder. There was a magnificent sense of movement in her parts, a delight in action as she trod the solid ground. She was alive. The sun shone in her red gold hair, fun sparkled in her eyes; she looked coquettishly across her shoulder and when she laughed her whole body thrilled at the easing of her mirth. Stopping a few yards away from them, she leaned on her fork with her firm slim legs astride, and looked down on them with a smile that shone like a pool in the autumn woods, but far more warmly.

"This man," she said, pointing to Kennedy, "he'll be the death o' me. God help ye lassie if ye mairry him for there never was sic a man tae speak o' beddin. And will it stop at speakin? Nae if I ken the licht in his bad black eyen."

She prodded Kennedy in the ribs with the end of her fork and went into a cry of laughter that made the quiet woods ring with its redoubling echo.

They laughed with her and their eyes grew brighter, for she warmed them with her generous spirit.

"We'll make you counsellor to the maids," Mr. Elphinstone said, "and you will warn them about the ways of men."

"And well I might," she replied, "for weel I ken ye. Mim and mild ye are in the licht o' day but lat the dark come doon and ye'll be creepin tae the window and tappin low and whisperin 'Lat me in. Lat me in.' O I'll advise the lassies tae draw the blankets ower their heads and nae lat on they hear ye. But what's advice to the like o' them. Advise them as ye like, the lassies come tae bairns in the end. And wha should ken better than me that hae had so mony."

She stayed chaffing them for a while, then an empty cart came rattling down the stony track between the fields. She picked up her fork again, hitched her coats more comfortably round her waist and marched away across the field, crying "Come on Maister Kennedy. Here's Leslie that holy, holy man. We'll tell him stories tae mak his puir thin bluid rin warm."

So the days of the harvest wore on, till the fields stood bare of the sheaves and the last load went home. Stephen and the old man were standing in the cornyard under the great moon as the load came creaking home in triumph. Young Jock walked at the horse's head with a spring in his step for he knew that this was an occasion of honour and on the top of the load the Merry Widow and Kennedy rocked about with their arms entwined and their forks across their shoulders. Somewhat inharmoniously but with tremendous feeling they sang what they thought to be the old song "Bringing Home the Sheaves". Passing Stephen and the old man they saluted them with a cheer and when the cart rocked to rest beside the stack they collapsed into each others' arms and exchanged a kiss that could be heard as far as the kitchen door. Stephen forked the last of the corn on to the stack and Tam built it neatly in and up to the crowning sheaf. Then they two that had fought so well for the harvest stood down together and looked at their work.

"We've done it," said Stephen.

Tam said nothing at all, for no words were needed. The many stout ricks stood about them in witness of the friendship that the season had made between them.

"Come in you twa lads and hae a dram," the old man said and he led them up towards the house.

Next night they celebrated the old feast of the Harvest Home.

Now in the olden days the Harvest Home had been one of the feasts most honoured in the countryside, for harvests were even more uncertain then than now and to have got the corn home was a real reason for thanksgiving. So it was the custom that the farmer should hold a supper in thankfulness to the gods, and invite to it all who had taken part in his harvest. But that pleasant custom had long been on the decline and the recent war had put an end to it entirely, even the old man had let it go, with so many other pleasant things; and, though he did give his men an extra good supper on the last day of the harvest, that was the palest ghost of the old time Harvest Home.

On this occasion, however, it was Mr. Elphinstone's honour to revive the festival in all its glory; and the old man, being always glad of an excuse to make merry, consented with enthusiasm, on the understanding that Mr. Elphinstone would not only provide a certain quantity of strong waters but would also lead off the ball with the Merry Widow. That having been arranged to their mutual satisfaction, Mr. Elphinstone devoted the last few days of the harvest to the feast with Aunt Elizabeth.

Now the feast, as Mr. Elphinstone saw it, falls naturally into three parts. First the supper, then the tasting of the meal and ale, and then the dancing in the barn. And so the feast was conducted on the appointed night.

A considerable party sat down to supper in the kitchen. The old man sat at the top of the table with Susan at his right hand and the Merry Widow at his left. Aunt Elizabeth sat at the foot of the table with Mr. Elphinstone at her left hand and Tam at her right. In the long space between them were Stephen and Kennedy, Willum and his wife, Mistress Tam, Jock and Sam; the holy Mr. Leslie with his wife, and two aged men, crofter friends of the old man who had harvested with him on Hillhead when they were boys and now considered themselves as it were his guardian angels. There was also Miss Carnousie, the devotee of the elemental in art, who had been invited by Mr. Elphinstone for reasons of his own.

It was a simple feast – a dish of good thick broth, cold salmon, a roast with new potatoes and a dumpling as big and round as Falstaff's belly, full of the richest living. Waited on by Bawbie, who under Aunt Elizabeth's eye directed two women hired for the occasion, the company ate mightily of what had been provided for them. They were a little shy at thus sitting down with the folks from ben the hoose but as they had little time for conversation their shyness was hardly to be remarked. Besides, whatever their deficiency in this respect was most amply made up by Miss Carnousie.

This lady who was in the flower of what Mr. Elphinstone called an ample thirty, was a fair person of a most enthusiastic nature. There was something Nordic about her, or so she liked to think, and indeed for those that liked them blonde and big she was, as Kennedy said, a bounding armful. She had very earnest blue eyes, a big scarlet mouth, magnificent breasts and a splendid bottom. When she spoke she was both confidential and superlative. She had a most unfortunate taste for mauve, which was the colour of her aura, and that may have been another misfortune. By breeding she was a woman of some private means; by persuasion she was a poetess; and at all times she loved the elemental, as Stephen found to his great embarrassment.

"Aren't they darlings," she said, waving her blood red finger nails in the direction of Willum and Andy and Davy. "So sweet and unspoiled."

"I don't know about that," Stephen replied, "Willum there has thirteen children."

"Thirteen, how splendid. What a man."

She turned her prominent blue eyes on the fount of so much elemental life and stared at him with such intensity that he choked and had to be thumped on the back. The clamour of thumping and coughing delighted Miss Carnousie.

"What unspoiled energies they have," she said. "How much happier they must be than we are. O Mr. Lee, if only we could get closer to the elemental ...'

She did not conclude the sentence but left it hanging in the air just over Davy and Andy's heads. Her thoughts were too tremendous to be expressed in words.

When the plum pudding had been eaten and the company were beginning to lose their interest in food the meal and ale was brought to the table.

Now in the olden days the meal and ale was the prime dish of the feast and it justified its name. For it was a compound of oatmeal and strong ale mixed up and left to ripen for a day or two. On the night of the feast further strong waters were added to it, in a great dish, and after the head of the feast had tasted it, the guests gathered round each with a horn spoon and ate their fill of it. Being made of meal, which is the inner substance of the corn and of ale and whisky which are the twin elements of its soul, the meal and ale thus symbolised the harvest. On this occasion Mr. Elphinstone desired the symbolism without the substance. Though he loved tradition he was not its slave; therefore though he was determined that the meal and ale should be enjoyed after the custom of the olden times, he also realised that the company would be in no mood for such a heavy dish after such a supper. It was in short ten parts whisky to one part of honey, with a handful of oatmeal thrown in for custom's sake. The mixture had then been warmed slightly to bring the parts into a proper union and had been set past to mellow in the coolest part of the milkhouse. Thence it was now brought by Aunt Elizabeth in a great china bowl and sat before the old man. The old man looked at it dubiously, helped himself to a little by means of a toddy ladle and tasted it. There was a hush in the kitchen as the sweet syrup spread across his palate and the company waited for the result with anxious looks upon their faces. Then he swallowed the syrup and sighed. It was a sigh of the deepest pleasure. Lifting the toddy ladle he fill his glass to the brim and sat back in his chair.

"Fire frae Heaven," he said with a laugh. "Drink up lads and daena spare the ladles."

Everybody laughed and beat upon the table with their silver ladles while the bowl circled the table. They

drank and as the strong syrup ran down their throats a
divine warmth spread through them. Their faces
glowed. Their tongues came loose. They laughed
without purpose and without ceasing. They cried to the
old man for a speech but he refused, saying that words
would be a waste of time when drink was on the table.
Then Mr. Elphinstone offered to speak but Susan re-
strained him; it was, she said neither the time nor the
place for the classics and far too early in the evening to
be indecent. At last the desire for an oration became so
strong that Tam rose and called on them to drink the
health of the master which they did, all of them, even
Leslie, that holy man, who had been drinking steadily all
evening to his own eternal damnation, against his will for
the look of the thing. By that time the bowl alas was
empty so that the old man rose and told them it was time
to go out to the dancing.

The barn, being in two parts, was a most conven-
ient place for a dance. The ground floor on which stood
the lower half of the mill was a dark enticing place with
many obscure corners. There sacks filled with straw had
been placed to sit on and the more public spiders had
been removed. The upper half of the barn was a loft
built around the top half of the mill, and approached by
a narrow stair. The wooden floor was highly polished by
many harvests of sheaves and therefore was ideal for
dancing on; and the top part of the mill, standing about
five feet above the floor and being as many feet in
breadth made an excellent gallery for the musicians.
From this part too the spiders and the other small tenants of the dark had been removed, more sacks filled
with straw had been placed along the walls, and the floor
had been treated with a substance that would make it
more grateful to the feet of dancers.

When the party from the house entered the barn
they found that the musicians were already tuning-up
their instruments. This band of music was a notable part
of the life of the countryside; it was indeed one of the

few traditions that had survived the war and in every way it was traditional if not wholly fabulous. The players were oldish men and they had the air of tradesmen about them; they were in fact journeymen all three, for one was a mason, the second a joiner and the third a smith; and journeymen they were in music too. They worked at music-making with all the zeal that they might have shown in their proper trades. The joiner worked at his fiddle as if he were sawing up a piece of the most enduring wood. The blacksmith brought from his string bass hollow sounds like the sledge of fate beating on the anvil of doom. And the mason scattered handfuls of notes from the cornet with the same careless and intermittent effect as if he had been harling a wall with harmony. They were well matched to look at; for the fiddler was a little amorous man with a whisky nose and a roving eye and the cornet was a round bald party swollen with wind and noisy laughter. In action they sat facing each other, scraping and blowing in concert. Behind the string bass towered and boomed, the man and the fiddle. The blacksmith was colossal, a vast unsmiling man who plucked the sound from the strings with a mighty hand. It was very seldom that he showed emotion but in the later parts of the evening he would get so intoxicated with the hollow sounds and with the refreshment that was his only fee, that he would occasionally rise from his high stool and clutch the fiddle with both hands as if about to tuck it under a chin that might well have held it. The band were unique both in themselves and in their music.

Having been refreshed first by the old man and then by Mr. Elphinstone, a piece of bad staff work of which however they made no complaint, they climbed on to the top of the mill and made impatient sounds with their instruments, a signal for the ball to begin. The company fell to partners for the Grand March and Circassian Circle which was the traditional prelude to the ball. It was the old man's privilege to open the March

with the lady of his choice but on this occasion, according
to their compact, Mr. Elphinstone led the way with the
Merry Widow. Then went the old man with Tam's wife;
then Tam with Aunt Elizabeth; then Stephen with Mrs.
Willum; the Kennedy with Susan; then the others
according to their choice and last of all, O wonder, Miss
Carnousie with Leslie, that holy man. The first dance
was a short one out of consideration for the older
people; the reels that followed were meant for heroes.

Led by the scraping of the fiddle, the reels swung
and spun then disintegrated into their breathless mem-
bers; but there was no rest for, obedient to the wayward
cornet scattering its grace notes to the rafters, the dancers two by two leaped and pirouetted before each other,
joined hands and swung then retired while two more
took their places. Then again the reels formed hands
and swung, the women between the men. The circle of
eight danced as one man, to the beat of the string bass,
till the floor sprang with them on its supple beams and a
cloud of dust, the flour of the corn and the fine small
notes of the air, hung before the lamps and turned their
light to the richest dusty gold. Between the reels they
danced the sweet old-fashioned waltzes. Now there was
grace when the band played, or thought they played, the
Lily of Laguna and Mr. Elphinstone led Aunt Elizabeth
to the floor. A little uncertainly perhaps, they started,
for the band had a nice beat in the waltzes; but soon the
memory of other days and more accomplished music
took them into a rhythm of their own and they swung
away into a private and most lovely world. Stephen and
Susan stopped to watch them with laughter touched by
tears, for who so gay and gallant, who so masterful and
yet so tender as Mr. Elphinstone with his silver hair and
his coattails flying; and who ever so kind and with so
sweet a smile as Aunt Elizabeth, swinging on his arm
while the swish of her black silk gown was the requiem
for a golden age. They were not alone on the floor for
Miss Carnousie and the holy Mr. Leslie, having been

mightily inspired, the one by close contact with the
elemental and the other by strong ale, had flared each
other to a waltz and now were steering an eccentric
course across the loft, locked in an embrace that was a
cross between a half nelson and that remarkable statue,
the Laocoon. Mr. Leslie, being of a puritan turn of
mind, did not believe in embracing his partner as closely
as she would have desired, but the spirit of kindness
which filled the hall had brought them to a compromise.
Miss Carnousie had her right arm tightly round Mr.
Leslie's neck and her chin in his stiff black hair; he kept
the lower part of his body as far from hers as possible
while he held her left arm stiffly in the air, with his
bottom sticking out like the bows of a coasting boat and
with her arm stuck high above them like a mast, they
lurched and veered like a most eccentric craft in a very
high sea.

So the hours passed quickly, the atmosphere in the
barn became more dusty golden and the dancing grew
more furious. Refreshed with tea and strong ale, the
men threw off their coats and waistcoats, and the women
whatever reserves of refinements they may have brought
with them. The dances spun faster and yet faster, till the
women were swept off their feet and flew round almost
horizontal, held in the arms of the encircled men. High
over everything else rose the Merry Widow's laughter
and her cries of wild excitement as she was carried away
in the reels. Her delight was demonic, a force of nature.
She was tireless, the very soul of pleasure. She danced
with all of them, especially with Stephen; and as he
danced his youth was so renewed that he wished that
night would never end. Between the dances he leaned
against the wall and looked at his friends. They were
inexpressibly delightful and dear; and they took their
pleasure with such splendid heart that they multiplied it
a hundredfold. There was such humour in them that it
warmed him to look at them; such energy that they
made the towns seem very old and tired; and such free

life that death would not bear thinking on. There, in the place of his own people, he knew he had found something that he must guard for all his days.

Then he missed the old man and Aunt Elizabeth from their places by the wall. Saddened to think that they were so old that they must leave before the end and creep to bed he went into the house to look for them. But even as he passed the kitchen door he heard a sound of laughter, and going through to the parlour he found the older men sitting round the table at cards with piles of coppers before them and the whisky jar at the old man's side. They were so intent on their game and they hit the table with such bangs of their fists as they played their master cards, that they did not see him, so he withdrew and closed the door and returned to the dancing. As he went through the close he heard a shriek and a woman came flying out of the stable into the starry night closely pursued by a man. As the woman passed the window the light fell on her face. It was Miss Carnousie in full flight from the elemental in the person of Leslie that holy man.

The dance went on till half past five. The old man and Aunt Elizabeth having won twenty three shillings between them, had gone to their beds; and Miss Carnousie had retired to hers some time before quite overcome. But even at half past five the dancers could hardly bear that an end should be made of the splendid night. But alas, the band, good honest men, were tired and no insults cried at them by the tireless Widow would bring back the beat of pleasure to their weary arms. They packed up their instruments and departed in single file into the night, first the fiddle making a wry face against the morning cold; then the cornet still puffing and blowing with his lips in a habitual embouchure; and last of all the string bass like a giant out of a fable with his monstrous fiddle across his shoulder. One by one they passed across the lighted door and then were lost into the darkness. The dance was ended. The dancers said good night and went home to bed. The world grew very quiet waiting on the dawn. And when they got up next morning the fields were bare of harvest. They set their faces to winter and the long cold dark.

A Scots farmer of a type that is now rare and soon may be forgotten

CHAPTER TEN

The Conflict

NOW THAT the harvest was over, a great peace fell on
Hillhead for there was little left but to tidy the place
against the winter. The men cut rushes in the moss and
thatched the ricks with them to keep the corn dry
through the long winter rains. The peats were brought
home and stacked at the end of the house, and on several days the carts went to the Lendrum woods for logs
that the men would split in the cartshed on stormy days.
The days grew short; the nights grew colder and every
morning had deepened the colour on the dying leaves.
Then the wind came snell across the river and the leaves
fell like hosts of birds homing to the earth. Nature was
drawing in upon herself for her long sleep. And so, it
seemed to Stephen, were the Brewsters. For instead of
making plans whereby the new year would come to a
braver flower than any year before, the old man was
dreaming of smaller and yet smaller things, as if the
virtue of his people were withdrawing upon itself for
ever. And every day the sense of imminent defeat became so intolerable to Stephen that he only waited the
appointed hour to take his proper place.

But if there was little cheer at Hillhead there was
plenty at Strathmuir where Kennedy and Stephen and
young Strath talked long into the night about the things
that ought to be.

Young Strath was thorough in all things and his
house was as modernised without as within. It was an
old house, older than the house at Hillhead but it lacked
no domestic device known to the ingenious mind of its
owner. There were electric switches everywhere and
plugs to which heaters, cleaners and musical instruments

might be attached. Young Strath had even a bed with a mattress heated by power; and on observing that wonder Kennedy remarked that when he took a wife she would no doubt be run on the same labour saving principle.

Sitting round the fire on the early November evenings, the three young men damned the obstinacy of the old that would have stood between the he countryside and the things that reason demanded should be done.

"Speak to them o' changes," Young Strath said, "and they'll tear the skin off your face. They think it's a deliberate insult when ye suggest there are better ways o' doin things than their grandfathers thought of."

"Just fear and laziness," said Kennedy. "Most people are not very clever; and when they've learned one way of doing things by very great pains, they're scared at the thought of having to learn a new one. Because they're afraid they can't. So they'll muddle along in the old ways and damn anybody that tries to stir them out of their blasted complacency."

"And what ways," Stephen said. "Tam – would you say he was a good man?"

"Better than average and willin tae learn," Young Strath said.

"Well he gets £60 a year from my grandfather, and the old man can't afford to give him more. He lives in three rooms without a kitchen or a bathroom. And Willum, O my god, Willum has £54 and thirteen bairns and his wife has to carry her drinking water from a pump a hundred yards away. Lord think of it, thirteen children and £54 a year. Yesterday I said to Mains that I didn't know how they managed and they still wouldn't have enough if they got twice as much."

"And what did he say?" Young Strath asked, with a laugh ready.

"He bristled up and said 'They've as much as they ken what tae dae wi. If they got ony mair they'd spend it in gaen tae the pictures.' Then he went down to the Doctor's to lose money at Bridge, for I know by the look of him that he's the kind of man that always loses."

"Waste, waste, waste," Kennedy said, "there's nothing but waste of human lives, waste through useless labour in businesses that have fallen behind the times, waste in houses where women have to struggle with dirt with a little money and a little thought, waste of men with ideas that cannot put them to work because some stupid fool is afraid to take a risk or afraid to be disturbed. We waste the only years we have in walking the old hard roads because the fools whose interest it is to help won't dare to try the new, and the rogues who have the power very rightly hang on to it with all the strength they can. Look at the farmers squeezed to death by the financial gents; or, if you prefer it, who are the victims of economic forces. But will they do anything to best the bankers or twist the economic forces to their own advantage? Lord no. The very hands that strangle them are sacred. Everything is sacred. Everything except human life. Property is sacred. It is money. But human lives are not sacred; they cost nothing but human suffering. If I were a woman I would not bear another child till I had made a sane world for it to live in."

Young Strath bit his pipe uncertainly.

"That's socialism and I daena like the sound o' it very much. I want to get on with the job."

"O socialism. What's in a name," Kennedy cried. "Call it anything you like. It's common sense. I don't care what you call it. I don't care how you do it. Only I want it done. What in Hell's the use of quarrelling about names when we want the same thing in the end. Socialism and capitalism aren't the word of God made eternal. They're ways of organising the world's wealth, and the plan that is good today may not be the plan that's good tomorrow. To Hell with principles. We've had too many principles that lasted too long. We want to trim the sails a new way. Lord god look at the winds that are blowing across the world – wealth, wealth, wealth; great golden winds blowing in from every quarter – and what do we get out of it?"

"There has been progress," Young Strath said. "Conditions are better."

Better, of course they're better. But that's nothing. Nothing at all compared with what they had ought to be with the resources that are lying to our hands. Of course there's progress and to the old it may seem a very wonderful thing. But what is that to us? We didn't see the old bad world. We that are young, we don't look back. We must look forward to the things that might and ought to be when we use all the wealth that is in the world to make a pleasant world to live in.

"But old people can say what they like, it has little to do with them. They're old and they want peace. But we have our lives to make, it is we who have to live in the future and it is we who must have the making of it."

Stephen, lying awake at night listening to the November rains on the cold roof, thought long about that future and at last there came to him a clear vision of what he must do as the latest generation of his people.

Next day he went to the old man with his plans.

Out of the many things he had discussed with Young Strath he had selected two – the buying of a tractor and the keeping of pigs; and finding himself alone with the old man in the parlour about mid morning he began to state a case for them. At first he was very nervous and hardly dared look at his grandfather while he detailed his estimate of costs and probable profits; but as the old man said nothing, and as his faith in his own schemes grew stronger, he gathered confidence and even dared a peroration in which he hinted that there might be greater schemes to come, then, having said his say he waited for the old man's reply.

He did not have long to wait. Turning a pair of grim eyes on him the old man held out his hand. "A fine story," he said, "and well tell't. Would ye give me thae

216

papers?"

Stephen handed over the sheets on which he had detailed his estimates.

The old man laid them on his lap, put on his spectacles with a great deal of ceremony, then read the papers, holding at arm's length the better to admire them.

"Bonny," he said. "O a bonny bit o' work. A' sae nicely figured out wi black lines and red lines and the pounds and shillings in their proper places. A bonny bit o' work, sae bonny that there's only ae place for't."

He rolled the papers in a ball and threw them on the fire.

"That's my answer; and ye can tell that tae Young Strath frae me."

Stephen burnt white as if the old man had struck him; then he jumped up and cried, "You can't do that".

"But I did it," the old man said with a short laugh, "and I'll dae it again; and I'll dae it as often as onybody tries tae meddle wi my business. For I'm the master here, and this is my place."

"It won't be long. You're growing poorer every day. In three years you'll be bankrupt. You'll be sold up, everything, everything, the chairs you sit in and the bed you sleep in – and where'll your pride be then?"

The old man laughed, a superior tormenting laugh. "Ye're somewhat hasty laddie. You hae your place but I hae mine and though my plans are maybe nae as braw as yours they're my ain. I thought o' them mysel, and they'll maybe keep a saft seat beneath me till the end o' my days."

"Plans, fine plans," Stephen said with his indignation rising. "Plans that'll put men out of jobs and keep wages down, all to save you the trouble of thinking."

"That would surely be my business," the old man said quite kindly, becoming more amused as Stephen became more angry, with intent to annoy him further.

"It's more than your business. It's Jock's business

and Sam's business and Willum's and Tam's. If you turn
Jock and Sam away because you won't think of a way to
keep them, where are they going to go?"

"God knows," the old man said, "but when the
Term comes that's an end atween me and them. What
for should I bother about them? I've paid them their
money as lang as they've worked for me. We're quits,
we're square – and we're finished."

"Aye, fine wages."

"They hadna the sense tae ask for better; and if
they're fools, that's nae business o' mine. If they and a'
their like had stood out for better they must hae got it;
but they didna; they got what they were willin tae tak;
and wha am I tae be sorry for them?"

"Because they were brought up to rely on you and
the like o' you for their living. Because you and the like
o' you never gave them the education to think for themselves. Because your kind have made them believe that
they had only to work for you and ask no questions and
their living would be sure to them till the end of their
days. Because they trusted you and you have betrayed
them. They've worked for you, they've kept their bargain for generations and you've lived easy on their
labour; but now that the times are out of your control
and ye haena the will tae mend them, ye'll turn the men
away to stand at the street corners with nobody to care
whether they live or die. You're a proud old man, aren't
you; you despise the rest of the countryside, don't you:
well there's something to be proud of."

"What a lot o' words," the old man said, mocking
him. "If ye gang on like that ye'll hae me greetin.
Maybe ye think I should be doon helpin Mrs. Willum tae
nurse her bairns."

"You might give her and them a decent house."

"Nae as lang as they'll live in the house they've
gotten. Ye've made a great sang, laddie, but it means
naething tae me, except that I'm wae tae see ony
Brewster botherin about folk that willna dae onything

tae help themselves. Na, na, laddie, ye'll hae tae play anither tune afore I dance tae your pipin."

If only he would get angry, Stephen said to himself. *If only he would show some feeling, but he treats me like a child and I can't get at him. It's useless, useless.*

But he did not give up, for he thought of all the plans that he and his friends had made for a new world and he turned to the old man again.

"Can't you think of the future? Are you going to let all the things you're so proud of just dwine away; the ploughed land go back into pasture, the pasture go into the rough, and the work of all those years into the waste where our people found it. O my god surely anything but that."

"It'll not happen in my time, and what happens after is nae concern o' mine, and, my man, I'd just like to suggest it's nae business o' yours."

"But it is," Stephen said. "It is my business and you'll admit it's my business afore I leave this room. It's my business because I've got to go on living after you're dead. The kind of world you leave me is my concern, my life depends on it, and I can't and won't stand by to see you play the fool with my inheritance. Not only mine but Tam's and Willum's and all the other men's and women's and the children's. You and your generation think they own the world; and a bonny world you're making of it. But you own little that the generations before you haven't made for you and once you're dead you'll own nothing but the hole you're buried in. You and your kind are sitting there thinking yourselves the master of the earth – you're only the tenants of a day."

"The world's wide," the old man said, "I've heard ye say that yoursel and if ye're nae pleased wi this bit o't, awa and dig a gairden o' your ain."

"The world may be wide but it's narrow enough for us, for we want only the bit that our people have lived in so that we can live in it and care for it as they did. What's the use of the wide world to me. Hillhead is the

Brewster's place and where ever should a Brewster be?"

"Brewster," said the old man with a laugh. "I thought your name was Lees."

"Whatever my name I'm a Brewster."

"Prove it," said the old man.

"Yes I'll prove it. You say you're hard. You believe you're hard. You're proud that you and all the Brewsters have been hard. Well I'll prove myself as hard as the rest of you. When your father died you went up the Knowes and looked down at Hillhead and said to yourself – 'It's mine, a' mine' – and you thought of nothing but your own pleasure and the fine things you would do. You've had your day of it but your time is nearly at an end. My turn is coming. I mean to take it. I'm a Brewster whatever I'm called. I'm a Brewster, the only one of my generation that knows Hillhead or cares for it. I'm ready to live for it and work for it and spend all my life on it. You had plans for it forty years ago. Well I have plans for it now, plans that will keep the land under the plough, that will keep the men in their work and give them the living that their work is worth. You can say what you like; you can sit there and glower at me; but be damned to you, I know what the land wants and I know what the land needs and nothing'll turn me from the work I intend to do. You can stop me as long as you live; but once you're dead I'll move the heavens to sit in your place. And when I'm there I'll look down on Hillhead and say 'It's mine'. So now what do you say?"

The old man turned round in his seat and looked at Stephen in a mixture of some amazement and wonder, as one who sees some by-ordinar folly.

"And if there's nae a road out o' the mess?"

"There's got to be a road and we'll find that road."

"Though ye pull the heavens doon about your lugs?"

"The heavens have looked long enough on stupidity and injustice that it'll do them no harm to fall; and if they do we'll build them new and better, or die in the attempt. But there's one thing certain – we're not going to be starved while praying to old gods that cannot help us. We've got to go on and I'm determined that Hillhead will lead the way, as it has always done. And now what do you say?"

He faced the old man, demanding an answer and daring him to avoid the issue. The old man still looked at him as if he were some world's wonder then he smote the table with his hand and laughed saying – "Ye're mad, man, ye're mad, but I see past a' question ye're a Brewster, for they've a' been mad about something. Ye want an answer dae ye? Then ye'll get it. What's the price o' a tractor?"

Stephen gripped the table in his excitement, "Ye'll do it?"

"Aye I'll do it," the old man replied, as if there could not be any question. "And what for no? If the Brewsters are gaun out they'll end as they've lived – in style. Man ye've spoken a lot o' nonsense the day, and many anither day, but there were some o' the things ye said that pleased. For I've aye liked a man that kent what he wanted and then made a dead set tae get it. I've been like that mysel, in my time. But man, I've begun tae think that I was the only ane that was left in the world, and afore ye cam here I was gettin lonely. I thought there was little need tae bother for there was nane o' my kind tae come after me. When ye did come I liked the look o' ye; and now that ye're here ye'd better bide; for ye're a Brewster and it's aye been in the nature o' Brewsters tae live by the laan. Aye, ye'd better bide and I promise ye ye'll never regret it."

Stephen lay back in his chair too exhausted to say more than, "I'll bide".

"Then that's that," the old man said, as if a long and difficult bit of work had been successfully ended. "I think we'd better drink a dram on't."

They drank to each other standing, then Stephen said with a laugh, "Ye'll put up wi the tractors and the pigs for my sake?"

"I'll put up wi the tractor for its ain sake," the old man replied. He looked through the window across the fields. "Man thae parks hae seen naething but horse and kye and corn a' their days. It'll be a michty thing whan your engines gang rivin through the yird. I've nae faith in the end o' them. Nane at a'. But man if we hae tae gang oot we'll gang oot wi a roar. Come on now lad sit down and tak your pencil; I'm an auld man but I'm nae yet ready for my grave; and afore I'm carried tae Lendrum we'll gae the countryside a lot tae think about, you and me and the tractors."

"Come on then," Stephen said, "I'm ready."

CHAPTER ELEVEN

The Beginning

THERE WERE two great occasions in the history of Hillhead – when the original Brewster turned the first sod and when the tractor drew the first furrow down the lea; and surely, Stephen thought as he watched the tractor ploughs ripping the green turf, all his ancestors must be present to watch the new beginning.

The circumstances were most fitting for a dramatic occasion, for the season had been a severe one and the work was far behind. The winter had come swift on the end of harvest, too swift for the backward farmers, and even now on Christmas Day the stooks were rotting in many fields. First there had been weeks of torrential rain; then a long frost that bound the earth. Only now a gentle wind had come over from the west and there was a heartening warmth in the sun. And only now the farmers were able to begin the ploughing. They had two months' work to overtake by the slow laborious horses that might not be hurried and many an anxious soul, who knew by long experience just how little the plough-ing weather could be trusted, must have feared that the two months' leeway might never be overtaken. But they had no such fears at Hillhead for the tractor sat ready in the shed and it was above all mortal weakness. "My god", Tam had said a dozen times with a kind of glorious impatience, "if only there was ploughin weather and this beastie could walk the laan, we'd show the countryside a ferly." Now its time had come.

It was a bright December morning when Stephen and the old man waited in the lea field for Tam to bring the tractor down from the steading. The land, released from the grip of the frost, was a gentle pattern of pasture and stubble where the ploughs were already drawing the long straight furrows and the jingle of the harness was like a little prelude to the spring of the year. Down in the Hillhead lea beside them Willum was already ploughing with three horses in the double furrow plough and whistling one of the old songs of the countryside while a flock of gulls come up from the sea wheeled over the black land behind him. It was a sight to make any man glad, but Stephen and the old man were too excited to enjoy it: the old man because he had a strong sense of the dramatic and knew that the countryside would be watching from a distance; Stephen because he felt that his real work was now beginning. But their excitement was nothing to the triumphant emotions that made Tam the king of men that morning.

"There she comes," the old man said, as the snore of the tractor was borne down the wind from the steading.

"Isn't she a beauty," Stephen replied when Tam drove the machine along the road towards them.

But Willum who was ploughing nearby just cried "Come up" to his horses and whistled defiantly out of tune. For the first time in his life he found no pleasure in ploughing weather. The tractor was an abomination in his eyes.

Tam however was in his glory as he felt the power of the machine obedient to his hand. Daring to take his eyes off the track in front of him, he looked across the land at the teams straining against the rise of the hills and he pitied them their old laborious ways. All his sense of frustration was gone. He no longer felt that the world was moving on while he was held in the grip of the past. Far otherwise; he was now moving on while his neighbours were standing still. There was a flourish, a touch of glory in the way he brought the tractor round and halted it beside Stephen and the old man, with its head towards the open field.

Like men who had not a moment to lose they

coupled on the three-furrow plough, while Willum
pretended not to watch them from a little distance where
he had stopped to do something quite unnecessary to his
coulter. When the plough was set, Tam mounted the
tractor, let in the clutch and with a jerk the ploughs bit
into the green sod. Tam was a little unsteady at first and
stopped after five yards or so at which Willum threw up
his hands in delight, called to his horses and moved away
whistling in triumph that the new fangled machine had
broken down while the old and immemorial ways still
held the field. But Tam soon recovered his confidence,
started the tractor again and held it straight for the far
side of the field. Midway to the other end he passed
Willum and waved gaily in passing. Willum's whistling
lost its triumph and took on a still defiant but somewhat
melancholy tone. Pleasure had gone out of the world
again.

Meanwhile Stephen and the old man had been
watching the tractor in silence but when it reached the
far end of the field, "It works," the old man said.

"And it'll keep on working," Stephen replied.

The old man laughed. "A body would be sorry tae
die wi all thae new things happenin. I was sorry tae sell
the horses, but I've had near on eighty years o' them and
it was maybe time for a change. Still it was a bad thing
tae be sending Jock awa tae mak a place for that machine."

"We'll bring him back again" Stephen replied,
"when we've learned new ways for him. Once we've
made some money we'll be able to make some more
work. We'll grow more of everything, and feed more
beasts and need more labour. We'll bring back Jock and
more like him. We'll double the crops and double the
labour and pay good wages and keep Hillhead the first
in the countryside as it has aye been."

"Stop, man, stop," his grandfather said. "I'm too
old for fairy stories, but I've made plans in my time and
it's time tae be makin plans again. I'll nae see much o'

them, though maybe I'll live lang enough tae keep ye frae ruinin yoursel in a twelvemonth." He looked round the countryside and said, "They're decent folk, my neighbours, but cautious, michty cautious. They've never liked me because in my day I was fond o' new things. Man, I had the first bath-room in Lendrum and the folk thought it sae immoral tae bath wi a' your body naked at one time that they nearly excommunicated me frae the Kirk. Now that I've gotten a tractor they'll expect me tae be consumed by fire frae Heaven as a punishment for ungodly presumption. But I've an idea that all that's happenin is naething tae what will happen when I'm deid and you get your head. I'll nae be here tae see that day, nor tae help ye, and that'll be a good thing for a man should hae the fun o' makin his own mistakes. But I've done the next best thing. I've made my will and left ye what there is, little enough that be, because – dammit man, you're a Brewster."

Without giving Stephen any time to reply he walked away towards the steading. Stephen was glad for he had been moved far beyond words. It was as if everything he could have wished for had been given him and he felt he must do something magnificent in celebration. But he only went over to Tam and asked him how he was getting on. Then the two of them went into raptures over the new machine while Willum, that loyal servant of tradition, glowered and grunted and whistled defiantly out of tune on the far side of the field.

Mr. Elphinstone went out to Hillhead in the afternoon to see how the new order was shaping; after he had listened to Stephen's endless plans he polished his glasses and said –

"Then you're going to be a farmer?"

"I'm afraid so," Stephen replied with a touch of pride.

"But what about seeing the world?"

"It's not so important now."

"And what about that liberty, that glorious freedom, the birthright of every man that you wanted some little time ago?"

"I've got it. I'm doing what I want to do."

Mr. Elphinstone put on his glasses and surveyed Stephen through them. "You may call that freedom if you like; but if you're wise you'll forget all about it. You'll never have freedom so long as you're here, and it'll never be worth anything to you if you go away."

Stephen would have interrupted him but he waved away the hint of objection.

"Because for a young man like you there can never be freedom. Freedom, if it means anything at all, means that you have no loyalties to anything but yourself. But you, my friend, are the kind that must have gods. And you'll only be happy when your gods are good."

He gave the landscape a patronising glance.

"As far as I can see you've chosen well enough. This is a good country that will reward them that care for it. You will have your work always before you and you'll be able to feel the work is of some value. You may even bring enlightenment to them that sit in darkness."

"By God, I will."

"Poor fellow, poor, poor fellow," Mr. Elphinstone said. "But it may be some consolation that you will not be the first missionary to be destroyed by those he would have saved."

"Tam won't destroy me."

"And Willum now? Even I see how much he hates the strange beast you've harnessed to the plough. If it blew up this minute he'd be the first to cheer. And for every Tam you find in the countryside you'll find a hundred Willums."

But Stephen said, "I don't care. I don't care a damn. This is my place and my living; it's my living and Tam's. We'll make it thrive in our own way and them that don't like our way can go and starve in a corner. This is my work. I'm going to do it the best way I can, and freedom and tradition and everybody that thinks

I'm a fool can go to hell."

"Then," said Mr. Elphinstone, "there's nothing left
for me but to wish you joy; and remember, when you
need a thousand pounds – at five per cent – just let me
know. And now I will leave you to your mission."

But Kennedy and Susan had come up on them
unawares and surprised them by saying –

"Stephen, congratulate me."

"Certainly," Stephen replied, "but why?"

"We're getting married," Kennedy said.

"Yes," Susan added, "I'm going to make an honest
man of him, it that's possible."

There was a deal of laughing during which Mr.
Elphinstone tried quite unsuccessfully to play the father.
Then, returning to his natural humour, he pointed to
Kennedy and Susan standing arm in arm and said –

"A foolish young people but charming. In fact I
don't think charming is quite the word; for he is heir to
all the knowledge in the world and she is heir to all the
understanding; and to see them married, my boy, it will
be as if all the ages of the world were going to bed together."

Stephen sighed, "I envy them" and when he saw
the happiness that bound them together he longed for
Jane.

"Don't worry, my dear," Susan said. "Remember
the farmer takes a wife."

"And even if he doesn't, the wife will take the
farmer," Kennedy added.

"After which," said Mr. Elphinstone, "they will live
together happily and fruitfully all the days of their lives."

Stephen laughed; but, looking at Kennedy and
Susan, he hoped that it might be so for him.

The short winter afternoon drew near the dark.
The sun went home into a gurly sky, the bright stars
came out and the waning moon hung low down in the
lift. Stephen went over to Tam and they decided that
enough had been done for a winter day. Together they

thought of what they had done and of how much there remained to do. Then Stephen, because he had come to respect Tam, spoke what had been in his mind for weeks.

"Some day this place'll be mine, Tam; and though I'll learn all I can, there'll be some things I'll not be able to learn. The place'll need you, Tam, and if you'll stick to me I'll stick to you. Together there's no end to the things we can do. What do you say?"

Tam thought for a moment rubbing his hands on his oily trousers. Then, "I'll stick by ye," he said.

They shook hands on the bargain. So a new partnership was made; and so a new part of the history of Hillhead began.

Before he went in to supper that night, Stephen climbed to the top of Brewster's Knowe and looked across the fields that lay almost invisible under the thin light of the moon. Slowly the fields took shape one by one before his accustomed eyes till he saw the whole farm lying as it were within the bright circle of his mind. These he knew were his heritage from the round knowe across the river the dead men had challenged him to take up that heritage and guard it with his life: he had accepted the challenge and now he was for the moment utterly content. He had no regrets for the things he had given up; and he had no fears for the future, for he knew that the spirits of his fathers stood at his shoulder. But he did not think of the past. He had work to do and he swore to do it so that one day he too might stand on Brewster's Knowe and say as his grandfather had said "This is mine, a' mine".

Glossary

Antrin .... occasional
Bein .... mellow, comfortable, douce, from the French for good
Cole .... small temporary hay rick
Darg .... wark
Dird .... bump
Drookit .... drowned
Dwinin .... fading
Endig .... either end of ploughed drills
Haflin .... apprentice farmhand
Joukit .... dodged
Lift .... ceiling
Midse .... where two bits of ploughing meet
Neeps .... turnips
Teuchat .... lapwing, green plover, peewit
Trump .... Jew's harp
Reeshle .... rustle
Rivin .... tearing
Sinsyne .... since then
Stot .... bounce
Stot .... steer, bullock
Stravaig .... wander
Wae .... sad, woe
Wame .... stomach
Yird .... soil